YOSEMITE FALL

Praise for the National Park Mystery Series

"What an extraordinary ride! You know when a reader says they couldn't put the book down? *Yellowstone Standoff* is one of those rare books . . . a *tour de force.*"
—WIN BLEVINS, *New York Times* bestselling author of *Stealing Fire*

"Bears and wolves in Yellowstone's backcountry don't hold a candle to the danger posed by the people sent there to study them . . . (*Yellowstone Standoff* balances) potential danger and shady characters."
—*KIRKUS REVIEWS*

"*Yellowstone Standoff* takes man versus nature—and man tangled up with nature—right to the brink of wild suspense."
—MARK STEVENS, Colorado Book Award-winning author of *Lake of Fire*

"Filled with murder and mayhem, jealousy and good detective work—an exciting, nonstop read."
—ANNE HILLERMAN, *New York Times* bestselling author of *Song of the Lion: A Leaphorn, Chee & Manuelito Novel*

"One of the most engaging mysteries I've read in a long while . . . delivers it all and then some."
—MARGARET COEL, *New York Times* bestselling author of *Winter's Child: A Wind River Mystery*

"Get ready for leave-you-breathless high country southwestern adventure."
—MICHAEL MCGARRITY, *New York Times* bestselling author of *Hard Country* and *Backlands*

"(*Mountain Rampage*) is tailor-made for those who prefer their mysteries under blue skies."
—*KIRKUS REVIEWS*

"Stunning setting, intriguing plot, and likeable characters make *Canyon Sacrifice* a bookseller's dream."
—ANDREA AVANTAGGIO, co-owner of Maria's Bookshop

YOSEMITE FALL

A National Park Mystery
by Scott Graham

TORREY HOUSE PRESS, LLC

SALT LAKE CITY • TORREY

This is a work of fiction set in a real place. All characters in this novel are fictitious. Any resemblance to actual events or persons, living or dead, is entirely coincidental.

First Torrey House Press Edition, June 2018
Copyright © 2018 by Scott Graham

Published by Torrey House Press
Salt Lake City, Utah
www.torreyhouse.org

International Standard Book Number: 978-1-937226-87-9
E-book ISBN: 978-1-937226-88-6
Library of Congress Control Number: 2017947291

Cover design by Kathleen Metcalf
Interior design by Jeff Fuller
Distributed to the trade by Consortium Book Sales and Distribution

The cover of *Yosemite Fall* features a portion of Thomas Hill's 1884 painting *Early Morning, Yosemite Valley*. The painting is reproduced in its entirety below, and is used by permission of the Chrysler Museum of Art, Norfolk, Virginia.

Thomas Hill
American (1829–1908)
Early Morning, Yosemite Valley, 1884
Oil on canvas, 53½ x 36 in.
Chrysler Museum of Art, Norfolk, Virginia
Gift of Edward J. Brickhouse

To all those dedicating their lives and careers to America's national parks, with gratitude

PROLOGUE

D awn.
A good time to cheat death.

He faced north in his wingsuit, his feet planted on the lip of Glacier Point, half a vertical mile above the shadowed Yosemite Valley floor.

The sun edged above the serrated peaks of the High Sierra to the east. Its slanted rays stirred the first of the morning's updrafts, precursors of the blustery, hot summer day to come.

He flexed his toes in his padded landing shoes, his arms pressed to his sides. The fabric airfoils of his flying suit flapped at his elbows and between his legs.

He was a small man at five foot six and a hundred and fifty pounds, still heavily muscled as he neared fifty, abs six-packed, biceps and forearms honed from decades of scaling El Capitan, Half Dome, and the dozens of other sheer granite faces walling the valley before him.

He took a steadying breath and focused inward. Even as he sought calm and the supreme confidence required to leap into the abyss below, his heart, hammering against his ribcage, betrayed him.

How many flights would this make for him this year? The number shouldn't matter, but it did.

Eight.

Far fewer than past summers, though more than any of the young fliers who'd jockeyed around him in the Wawona campground since May, asking what they could do for him, anything, anything at all, he had only to name it.

And he, ever magnanimous, telling them thanks, but, really,

1

no, there was nothing they could do—unless the offer came from one of the few female fliers, they with their lithe, supple bodies. As long as his girlfriend didn't find out, there was always something they could do for him in his camper van, after the campfire burned to coals and the tangy scent of pine replaced the fog of woodsmoke in the air.

He sensed Ponch's presence behind him, providing silent, necessary peer pressure—not that he ever would admit he needed it. He assured himself Ponch was on hand simply to film the initiation of his flight off the point, nothing more.

He glanced down between his feet at the floor of the valley below. Through breaks in trees, the concrete huts of Housekeeping Camp shone with silvery fluorescent light, while Majestic Yosemite Hotel radiated its luxuriant, electric-yellow glow on the opposite side of the river.

He looked left, focusing on the dark gap in Sentinel Ridge. He hadn't yet determined if he would enter the narrow slot, a flying dart threading the rock-walled breach at 120 miles an hour. He couldn't decide, in fact, until he dropped into the yawning void and the first of the day's rising thermals gathered in his wings. Still, having curled away from the notch his previous three flights, the need to rocket through it sometime soon, as the end of summer drew near, was growing impossible to ignore.

Half Dome skylined the eastern horizon. The morning sun silhouetted the hulking granite dome's sheer north wall. Movement rippled along the wall's few narrow shelves—climbers, outside their portaledge tents, their headlamps winking in the early morning shadows as they prepared breakfast and sorted gear in anticipation of the day's upward push.

The sun rested just above the hunchbacked dome of granite in the dusty, brown-streaked sky, bathing the topmost reaches of El Capitan, opposite him, in orange and red. His eyes tracked to the shadowed base of El Cap's three-thousand-foot face, where the gravel Camp 4 parking lot, his triumphal landing spot, formed a smoky gray rectangle on the flat valley floor.

His stomach fluttered at the notion of his surprise landing in the Camp 4 lot. His appearance there in a minute or two from out of the dawn sky would be that of a spirit, a specter, an apparition from beyond.

The flecks of quartz at his feet glimmered in the slanted rays of the low sun, as if he stood not on stone but on stardust, poised to fly up and away into the morning light, unencumbered by the bonds of gravity. The setting was perfect—the shimmering lip of stone, his Superman-red wingsuit aflame in the day's initial burst of sunlight, his body still and erect, high above the valley floor. He took quick breaths, boosting the oxygen level in his brain as he sought the mental fortitude required to initiate his flight.

He began his silent countdown from five. On three, the pounding of his heart rose from his chest into his throat. On two, he didn't so much lean forward as simply begin the process of falling, his weight shifting out and over the edge of the cliff.

On one, he lifted his arms, raising his wings into place. On zero, he bent his knees and leapt off the point of rock.

He plummeted straight down, a hundred feet, two hundred, the stone face scant meters away, his arms and legs spread, until the air rushing past him filled his airfoils and he soared away from the wall, a human missile slicing through the sky.

He lowered one wrist, then the other, angling left, right, the roar of the wind loud as a jet engine in his ears as he shot across the canyon. No gusts of wind buffeted him. The gap? Yes, a go, the need to increase his viewership numbers announcing itself from deep in his cerebral cortex.

Bending his spine, his arms and legs fanned wide, he described a sweeping arc and lined up with Sentinel Ridge. He focused through his goggles on the dark notch in front of him, aiming for the narrow break in the forested ridge. The slot, sixty feet wide, angled downward and to his left, requiring a dead-center entry and a continued, precise leftward turn its entire length. At a hundred-plus miles per hour, the slightest deviation would send him rocketing into one or the other of the gap's granite walls.

Judging himself too low as he sped toward the notch, he lowered his legs, angling his body upward to catch more air and moderate his gliding descent. The added blast of wind from the maneuver ripped at a loose thread dangling from the airfoil between his legs at the bottom of his suit. The thread popped free from needle hole after needle hole beside his right ankle, lengthening up the seam of his lower airfoil.

He bowed his body to initiate his turn as he neared the slot. The force of the maneuver caused the thread to lengthen further, separating the airfoil at its seam and exposing one of the foil's stiff plastic stays. The exposed stay flapped next to his foot like the blurred wing of a hummingbird, setting off an undulating vibration along the bottom hem of the airfoil. The buzzing plastic rod slashed through his sock and bit deep into the skin of his ankle. At the same instant, the vibration along the hem of his wingsuit progressed to his right leg, which bucked violently from ankle to hip and back again.

Fear flared white hot in his brain. He tightened his right quadriceps, attempting to still his rocking leg, but it continued its fierce shimmy. As he entered the gap, the intense bucking of his leg caused him to veer wildly out of control.

PART ONE

"Yosemite Valley, to me, is always a sunrise,
a glitter of green and golden wonder in a vast
edifice of stone and space."

—Renowned Yosemite photographer Ansel Adams

1

Caught off guard by Carmelita Ortega's speedy ascent, Chuck Bender didn't react until his twelve-year-old stepdaughter was fifteen feet off the ground and climbing higher, her yellow T-shirt incandescent in the morning sun.

Chuck retrieved the growing slack in Carmelita's climbing rope, sliding the line past his brake hand and through the belay device attached to his waist harness. The rope's braided sheath warmed his skin as it slipped through his cupped palm.

Thin as a whiffle bat, her navy tights hanging in loose folds from her tiny thighs and calves, Carmelita balanced the rubber soles of her climbing shoes on the resin holds bolted to the climbing tower and grasped additional holds above her head with chalked fingers, hoisting herself up the wall.

"Take it easy," Chuck called to her, pride edging his voice, as he took up the last of the slack in the rope. "Give me a chance to keep up, would you?"

She hesitated for only a heartbeat, then shinnied skyward, her helmeted head back, her moves smooth and fluid as she moved from hold to hold up the vertical tower.

Chuck shot a grin at Janelle, who stood beside him in a form-fitting fleece top, black yoga pants, and white sneakers. "You sure she hasn't snuck off and done this before without our knowing it?"

His grin widened as he looked back up at Carmelita. A sweet spot, that's where he found himself, three years into parenthood, on a working vacation with his family in beautiful Yosemite Valley in the heart of California's Yosemite National

Park. Everything was right in his world on this sunny mid-August morning. Perfect.

A loner turned sudden husband to Janelle and stepdad to Carmelita and Rosie three years ago, Chuck was well settled in his new life by now, taking off for morning runs with Janelle before the girls awoke, working at his computer in his small study in the back of the house during school hours, helping Janelle with household chores and the girls with their homework in the evenings. He mostly bid nowadays for archaeological work close to Durango, in the mountains of southern Colorado, assuring he made it home on weekends while he conducted the fieldwork portion of his contracts.

His morning runs kept him fit at forty-five, fifteen years Janelle's senior, even as gray spread from his sideburns through the rest of his scalp, and new wrinkles pleated the edges of his mouth, mimicking the crow's feet that for years had creased the sun-scorched corners of his eyes.

Carmelita continued her smooth ascent up the portable, forty-foot climbing tower, which was raised on hydraulic arms from the bed of a flatbed trailer attached to a parked semitruck at the edge of the Camp 4 parking lot. Her bravura climb in front of the couple dozen onlookers at the foot of the tower, so out of character for her, took Chuck aback. Such brash public displays weren't like her. Rather, they were the province of her openly exuberant ten-year-old sister, Rosie.

Chuck took in an arm's length of rope. Another sidelong glance revealed a happy smile splashed across Janelle's face as she watched her older daughter's confident moves up the tower.

Janelle's smile reinforced what she'd told Chuck in their crew-cab pickup truck late last night, after the girls had fallen asleep in back as they'd driven from Colorado. She'd spoken softly, so as not to awaken the girls, of her pride at having passed the last of her paramedic training courses and the national certification test, her application now pending with the Durango Fire and Rescue Authority. Since moving north from Albuquerque to join Chuck in Durango three years ago, she'd taken fully to the outdoor lifestyle of the Colorado mountain town, hiking and camping with him and the girls, shopping at the local farmers' market, and participating in the many group trail runs hosted by the Durango Running Club in the forested hills above town.

"She must have gotten this from you," Janelle said at Chuck's side, her olive face turned to the sky. Her dark hair, long and silky, hung free down her back, and a tiny, pink gemstone winked in the side of her small, pointed nose.

"Not me." Chuck took up more slack, maintaining slight tension on the climbing rope to assure it would catch Carmelita the instant she fell—*if* she fell. "I was always a grunter. I climbed by force of will. But look at her. She's defying gravity, and she's doing it with pure grace."

Carmelita passed the tower's halfway point, moving higher despite the decreasing size and number of holds on the top portion of the structure. She grasped the undersized resin grips, dyed a rainbow of colors, with the tips of her fingers while keeping most of her weight on her toes. The climbing rope extended from her harness to a pulley at the top of the wall and back down to Chuck in the parking lot below. Her chestnut hair, gathered in a ponytail, gleamed in the sunlight beneath the back of her helmet. She showed no hint of fear as she passed thirty feet off the ground, nearing the top of the tower.

"You go, girl!" Janelle's brother and Chuck's assistant, Clarence, called to Carmelita from where he stood forty feet back from the base of the tower with the other onlookers, several of whom waited their turn to climb when Carmelita finished.

Clarence tucked his shoulder-length black hair behind his silver-earring-studded ears and raised his hands in a two-fisted salute, the sleeves of his black T-shirt climbing his pudgy upper arms, his jeans riding low on his hips beneath his sizable gut.

"Yeah! You go, girl!" Rosie echoed from where she stood at her uncle's side.

Rosie's stocky frame contrasted sharply with that of her slight sister. She could have been her uncle's twin, however, with his squat physique and potbelly, if not for the difference in their ages.

"No way am I going up that thing," Rosie declared. She hooked her thumbs through the belt loops of her shorts. "No frickin' way."

"Rosie!" Janelle admonished. Her reprimand was halfhearted, however, focused as she was on Carmelita three stories overhead. Janelle put her hand to her brow, shielding her eyes from the sun. "Isn't that high enough?" she asked Chuck.

"She might send it," Chuck replied, agog. "She might actually top out."

Carmelita continued her ascent, the widely spaced holds at the top of the tower presenting her no discernible difficulty until, as if by levitation alone, she was forty feet off the ground and there was no more climbing to be done. After giving the top of the fiberglass tower a tap, she leaned back in her harness as Chuck had instructed, her feet spread wide on the wall. She shook out her hands at her sides while he held her in place, his brake hand gripping the rope.

"How's the view from up there, sweetness?" he called up to her.

She looked at the granite cliffs lining the valley thousands of feet above the tower. "I've got a ways to go."

At Chuck's side, Janelle shivered. "Don't get any big ideas, niña."

Chuck relaxed his grip and lowered Carmelita, the rope running through his palm. "I'm glad I belayed her," he said to Janelle as Carmelita walked backward down the wall while he played the rope past his brake hand. "As light as she is, I wouldn't have wanted to trust the auto-belay to kick in and catch her."

When Carmelita reached the ground, the tower attendant, blond haired, thickly bearded, and in his mid-twenties, approached from where he'd been talking with a female climber his age. The attendant's broad shoulders extended from his tank top straight as a crossbeam. His powerful quads filled the legs of his shorts. The woman climber, waiting her turn on the tower beyond the line of waist-high boulders between the parking lot and campground, wore a magenta bikini top and shiny black climbing tights cut low across her hips. Her bare stomach was tanned and flat. A gold ring sparkled where it pierced the skin above her navel.

At the foot of the tower, the heavily muscled attendant untied the rope from Carmelita's waist. "Good going," he praised her, offering his meaty palm for a high-five.

Carmelita slapped his hand and pranced over to Janelle and Chuck, a grin plastered on her face. "That was a blast."

"You made it look easy," Janelle said.

"It *was* easy."

Chuck lifted an eyebrow at the bright-eyed youngster before him. "Not for mere mortals."

He freed the climbing rope from his harness, allowing the attendant to set about reattaching the rope to the cylindrical auto-belay mechanism at the tower's base.

Carmelita's white teeth flashed in a smile. "When can I do it again?"

Chuck cocked his head at the climbers grouped and waiting behind the line of boulders separating the parking area from Camp 4. Jimmy O'Reilly stood at the front of the group, deep in conversation with Bernard Montilio, the two men clearly enjoying the opportunity to catch up with each other this morning, as the planned reunion of old climbing buddies, including Chuck, got underway.

With Jimmy and Jimmy's longtime climbing partner Thorpe Alstad as their unofficial leaders, the other aging climbers attending the reunion this weekend had spent entire summers and significant portions of falls, winters, and springs at Camp 4 twenty years ago. They'd teamed with each other in twos, threes, and fours to put up ever-more-challenging routes on the valley's towering walls, all the while bickering like family over who among them was the most talented climber and whose completed routes were toughest.

"The line got pretty long behind Jimmy while you were up there," Chuck said to Carmelita. "I'm glad we came over first thing this morning." He hesitated, avoiding Janelle's gaze, the idea coming to him even as the words formed in his mouth. "The only way you're going to get to climb any more this weekend is if you enter the Slam."

"The what?" Carmelita asked.

Janelle stiffened beside Chuck as he continued. "The Yosemite Slam, Camp 4's big climbing competition. It starts tomorrow and runs for two days, through Sunday. That's why the tower's here. Jimmy started the Slam a few years ago to raise money for his nonprofit organization, the Camp 4 Fund, which supports the campground. The competition has gotten bigger every year. Once it begins, entrants will be the only ones allowed on the tower."

The reunion was Jimmy's idea, timed to coincide with the Slam. Chuck had scheduled his Yosemite work, which called for him to explore a pair of confounding 150-year-old murders in the valley, to overlap with the get-together, too.

None of the reunion attendees had taken Jimmy up on his suggestion that they sign up for the Slam. In declining Jimmy's offer, the climbers, all well into their forties, cited creaking joints and declining fitness. Chuck cited, as well, the tight timeframe he and Clarence faced to complete their work in the valley.

Carmelita begged Janelle. "Can I do it, *Mamá*?"

Janelle turned to Chuck, her smile replaced by a wary frown. "A climbing competition? Aren't those for adults?"

"The best sport climbers in the world these days are teenagers. Their strength-to-weight ratios are off the charts thanks to the fact that—" he encircled Carmelita's upper arm with a finger and thumb "—they're so skinny."

"But that's teenagers you're talking about."

"I'll be thirteen in December," Carmelita reminded her mother.

"I don't want to think about that."

"Uncle Clarence said I'll be driving in two years, with my learner's permit."

Janelle glared at her brother, who ducked his head, hiding a grin. She turned back to Carmelita. "Remember what we always say, *m'hija*. Cars are weapons. You have to be very careful with them. And two years is a long time. A very long time." She shot another glowering look at Clarence, her brows furrowed.

He raised his hands in defense. "Carm's getting to be a big girl. Like it or not, *hermana*, two years from now, your daughter's gonna have a steering wheel in her hands. She's gonna be one weaponized young lady."

When the furrow between Janelle's brows deepened, Clarence raised his hands farther, his palms out. "Just talking the truth to you." He lifted his shoulders close to his ears in an exaggerated shrug. "What can I say?"

Janelle turned her back on her brother and crossed her arms in front of her.

"Carm was a natural up there," Chuck told her.

She shifted her elbows, loosening her arms. "Do they actually have a kids' section?"

"Maybe. Either way, though, I'd say she should enter the open division. The way she climbed that tower just now, you never know."

Carmelita's face glowed, but Janelle pursed her lips. "You mean, where she'd be going up against anybody and everybody?"

"All the other female climbers, anyway."

"But that was the first time she's ever climbed anything in her whole life. You just got her the helmet and climbing shoes last week."

Chuck glanced up at the tower. "This is why we got them for her. Besides, I can't imagine she'd have any chance of winning. Although I will say, climbing isn't as much about experience and repetitive practice as other sports. It's a matter of body control and sense of balance—which, clearly, Carm's got by the bucketful. From what I just saw, I don't think she'd have anything to be ashamed of."

Carmelita beamed at him. "Really?"

Chuck cupped the back of her head in his hand and looked into her luminous, hazel eyes. "Really."

"Cool," Rosie declared. She jigged at her sister's side, her arms swinging. "You should do it for sure, Carm."

Janelle rested her hand over Chuck's at the back of Carmelita's head. "You really think you want to try it?"

Carmelita nodded, bouncing up and down on her toes.

"You won't be sad when you lose?"

"*If* she loses," Chuck said.

"No," Carmelita told her mother. "I won't. I promise."

Rosie chimed in. "But I'll be sad for her. Would that be okay, *Mamá*?"

The corners of Janelle's mouth ticked upward and her face softened. "Okay," she said. "You guys win."

At the base of the tower, Jimmy tied a re-woven figure eight into the end of the climbing rope with a well-practiced flip of his fingers. He clipped the loop into his harness. Still exchanging small talk with Bernard, he gave the rope a tug, assuring it ran from his waist, up through the pulley at the top of the tower, and back down to the auto-belay mechanism.

Faded tattoos purpled Jimmy's sinewy forearms below the short sleeves of his plaid, cotton shirt. A long, braided beard, cinnamon cut with silver, curved outward from his jaw like a scorpion's tail. Stringy, gray-streaked red hair fell to his shoulders from the back of the battered straw cowboy hat he wore low over his eyes like a country singer. His brown canvas carpenter pants clung to his narrow waist, and the top buttons of his shirt were undone, revealing a thick nest of chest hair. A red bandanna—his signature style statement for as long as Chuck had known him—was knotted around his neck.

"Show us what you can do, Jimmy," Chuck called to him.

"You're the man," Bernard cheered from behind the line of boulders. He tapped the sides of his legs with his hands, a quick rat-a-tat beat. "Let's see how much gas you've got left in the old tank."

Bernard's pasty face and jowly cheeks spoke of his current life as an office-bound attorney for a downtown San Francisco law firm, as did his trendy, turquoise-framed glasses. His ample waistline pressed at his pleated khaki shorts and short-sleeved dress shirt, while his short brown hair showed only a hint of gray.

He turned to Carmelita. "And you're the climbing-est girl of them all," he congratulated her. He continued to tap his legs with his hands and counted off in time with the taps, "One . . . two . . . three, four, five. You're the girl who's got the jive."

Jimmy settled his fingertips on two holds above his head. "You guys are next," he called over his shoulder to Chuck and Bernard.

"Not me," Chuck said. "No way."

"I'm ground-based these days," said Bernard.

"You're scared you can't do it anymore," Jimmy chided.

"You got that right," the two of them said in unison.

Jimmy tightened his grip on the holds at the base of the climbing tower and lifted himself off the ground. He ascended the large, easy-to-grasp holds on the lower portion of the tower smoothly, the belay mechanism automatically taking up the slack in the rope as he climbed. Each of his moves was precise, his fingers set, his feet poised on holds beneath him. He angled left and right, scaling the wall with no apparent strain, his decades of climbing experience evident.

He passed the halfway point on the tower and reached above his head for a small hold thirty feet off the ground. Only two of his fingertips fit atop the tiny protrusion, which sloped outward, providing little purchase.

He grunted as he transferred his weight to the hold, revealing his first sign of effort. His knuckles turned white as he clung to the tower. Then his fingertips slipped from the hold and he fell.

The ratchet in the auto-belay mechanism should have kicked in, catching him when he dropped no more than a few inches. Instead, he cartwheeled away from the wall and plummeted toward the ground, his arms and legs flailing.

He screamed as he fell, the climbing rope zipping unimpeded through the mechanical belay device bolted to the base of the tower.

2

Jimmy's scream echoed across the parking lot as he plunged headfirst toward the ground. Chuck charged forward with Janelle at his side, but they were too far back to reach Jimmy in time to break his fall.

At the last possible second, Jimmy spun himself upright and struck the gravel parking lot feet-first. The sharp *crack* of breaking bone echoed off the tower wall, followed by a howl of pain from Jimmy. He crumpled on the gravel at the base of the tower, the rope still attached to his waist. He gripped his left leg with both hands, his face contorted.

Janelle knelt at Jimmy's side while Chuck slid to a stop in the loose rocks and stood over them. Clarence and Bernard and the other onlookers formed a circle around Janelle and the fallen climber. Carmelita and Rosie peered around Chuck from where they pressed at his back.

Jimmy took quick, gasping breaths. He moaned, the sound coming from deep in his throat. Janelle slid his jeans up his leg. Chuck bit his knuckles to keep from gagging at the sight of Jimmy's foot turned sideways from his ankle at a ninety-degree angle.

"Ouch," Rosie said.

"Rosie!" Janelle scolded without looking up. Then, to the group, "Someone call 911."

Clarence plucked his phone from his pocket. "I'm on it."

"Goddammit," Jimmy muttered. He grimaced, his eyes squeezed shut.

"Appears to be a fracture and dislocation of the ankle," Janelle said. "No way to reset it here."

She shifted to put her knees on either side of Jimmy's head, bracing his neck. "Do you hurt anywhere else?" she asked him.

"I think my leg took all my weight," he said through clenched teeth. He exhaled, his breath morphing into a groan.

"Good."

"Good?" His pupils glinted between his slitted lids as he squinted up at her. He breathed hard and fast, chuffing like a steam engine.

Clarence jabbed at the face of his phone. "I can't believe it. No service."

"That's not a surprise," the climbing tower attendant said as he arrived from the tiny A-frame building set between the parking lot and campground that served as the Camp 4 office. "It's okay, though. I called in on the campground radio."

The shriek of a siren sounded from up the valley in the direction of Yosemite Village. The number of gawkers around Jimmy grew as campers arrived from their sites beneath the firs and black oaks towering over the campground.

Members of the Yosemite Search and Rescue team, stationed in a ring of canvas tents west of Camp 4 in the heart of the valley during the park's busy summer climbing season, arrived at a jog. They wore T-shirts, shorts, flip-flops, and ball caps bearing the YOSAR logo. The rescuers were in their twenties and early thirties, tanned and buff, mostly males with a smattering of females. They elbowed their way to the front of the circle as an ambulance turned from Northside Drive into the Camp 4 parking lot. The vehicle braked to a stop next to the climbing tower, raising a cloud of dust.

From where she knelt at Jimmy's head, Janelle reached to rest a hand on the storied climber's tattooed forearm. "They're here."

"Thank God," Jimmy said through compressed lips. Sweat beaded his brow.

The onlookers fell back as a pair of attendants approached from the ambulance.

"I'll go with him," Bernard told Chuck.

"Where will they take him?"

When Bernard shrugged three times in a row, raising and lowering his shoulders in quick succession, a YOSAR team member said, "He won't go to the valley clinic, that's for sure. I bet they'll take him straight to Merced. Believe me, they know the way."

"His foot sure was twisted," Rosie said thoughtfully, a finger pressed to her chin.

She walked with Chuck, Janelle, Carmelita, and Clarence on the gravel path through the middle of Camp 4, returning with them to their campsite from the climbing tower. West of the campground, the wail of the ambulance siren died away, marking the vehicle's departure as it bore Jimmy and Bernard down the valley.

"That is so gross," Carmelita told her sister.

"But true," Janelle said. "One of the things I've learned in my classes is that the human body can get really pretzeled in an accident."

Picturing Jimmy's injured ankle, Chuck clamped his jaw, his muscles growing tense. Thank God he'd belayed Carmelita himself; the thought of her leg mangled like Jimmy's, or worse, made his stomach queasy.

Their campsite came into view through the trees ahead. Camp 4 offered only walk-in tent sites, with vehicles restricted to the large parking lot at the campground's front entrance. Campsites were arranged side by side in long rows, accessed by pathways linking the sites to the parking lot and central bathroom. Beneath the tall pines and oaks looming overhead, the campground was open and dusty, the only ground cover a few hardy bunches of buffalo grass, with campsites in full view of one another among the tree trunks.

Chuck had erected their two-room family tent in the dark last night at the edge of their reserved research-team site, while Janelle wrestled the half-asleep girls into their pajamas, and Clarence set up his own small, solo tent. Early this morning, Chuck had hauled the last of their supplies from the pickup truck via the graveled footpath past the other campsites to their assigned site, using one of the oversized wheelbarrows provided by the campground. As his family slept, Chuck had propped open his multi-pocketed gear duffle, the words "Bender Archaeological, Inc." stenciled on both sides, and double-checked its contents for the week's work to come. He also had opened the cookstove on the picnic table and connected it to its propane tank, and had assured the latch was fastened on the metal cabinet next to the table that contained their food, as required to keep the park's notoriously nosy black bears at bay.

Carmelita had spied the climbing tower at the edge of the parking lot when she'd stepped out of the zippered family tent that morning.

"Can I climb it?" she begged Chuck, eyeing the tower through the trees. "Pleeeeeease."

He gaped at her. Carmelita rarely made such requests, particularly with such ardor.

She added, "That's why you got me my new climbing shoes, isn't it?"

He studied the fiberglass tower, rising beyond the trees at the front entrance to the campground. Only a few campers waited their turn to climb it this early in the morning. But the line was sure to grow as the day wore on and more climbers arrived in the valley for the start of the Slam tomorrow.

Janelle ducked out of the tent. "Are you okay with it?" Chuck asked her, warming to Carmelita's interest in the sport that had consumed him as a young man.

Janelle stood at Carmelita's back and combed her fingers through her daughter's long, sleep-tangled hair. "You want to be like Chuck, do you?" she asked Carmelita.

"Like me a long time ago," Chuck clarified.

Now, as Carmelita reached the campsite with the others in the wake of Jimmy's fall, she spoke while looking at her feet, her voice soft but firm. "I still want to do it," she said. "I still want to be in the Slam."

Chuck took Janelle's hand in his and gave it a squeeze. Carmelita's first year of middle school hadn't been all they'd hoped. Shy and reserved, Carmelita had made few friends and refused entreaties from Janelle and Chuck to try after-school clubs and sports. The good news, at least, was that she'd done well in her classes. Very well, in fact. But she'd spent a lot of her free time alone.

"You're crazy, Carm," Rosie declared. She swung her hiking boot at a stone, kicking it from the path. She teetered at the end of her kick, her foot nearly as high as her head. Only Clarence's quick grab kept her from tumbling backward to the ground.

"I was good at it," Carmelita said. "I was really good. Wasn't I?"

"That's stating the obvious," Clarence told her. "You were *estupenda* up there."

Janelle slipped her hand out of Chuck's grip and turned to him as they walked. "They'll cancel the competition because of Jimmy's accident, won't they?"

"I doubt it. People come from all over to compete in the Slam. It's turned into a big money-maker for the Camp 4 Fund. Jimmy told me last year's entry fees paid for a whole new set of gear-hauling wheelbarrows. They're already planning to use this year's proceeds to remodel the bathroom. They might even raise enough money to add showers, which they've needed forever."

Janelle slid her hand into the crook of Chuck's arm. "What happened to him back there?"

"The auto-belay device failed. They'll fix it, of course—not that Carm would use it. If she competes, I'll belay her again myself, just to be completely safe."

"Completely safe?"

"People think everything having to do with rock climbing is dangerous. But big-wall climbing and sport climbing are entirely different animals." He pointed up through a break in the trees to the top of El Capitan, rising half a mile above the valley floor. "Big-wall climbing comes with unavoidable risk. The potential for accidents on massive cliffs, here in Yosemite or anywhere else, is part of the game. There's simply too much that can go wrong on multi-day, multi-pitch climbs—sudden weather changes, equipment problems, fatigue, personality issues between team members. It's impossible to control for all of them." He aimed a thumb behind him at the tower. "But climbing on a bolted wall is one of the safest sports there is."

Clarence pooched his lips. "Despite what just happened to Jimmy?"

"Despite that," Chuck confirmed.

Janelle asked Carmelita, "You're not scared?"

Carmelita shook her head. Then she nodded. "Sorta. But that's why I want to do it."

Clarence wrapped one of his beefy arms around Carmelita's narrow shoulders, drawing her to his side. "*Esa es mi sobrina valiente*," he said. "That's my brave niece."

Janelle's fingers tightened around Chuck's arm. "*Bastante bien*," she said, acceding to Carmelita with a sigh. "As long as Chuck says it's okay."

Carmelita leaned around Clarence and grinned at Chuck, but Rosie said to her sister, "I'm telling you, Carm, you're craaaaazy." She swung her boot at another stone, sending it flying into a neighboring campsite.

"Careful," Chuck warned her. "It wasn't easy for me to reserve one of the researcher sites here. We don't want to get thrown out our very first day."

They continued along the path. In campsites on either side of them, campers prepared breakfast and arranged gear. Some organized overnight camping supplies. They packed duffle bags, tied guy lines to tent poles, and tossed sleeping bags over their tents to air the bags in the sun. Others, obviously climbers, sorted through their climbing kits. They counted out carabiners, coiled ropes on tarps, and arranged cams and bolts and quickdraws on picnic tables, grouping the pieces of milled-alloy climbing hardware by size and type. Still other Camp 4 campers were Latino families, middle-aged men and women with children who occupied sites ringed with inexpensive hoop tents. The adults' worn jeans, denim shirts, long skirts, and cafeteria-worker blouses and slacks marked them not as park visitors but park concession employees.

Block-shaped Columbia Boulder, the size of a two-story house, sat just beyond the north boundary of the campground, where it had come to rest on the valley floor after tumbling eons ago from the cliffs above. For decades, the short, demanding climbing routes up the boulder's vertical sides had provided a rope-free proving ground for Camp 4 climbers. These days, in an attempt to improve the often frayed relations between Camp 4's free-spirited climbing community and Yosemite's staid ranger staff, the park service provided free coffee and donuts to all comers every Sunday morning at the base of the boulder, where the two groups mingled and hashed out any outstanding grievances.

After so many years away, Chuck gazed around him with a sense of nostalgia. No campground in the national park system was more famous than Camp 4. From its position on the north side of Yosemite Valley, the campground had served since the 1960s as the base of climbing operations for hypercompetitive climbers bent on putting up ever more difficult routes on the valley's surrounding faces. In those early years, the original occupants of the campground included pioneering rock climbers like Yvon Chouinard, Doug Tompkins, Royal Robbins, Ron Kauk, and—among only a handful of accomplished female climbers at the time—Lynn Hill. The early Camp 4 denizens assumed mythic status as climbing grew to become a global sport. During Chuck's summers at Camp 4 decades later, the campground had remained home to an ever-changing cast of big-wall climbers, still predominantly male, all competing for the unofficial title of Best Rock Climber on Earth.

Chuck looked from side to side as he walked along the central corridor through the campground with his family. Camp 4 was a different place now than when he'd spent so much time here twenty years ago. The campground's sites were occupied by a roughly equal number of males and females, and by a far more diverse crowd as well. Rather than almost exclusively white, Camp 4's current climber occupants embodied a healthy mix of the multiethnic stewpot representative of modern-day America and the world, with Anglo as well as Asian, African American, and Latino climbers sorting piles of gear. Signaling the biggest change of all, in addition to the walk-in campsites occupied by climbers preparing for ascents and the numerous sites taken by tourists organizing camping supplies, a third of the campground's sites were occupied by park workers and their families.

As Chuck, Janelle, Clarence, and the girls passed one of the worker-occupied sites, a middle-aged Latina woman looked up from a camp stove positioned at the end of a picnic table in front of her. The smell of frying bacon wafted from a skillet on the stove. The woman looked through the steam rising from the pan, taking in Janelle, Clarence, and the girls.

"*Hola, amigos,*" she greeted them. Her deep, gravelly voice reminded Chuck of the rough, sandpapery tone shared by Rosie and Rosie's grandfather, Janelle's Mexican-immigrant father.

"*Hola*," Janelle responded.

The Latina woman went back to flipping strips of bacon in the pan with her spatula.

Janelle winked at Chuck. "You said you were bringing us to Yosemite Valley, not the South Valley. It's nice to see the diversity in the park."

In the years after their arrival in New Mexico from Juarez as newlyweds, Janelle's parents raised her and Clarence in Albuquerque's South Valley, the only neighborhood they could afford with their meager, blue-collar incomes. In her teen years, Janelle fell in with a rough set of friends, dropped out of high school, and bore Carmelita and Rosie with a local drug dealer, now deceased.

Clarence sidestepped the violent culture of the South Valley, completing high school and attending the University of New Mexico School of Anthropology. He joined Chuck's firm, Bender Archaeological, as a temporary employee after graduation. Chuck appreciated Clarence's boisterous ways, which contrasted with his own taciturn manner, and named Clarence his right-hand man on contract after contract.

When Chuck met Janelle through Clarence, their courtship led to a quick marriage and Janelle's move with the girls to Chuck's hometown, just north of the New Mexico border in Colorado's rugged San Juan Mountains.

"Looks like they're here to work instead of play, doesn't it?" Chuck said of the Latino campers. "Then again, so are we."

The site he'd reserved, one of a handful of Camp 4 sites set aside for teams conducting research in the valley, abutted the far west end of the campground. Next to the site was the campsite reserved by Jimmy, using his many personal connections in the park, for himself and the other men attending the reunion.

Besides the two solo pup tents already erected by Jimmy and Bernard, the reunion site was empty.

The YOSAR team's steepled white tents ringed a small meadow outside the campground to the west, beyond the Bender Archaeological and reunion campsites. Cruiser bikes rested against wooden platforms on which the search-and-rescue team's wall tents stood, and an array of lawn chairs faced each other in a circle in the center of the meadow.

Of the former Yosemite Valley climbers who had accepted Jimmy's emailed invitation to attend the reunion, Chuck considered himself the furthest outlier. In the years after his graduation from the Fort Lewis College School of Archaeology in Durango, he'd focused on building Bender Archaeological into a viable archaeological services contractor. Only during breaks between projects had he driven to the valley to climb with the others, freeing himself for a week or two from the ongoing stress of winning and working his contracts.

Bender Archaeological started out as, and largely remained, a one-man operation. Chuck was the only full-time employee of his firm. He hired part-timers like Clarence to complete specific projects as necessary, and maintained only superficial contacts with other archaeologists, a fact that had served him well professionally. By working his contracts on his own, fame within the archaeological community for the many discoveries he'd unearthed over the years accrued directly to him. That fame led to the stream of work that had flowed his way month in and month out over the years—straight through to the intriguing contract from the Indigenous Tribespeople Foundation that brought him to the valley this week.

Chuck knew his ability to create and run his own business derived from his isolated upbringing in Durango as the only child of an entirely absent father and mostly absent mother. It was as a direct result of that lonely upbringing, in fact, that he'd so appreciated the camaraderie of the tight circle of fellow climbers with whom he'd based out of Camp 4 and climbed the cliffs around the valley each summer as a young man.

Chuck stopped in the path with Janelle, the girls, and Clarence when brakes squealed on Northside Drive outside Camp 4. A large truck pulling a flatbed trailer stopped on the shoulder of the road adjacent to the campground. Three dozen tourists in broad-brimmed hats and long-sleeved sunblock shirts sat in rows of bench seats bolted the length of the trailer. A tour guide in walnut slacks, beige shirt, and a billed cap faced her charges from her perch in a tall chair affixed to the trailer bed behind the truck's cab.

The guide addressed the tourists through a microphone hooked over her ear and running from the side of her head to her mouth. Her voice issued from speakers mounted on the cab's roof as the tourists peered through the trees at the campsites.

"Before you is Camp 4," the guide announced, her amplified voice reaching her tourist charges as well as every camper in the campground. "For decades, the best rock climbers in the world have made names for themselves climbing demanding routes around Yosemite Valley while based out of this camping area. Camp 4 is considered the birthplace of big-wall rock climbing, and was added to the National Register of Historic Places in 2003."

The tour guide adjusted the arm of her microphone at her cheek. "Today, Camp 4 is more than just a climber hangout. Climbing teams still use the campground as their temporary living quarters between ascents. But they face stiff competition for campsites from non-climbing park visitors and seasonal employees in the valley. To secure first-come, first-served sites in the campground, would-be campers begin lining up as early as three o'clock in the morning—about the time the infamous, hard-partying Camp 4 climbers of old would have been going to sleep."

Her spiel complete, the guide tapped the cab of the truck behind her. The tour vehicle jerked into gear and rumbled on down the road.

"You're famous," Janelle told Chuck as they resumed their walk.

"I think she said 'infamous.' I like that better."

Rosie hopped from foot to foot when they reached their campsite. "I have to go, go, go," she said, her voice strained and her face turning purple.

"I'll take her," Carmelita offered.

"*Gracias*," Janelle said.

Rosie and Carmelita set off for the bathroom at a jog.

Clarence sat sideways in a hammock he'd tied between the trunks of two trees next to his tent. He dug his toe into the dirt to swing himself back and forth, using the woven-mesh sling as a chair. "I'm impressed," he said to Janelle. He rested the back of his head against the side of the hammock as he swung. "You're letting Carm climb tomorrow."

"She just . . . she looked so good up there. Like she was lighter than air."

Clarence patted his round belly. "Lucky for her, she takes after you, not me."

"Ahoy," a tall, lanky man Chuck's age called out as he approached on the gravel path from the front of the campground. He pushed one of Camp 4's shiny aluminum wheelbarrows loaded with duffle bags. "Where is everybody?" he asked Chuck, stopping in front of the reunion campsite next door.

"Hello to you, too, Ponch," Chuck said. He walked over and offered his hand. "Been a long time."

Ponch Stilwell settled the legs of the wheelbarrow in the dirt at the edge of the site and took Chuck's hand. "Twenty-some years," he agreed.

Ponch's high forehead gave way to thin tendrils of blond hair combed from the front of his head to the back. His black jeans, polo shirt, and loafers were far removed from the beaded leather vest, woven headband, and silk drawstring pants he'd sported in Camp 4 twenty years ago. Back then, as the group's hippy wannabe, he'd given himself over to mystical dances, transcendent chants, and spooky fortune tellings, his Buddhist thumb cymbals, dried-gourd maracas, and deck of tarot cards always close at hand.

Chuck briefed Ponch on Jimmy's accident, concluding, "He's on the way by ambulance to the hospital in Merced."

"Geez. What a way to start the reunion." Ponch rested his palm on the handle of his gear-filled wheelbarrow. "Did Thorpe go with him?"

"Bernard went. I've got his cell number to check in with him when they get there."

Ponch turned to the reunion campsite and surveyed the two tents. "Where is he, then?"

"Thorpe? I haven't seen him yet. Jimmy and Bernard were the only ones here when I showed up with my family last night. You're the first to get here this morning."

"He should be here by now."

"The way I understand it, everybody's trickling in throughout the day today."

"No," Ponch insisted. "You don't get it. Thorpe was supposed to come in at dawn. Right here, to Camp 4." His eyes roamed the deserted campsite. "Jesus," he moaned. "What have I done?"

"Say what?" Chuck asked, bewildered.

"Thorpe's dead," Ponch said, his eyes clouded and voice shaking. "And it's all my fault."

29

3

Chuck took a backward step, the muscles on either side of his spine drawing up tight. "What in God's name are you talking about?"

"The cards." Blood drained from Ponch's face. He pounded his cupped palm with his fist. "I should have told him."

"Your tarot cards?"

Ponch nodded. "I should've spoken up."

"They told you something might happen to Thorpe?"

"Not might. *Would.* Something awful would happen to him, at the hands of someone else."

Chuck's back muscles loosened. "I can't believe you're still into those things." He shook his head. "You're saying your cards are telling you Thorpe is in some sort of trouble, is that right?"

"I laid them out a few days ago, alone at my place. I figured I'd get a sense of what was up with him since he'd asked me to be with him this morning when he flew."

Chuck raised his arms, imitating a soaring bird. "You mean . . . ?"

"That's exactly what I mean. In his wingsuit."

Chuck's back again grew tense. Tarot cards or not, he knew the risks of Thorpe's chosen sport.

"The cards told me he was in danger," Ponch said. "I did a Two Paths spread. The major Arcana cards were fine, but the Death card was upright instead of reversed. The danger was clear as could be, but I convinced myself not to say anything to him. I mean, come on—he's a wingsuit flier."

"Danger is what he does," Chuck concurred.

"I figured I hadn't heard anything yet because of the bad

reception in the valley." Ponch dug his phone from his pocket, punched its face, and turned it to Chuck. "See? Nothing." Again, he scanned the empty campsite. "But he's not here." He pointed skyward, toward the head of the valley. "I was with him at sunrise on Glacier Point."

"He jumped?"

"He flew." Ponch's jaw muscles twitched, his face still white. "He dropped off the point into the shadows and then out across the valley. I lost sight of him pretty quick." He stared up through the trees, where the valley's south wall showed between outstretched branches. "He planned to shoot Sentinel Gap."

Chuck sucked a breath. "The notch in the ridge?"

Ponch lifted and dropped his chin, a grim up-and-down movement. "If conditions were right, he was going to fly through it, then swing around and pop his chute to land here, in the parking lot. It was supposed to be a big surprise. He figured the helmet-cam footage of his fly-in to the reunion would make for a great online post. But it all depended on the wind—shooting the gap, landing here, the whole thing. If the winds were too strong after he jumped, he could have landed anywhere, even outside the valley altogether." Ponch looked around him. "But if he's not here by this—"

A male voice broke in from behind Ponch. "Chuck Bender?"

A park ranger approached on the path through the campground. The ranger carried a metal clipboard thick with papers. He looked eerily familiar to Chuck. The uniformed man was in his early thirties, his regulation gray shirt and evergreen slacks crisply pressed. A flashlight, walkie-talkie, and holstered pistol hung from his black leather belt. Buzz-cut hair showed beneath the circular brim of his straw, Smokey Bear ranger hat. He was clean shaven, his piercing gray eyes set close on either side of a long, hooked nose.

The broad-shouldered climbing tower attendant walked

with the ranger, their feet crunching on the graveled path.

Chuck lifted a hand. "That's me."

The two men stopped next to Ponch. The tag pinned to the ranger's chest above his brass badge was inscribed with the name Owen Hutchins. Chuck stared at the engraved name. He should have known—the hooked nose; the eyes the same slate gray color as the ranger's shirt.

"Would you come with us, please?" the ranger, Owen, asked Chuck without introducing himself.

"I'm pretty busy right now. What is it you need?"

Owen indicated the tower attendant beside him with a tilt of his head. "Alden here tells me you belayed a youngster on the climbing wall immediately preceding the accident. I tracked down your name on the campground register."

"I'm not sure I—"

"Did you or did you not," the ranger broke in, his face set, "adjust the auto-belay mechanism when you tied yourself into the climbing rope?" He tucked the bulky clipboard beneath his arm, his eyes on Chuck.

"I didn't touch the auto-belay," Chuck said, meeting the ranger's gaze. "As light as my daughter is, I was afraid it wouldn't kick in if she fell. All I did was release the rope and belay her off the top pulley myself."

The attendant, Alden, said, "You're supposed to let me detach the rope from the auto-belay for you."

While Chuck had released the rope from the device and set up his own belay for Carmelita, Alden had chatted with the female climber on the far side of the line of boulders, his gaze fixed on her bikini top.

Chuck looked the attendant up and down. "You were otherwise occupied, if you recall."

Alden's eyes darted away.

Owen stepped forward. "I'm performing a preliminary Q&A

to determine if a special agent from the Investigative Services Bureau should be assigned to investigate the incident."

"A special agent?"

"The National Park Service takes all accidents that occur in its parks seriously. The agent, if assigned, will determine whether an SAIT should be formed."

"An SAIT?" Chuck asked, repeating the letters.

"A Serious Accident Investigation Team."

"A whole team of investigators? Sounds pretty over the top."

"The park service will decide what's over the top and what's not." Owen pulled the clipboard from under his arm. "You claim you did not turn off the auto-belay device, is that correct?"

"I just told you, I didn't touch it. I had no reason to."

"But you took it upon yourself to—"

"Look," Chuck cut in. "I belayed my daughter myself, that's all. People do that all the time on sport walls." He turned to Alden and waited until the tower attendant met his gaze. "You know I'm right . . . Alden, is it? Everybody knows. That's why you didn't have any problem with what I did." Chuck pivoted back to Owen. "The only thing I touched was the climbing rope."

"Which was attached to the auto-belay mechanism."

Chuck's voice quivered. "I simply released the rope from the device to belay my daughter myself."

"I want you to show me exactly what you did."

"I already told you what I did."

"There's no need to get defensive, Mr. Bender."

Chuck felt his face growing hot. "All I did was—"

Owen held up a palm. "Please." He turned sideways, his black boots grinding in the path's chunky stones, and indicated the direction back through the campground to the parking lot with an outstretched hand. "If you'll come this way."

Chuck said to Ponch, "I'll be right back. We'll figure out what to do next."

Falling into step with the ranger and tower attendant, Chuck bit down on the inside of his cheek to control his anger. There was more going on here than just Owen Hutchins' undue suspicion regarding the auto-belay device, and Chuck suspected what it was.

"Here we are," Owen announced, halting at the base of the climbing tower with Chuck and Alden.

Chuck looked past the tower. Sedans and SUVs glittered beneath the sun in the parking lot, the oversized Bender Archaeological pickup truck among them. Presumably, Thorpe had planned to end his dawn flight by landing in one of the open stretches between the rows of parked cars. Instead, Chuck assured himself, Thorpe had touched down safely somewhere else. As for Ponch's overwrought concerns? Nothing more than tarot-card-inspired paranoia.

"Let's take a look at the auto-belay mechanism together," Owen suggested.

Alden squatted next to the device, a metal cylinder six inches around and eighteen inches long bolted to the climbing tower two feet above the ground. A wire cable ran from the top of the cylinder to a pulley affixed to a steel stanchion extending three feet from the top of the tower. "The disable switch is under here," Alden said, pointing to the base of the cylinder.

"Did you check it after Jimmy fell?" Owen asked him.

"Yes."

"And?"

"It was turned off, deactivated."

"Meaning?"

"The rope had no tension. With the device disabled, the rope spools in, but the ratchet doesn't engage when a climber falls." He pointed at the top of the wall. "It's used for retrieving the rope at the end of a climbing session."

"But if it's turned off when someone is climbing . . . ?"

Alden aimed a thumb at the ground and whistled through his two front teeth, a single, descending note, imitating the sound of a falling bomb. "That's why the switch is underneath the cylinder, where it can't be turned off by mistake."

Owen turned to Chuck. "You say you didn't touch it?"

Chuck thrust out his chin. "I keep telling you, I released the rope and tied myself into it. That's all I did."

Owen asked Alden, "How closely did you observe his actions?"

"Not very," Alden admitted.

Chuck pointed past the line of boulders. "He was back there, under the trees."

"Is that true?" Owen asked the tower attendant.

"I was making sure no one cut in line," Alden said, his face coloring. "People get pissed off when that happens."

"You say you found the auto-belay in the off position when you checked it after the accident?"

"Right."

"So someone had to have turned it off."

"Or," Chuck said, "it's broken and it switched off by itself."

Owen appraised Chuck with cold eyes. "That's possible, I suppose." He faced Alden. "Whatever the case, we can't allow the Yosemite Slam to take place tomorrow without knowing what happened."

"I've got an extra auto-belay along," the attendant said, aiming his square jaw at the semitruck attached to the portable tower's flatbed trailer. The words "Sacramento Rock Gym" emblazoned the front door of the truck in gold letters above the stenciled silhouette of a climber leaning back from the face of a cliff. "I'll switch out the old one and test everything to make sure we're good to go."

"Correction," Owen said. "I'll be the one who will test everything, before the start of the Slam tomorrow morning. If there's any question things aren't right, I'll shut the whole competition down. Understood?"

"Sure," said Alden. "But Jimmy . . ." His voice trailed off.

The ranger snapped, "He's the whole reason I'm doing this. An hour ago, Jimmy O'Reilly, the man everybody in Yosemite Valley knows as Camp 4's best friend, nearly died on your climbing wall. My job is to figure out what happened, to recommend whether an ISB special agent should be assigned, whether we need an SAIT. The way I see it, either something made the auto-belay mechanism turn off—" he directed his gray eyes at Chuck "—or someone turned it off."

Chuck raised his hands with his palms out. "I'm as upset about what happened as you are. Jimmy and I go way back. I'm here for the reunion."

"The reunion," Owen repeated, his brows drawing together. "Of course."

Chuck lowered his hands. "I assume you've heard about it."

"Jimmy mentioned it to me. I know all about you and your old friends. My father was a ranger here before me."

As Chuck already had deduced. "So you're Owen, Jr."

Time unspooled in Chuck's mind. Owen Hutchins, Sr., had been one of a handful of rangers known unofficially as the Yosemite mafia. Allegedly, the small group of rangers had formed a secret, unspoken fraternity dedicated to ridding Yosemite National Park of visitors such as hippies and drug users considered less than desirable by mafia rangers, who even had been accused of illegally bribing informants to implicate suspected drug dealers in the valley. Nowhere in the Yosemite mafia's vision of the valley had there been room for the unshorn, dirtbag climbers who populated Camp 4.

"Dad retired a long time ago," Owen, Jr., said. "He died a year later. I've been a ranger here for five years now."

Of the members of the Yosemite mafia, Hutchins, Sr., had been known for his particularly intense devotion to the cause. "You probably know your father wasn't the most popular guy in the park," Chuck said.

Owen's eyes grew flinty. "He did his job, just like I do mine."

"He rode climbers in the valley pretty hard, especially those of us who hung around with Jimmy O'Reilly and Thorpe Alstad. The way I remember it, he wrote us up for pretty much anything he could think of—noise infractions, open container violations, campsite fee payments that were just a few minutes late." Chuck glanced past the tower where Thorpe had planned to land in the parking lot; Ponch was waiting back at the reunion campsite.

Owen's lips flattened. "He kept guys like you in line. He had no choice. It's the same now. Four million people visit Yosemite Valley each summer, with more coming every year, all of them trying to squeeze into a place not much bigger than an over-sized bathtub. The only way that works is with a lot of planning, a lot of control."

"Planning I'm okay with," Chuck said. "But control? A lot of people thought your dad was a total control freak."

"He kept a lid on things. That was his job. When something bad happened, like with Jimmy this morning, he jumped on it right away, hard. That's the right thing to do—get it figured out before the evidence disappears."

"Evidence? It sounds like you think someone was out to get Jimmy."

Owen's face hardened. "I don't work with what I think, I work with what I know. And what I know is that sport climbing on walls with bolted holds is, or should be, one-hundred-per-cent safe. The YOSAR team rescues people off the big walls around the valley all summer long. But sport climbing? Nothing should go wrong with that." The ranger looked at the auto-belay mechanism at the base of the tower, then said to Chuck, "Maybe the switch is faulty. Maybe it turned off by itself somehow. That's possible, sure. But the odds of it happening? Astronomical. Whereas, the idea that somebody turned off the switch by mistake—or maybe, even, on purpose?—that's what makes the most sense to me."

"I understand you need to look into what happened to Jimmy," Chuck told the ranger. "I get that." He extended a stiff finger at the auto-belay device. "But there's no need for me to examine that thing with you. I didn't do anything to it, and, to be perfectly honest, I resent any insinuation that I did."

He spun on his heels and strode past the small A-frame office at the entrance to the campground and back into Camp 4. Halfway to the campsite, he came up short.

Owen Hutchins, Jr., was convinced someone—specifically, it seemed, Chuck—had deactivated the auto-belay mechanism on the climbing tower in an attempt to kill Jimmy. But what if someone had switched off the device earlier—not before Jimmy's climb, but before *Carmelita's* climb? That someone could not have predicted Chuck would detach the rope from the mechanism and belay Carmelita on his own.

Chuck gritted his teeth. No one who knew the ins and outs of an auto-belay device could possibly have anything against twelve-year-old Carmelita. Rather, if the mechanism had been turned off before her climb, it was because someone had it in for Chuck—and had come at him by attempting to harm his family.

4

An icy band tightened around Chuck's midsection. Who, possibly, could be out to get him? With the question came the immediate answer: nobody.

He was here to investigate a pair of killings in the valley that had occurred in 1852. No one could be worried about what he might discover about the killings more than a century and a half later. Nor could he think of any potential enemy he might have made during the summers he'd climbed in the park, particularly someone still carrying a grudge after all these years.

A beam of morning sun broke through the trees, warming his back. The scent of fried bacon drifted through the campground.

He popped his tongue off the roof of his mouth. Other than the climbers preceding Carmelita, he couldn't recall anyone coming near the tower before her turn on the wall, nor did he remember anyone other than Alden approaching the base of the tower after her ascent.

He resumed his walk through the campground. Just because Owen Hutchins, Jr., appeared to be a conspiracy theorist of the first order didn't mean Chuck had to succumb to such irrationality himself.

Jimmy's fall from the climbing tower was an accident, simple as that. There was no evil scheme aimed at Chuck or Jimmy or anyone else. And as for Thorpe—it was time, right now, to learn where he'd flown.

* * *

Janelle and Clarence stood with Chuck in the reunion campsite and listened to Ponch.

"I caught a red-eye into Fresno from LAX and met Thorpe at Glacier Point before dawn," Ponch explained to the three of them. "After he jumped, I drove into the valley. I kept trying to reach him on his phone. They say the signals bounce all over the place off the cliffs, so places in the valley that have five bars of service one minute have none the next. The couple of times I did get through, there was no answer." He held up his phone. "I'm still trying, and still nothing."

"Did you feel any gusts of wind after he jumped?" Chuck asked. He was no expert on wingsuit flying, but he knew that even a slight breeze would have been enough for Thorpe to abandon his planned flight through the granite-walled notch in Sentinel Ridge, and that stronger gusts might have forced him to seek calmer winds over the Sierra foothills outside the valley altogether before pulling his ripcord and parachuting to the ground. Had that been the case, Thorpe would have landed in a meadow somewhere outside the park to the west, perhaps far from a road—in which case, he might still be making his way to the nearest highway.

"I know what you're thinking," Ponch said. "But when he caught enough wind to take flight, he didn't swing out over the valley. He turned and aimed straight for the ridge. He dropped into the shadows at that point and that was the last I saw of him."

Chuck exhaled, jetting air between his lips. "That's where we've got to go, then."

Ponch nodded, his gaze downcast.

"Should we report it?" Chuck asked him.

Ponch looked up. "It'll go viral the instant we do. If he flew out of the valley and hasn't been able to contact us yet, he'll kill us for damaging his brand."

Janelle's eyes narrowed. "His brand?"

"That's what he lives for," Ponch explained. "His brand, his image."

Chuck said, "From what I hear, that's *all* he lives for."

Clarence raised a hand to break into the conversation. "You're not going to call anyone?"

"If we don't find anything up on the ridge," said Chuck, "and we still haven't heard from him . . ."

". . . then," Ponch finished, "it'll be time to put out an APB."

Janelle asked, "You're going to look for him yourselves?"

"Our very own mission," Ponch confirmed.

"You mean, search-and-rescue mission?"

Ponch nodded.

Janelle faced Chuck. "I'm coming with you. With my paramedic kit."

Chuck thought about Thorpe's plan to fly through Sentinel Gap, and the fact that Thorpe had turned toward the ridge before Ponch had lost sight of him. "Good idea."

"Clarence can stay with the girls." She turned to her brother. "Right?"

"*Por seguro*," Clarence said.

"You understand, though," Chuck said to Janelle, "we probably won't find anything."

"I hope to God we don't," Ponch said, a tremor entering his voice. "But that's not what the cards told me."

They left the campground after changing into lightweight hiking pants and long-sleeved cotton shirts. The already-hot mid-morning sun promised a blazing afternoon to come. Chuck and Ponch carried daypacks weighted by bottles of water. Janelle shouldered the medical-kit backpack she'd outfitted piece by piece over the last few months as she neared the completion of her coursework.

They crossed the road outside the campground when a break in traffic presented itself, then traversed the pedestrian bridge over the Merced River. The stream, low and calm in late summer, flowed beneath the bridge on its winding journey down the valley.

They hurried across Southside Drive and through a parking lot filled with cars to the start of Four Mile Trail at the base of Sentinel Ridge. A topo map tacked behind plexiglass on a signboard showed the trail climbing up and around the ridge on the south side of the valley to an overlook of Sentinel Falls, and on and farther up from there to the trail's end at Glacier Point, four steep, switchbacking miles from where they stood at the head of the trail.

"Thorpe wanted to make a statement," Ponch said as they set out from the trailhead. "He had this whole picture in his head of how great it would be to drop in on the reunion from out of the ether."

Janelle took the lead, Chuck hiked in the middle, and Ponch brought up the rear.

"But no one would have been awake to see him," Chuck said.

"He wanted it to be a surprise, unannounced. He was counting on a big viewer bump from posting the video online."

"I take it you've stayed in contact with him over the years?"

"I've been one of his YouTube followers forever. I've always been fascinated by his flying. He didn't miss a beat after he and Jimmy had their big split. The Pied Piper of Yosemite, they call him."

"'Big split'?"

"You know all about what a fixture the two of them became in the valley after the rest of us got on with our lives, right? They put up new routes on El Cap and Half Dome all the way into their forties. It wasn't until age finally caught up with them and they couldn't keep up with the younger climbers anymore that they went their separate ways. To hear Thorpe tell it—which he did online, regularly and loudly—Jimmy went over to the dark side. Jimmy and Thorpe had prided themselves on being the most rebellious Yosemite climbers ever. They went *mano a mano* with the rangers, protesting route restrictions, fighting bolting regulations, leading rallies in favor of limiting the number of tourists allowed in the valley in the summer months. Then, about the time the old-school Yosemite mafia rangers were giving way to a younger, more personable bunch, Jimmy flipped. He became an unofficial spokesman for what he called the new face of the climbing community, one that worked with, instead of against, the park and the rangers. He said his goal was to make sure there always would be room for climbers and climbing in the valley along with the increasing gazillions of tourists mobbing the place. He really threw himself into supporting Camp 4 in particular."

The trail climbed through a thick stand of pines above Sentinel Creek. In minutes, Ponch was breathing hard. Even so, he kept up with Janelle as she took long strides up the trail, passing slower groups of hikers, her orange paramedic-kit backpack high on her shoulders.

Where the trail climbed through a cliff band, Chuck followed her up a short flight of hand-hewn stone steps. "Didn't I see Jimmy on Facebook or YouTube or somewhere a year or so ago?" he asked Ponch. "In nice clothes, no less?"

"Yep. The footage bounced around online for a while. He attended the park superintendent's holiday gala." Ponch drew a deep breath after every few words. "He said he was willing to do whatever it took, including renting a tuxedo, to work with the park on behalf of climbers' rights in the valley."

"But Thorpe went the other way?"

"He's always considered himself the ultimate rebel, to the

point of being pretty uppity about it. It's part of his persona."

"His brand, you mean."

"Yeah, that. After the rest of us moved on, Jimmy and Thorpe needed each other for the climbs they still wanted to complete. After they split, though, Thorpe, being Thorpe, wasn't about to devote his time to anything that benefited anything or anyone but himself. With his big-time climbing days done, he had to find something else to keep his name in the public eye and hang onto as many of his sponsorships as he could."

"So he started flying."

"It turned out to be perfect for him. Instead of fighting gravity to climb cliffs, he put on a wingsuit and used gravity on the way down instead. Plus, wingsuit flying turned out to be ideal for the internet. He started flying at the beginning of the extreme-sport craze, when helmet cams were brand new. All his videos play up the rebel thing, which his viewers love. He capitalizes on the fact that it's illegal to fly wingsuits in Yosemite. His most famous clips are the ones where he lands out in the open and gets arrested. When he had himself filmed while reporting to jail the first time—accompanied by one of his ever-present babes, of course—his viewer numbers went through the roof. That video spurred other fliers, all of them a lot younger than him, to come to Yosemite and try to outdo him with their own flights."

"I assume that's where his Pied Piper nickname came from."

"It came later, actually, when the younger fliers started getting killed—or killing themselves, as Thorpe would say—by trying increasingly dangerous stunts. 'I'm still here,' became Thorpe's tagline after each of his flights, while the body count built up around him. The rangers blamed him for the young fliers' deaths. They said he set a bad example. But he kept flying, and the rangers got more and more frustrated with him until, finally, they zapped him with a Taser after one of his flights. The whole incident was caught on video by an onlooker, including the part where, after Thorpe was tasered and fell to the ground, he jumped to his feet and announced, 'I'm still here!' while the rangers led him away. The video went nuts online."

From in front of Chuck, Janelle said, "So Thorpe and Jimmy went in opposite directions."

"They're not shy about it, either," Ponch replied. "They trade barbs on their Twitter feeds, rip at each other on their YouTube channels. It's a very public catfight."

"But Jimmy invited Thorpe to the reunion," Janelle noted.

"Of course. They're smart guys. You don't survive for long in Yosemite Valley if you're not. Their feud keeps their names in lights. I'm sure both of them will play it up big time this weekend. It wouldn't surprise me, in fact, if that's not part of the reason Jimmy decided to get all of us together in the first place."

Janelle rounded a switchback in the trail and stopped. She looked down at Chuck and Ponch, who halted on the stretch of trail below. "What, exactly, is wingsuit flying, anyway?" she asked.

Ponch hunched forward, breathing hard, his hands on his hips. "It's pretty much just what it sounds like," he said. "Fliers jump off cliffs, bridges, skyscrapers, that sort of thing. They fall straight down until their wings fill with air and they're transformed from falling rocks into flying squirrels."

"Except," Chuck added, "they're not really flying at all. They're always going down."

"But in controlled fashion," Ponch said, straightening as his breathing calmed. "They're gliding while they fall. They're able to turn and adjust their flights and complete maneuvers until they get close to the ground, at which point they parachute in for a landing."

"Sounds dangerous," Janelle said.

"It's extremely dangerous. Or, it was, then not so much, and now, today, it's dangerous all over again."

"How's that?"

"In its first years, wingsuit flying was one hundred percent fatal. The first flier sewed some cloth between his arms and legs and jumped off the Eiffel Tower straight to his death. Other early fliers met the same fate. Then somebody had the bright idea of substituting airfoils for cloth wings. The foils—layers of fabric held apart by plastic rods—fill with air at high speeds and create lift. This was in the 1990s. All of a sudden, winged fliers could actually, in a sense, fly while they fell. The foils gave them a glide ratio of two to one, even two point five to one in perfect conditions."

"Glide ratio?"

"How long they could stay in the air. A two-to-one glide ratio means fliers move forward two feet for every foot they descend."

"So airfoils made the sport safe."

"For a while, anyway. Fliers could glide for long distances and control their speed and direction. The sport really took off."

"But then . . . ?"

"They got bored. By definition, wingsuit fliers are adrenaline junkies. And with so many fliers like Thorpe trying to make names for themselves, the ante kept going up." Ponch pulled a liter of water from a side pouch of his daypack, unscrewed the top, and took a swig. "It's testosterone-plus with them, the men as well as the few women fliers. It didn't take long for someone to come up with the idea of proximity flying. Pretty soon, they were all doing it, Thorpe included."

"Proximity flying?"

"That's where they do fly-bys as close as possible to stationary objects. Videos of fliers zipping within a few feet of ridges and cliffs and trees and buildings became internet sensations, and the fliers who starred in them started making real money. The whole thing became a game of can-you-top-this."

"Which is when things got dangerous again?" Janelle asked.

"Right-o. And have stayed that way ever since. There's even a world championship of proximity flying in China, where fliers complete a set course in the shortest time—or, often as not, die trying. The life expectancy from when a wingsuit flier takes up the sport until he or she dies doing it is roughly six years."

"Sounds suicidal."

"It *is* suicidal."

"But Thorpe would disagree with you."

"Thorpe Alstad is an anomaly in the flying world, the same as he was as a rock climber. When he and Jimmy climbed together, they never had accidents, never even got hurt. They said it was because of their intense focus combined with their willingness to turn back from a climb for any reason. They could do that because they were full-time climbers. They made money through their sponsorships. If a certain route didn't go one day, they could always try it again later. Amateur, part-time climbers—which is to say, all but a small handful of climbers—don't have that luxury. When they're on a route, they face the pressure of knowing their attempt probably will be their only chance at it. They push things when they shouldn't, and get in trouble as a result."

"But Thorpe has stayed alive all these years as a wingsuit flier, too," Janelle said. "That doesn't seem possible."

"He approaches each flight, especially each proximity flight, the same way he approached all his climbs with Jimmy. If things aren't perfect, he turns away." Ponch took another swallow from his bottle. "This year hasn't been a good one for him, though. He's known for his Yosemite flights. But his videos have become repetitive and his viewership is way down. The rangers don't even bother to bust him when he lands anymore. That's the worst thing they could do to him." Ponch screwed the lid back on his bottle and returned it to the pocket of his pack. "He called me a month ago saying his sponsors were threatening to

leave him. When I suggested maybe it was time to give up flying, he about shot me through the phone."

"So you helped him instead," Chuck said. "You were with
him on Glacier Point this morning."

Ponch blanched. "I shouldn't have been there. The hand
was as clear as any I've ever dealt, but I went anyway. He asked
me to support him. I agreed. It's as simple as that. I kept trying
to find a way to bring up what the cards said, but I couldn't."

"Because you know they're a bunch of hooey."

"No," Ponch said, his voice sharp. "Because I know what
people like you think."

"And people like Thorpe."

Ponch dipped his chin. "And people like Thorpe," he acceded.
He tilted his head back and studied the ridge above them.

Chuck followed Ponch's gaze. Somewhere up there was the
rock-walled gap toward which Thorpe had been aimed when
Ponch last had seen him. The sooner they got up there, the
sooner they could put to rest the hogwash about the hand of
tarot cards.

"Ready when you are," Chuck said to Janelle.

She led the way on up the footpath. Where the established
trail angled west around the base of the ridge toward Sentinel
Falls, Chuck called ahead for her to leave the path and bush-
whack straight up the mountainside. She hiked upward through
the pines, quickly outdistancing Ponch. Chuck split the difference between the two of them, anxious to reach the gap but
unwilling to leave Ponch too far behind. The mountainside
steepened as they climbed. The distance between the three of
them increased until Janelle reached a spot near the top of the
ridge where the forest gave way to bands of granite stacked one
atop another like the layers of a wedding cake.

"Follow along the base of the lowest cliff band," Chuck
yelled up to her from a hundred yards below, basing his

recommendation on his memory of the map at the trailhead. "The notch should be just ahead of you."

Janelle disappeared around a bulge in the cliff, turning sideways to slip past the trunk of a ponderosa pine tree growing close to the granite wall. Chuck reached the base of the cliff a minute later. He waited for Ponch, then led the way between the tree and cliff face, following Janelle's bootprints in the dusty soil.

A cry from Janelle reached him from around the rock outcrop ahead.

"What is it?" Chuck called to her.

"A leg." There was a long pause before she spoke again, her voice shaking. "A human leg."

5

Chuck sprinted around the base of the cliff with Ponch a step behind him. He came to an abrupt halt beside Janelle, who stood where the cliff band gave way to a sun-splashed slope of tufted grass, spindly brush, and scattered ponderosas. Granite walls boxed the slope on both sides, forming the notch in the top of the ridge known as Sentinel Gap.

The leg was wedged ten feet off the ground between the trunk and lowest branch of a ponderosa growing in the middle of the gap, thirty feet ahead. Janelle reached toward the append-age, her hands arrested in midair.

Sunlight broke through the tree's branches, speckling the human limb. The leg had ripped away from its body below the hip. A white sock and thick-soled landing shoe clad the foot. Otherwise, the leg was bare, its skin battered and bruised. Blood from a deep cut in the ankle soaked the sock and shoe. More blood from the place where the leg had torn free from its body coagulated on the pine-needle-covered ground at the base of the tree.

Chuck pressed his forearm to his mouth.

Beside Chuck, Ponch spoke, his voice trembling. "I should've stopped him."

Chuck lowered his arm. "You suggested he quit."

"He wouldn't hear it."

"He never listened to anyone when we knew him twenty years ago. I'm not surprised he wouldn't listen to you now."

"I should have told him what the cards said."

"He wouldn't have listened to that, either." Chuck didn't add that no one else in their right mind would have listened to

Ponch's tarot-card nonsense as well.

Ponch dug his phone from his pocket while Janelle approached the wedged leg, her steps slow but purposeful, her hands at her sides.

"We have to find him," she said. "We have to make sure he's . . . he's . . ."

Chuck trailed after her, his legs shaky. He said over his shoulder to Ponch, "She's right. Then we'll call."

Janelle stopped beside the thickened pool of blood below the suspended leg. She turned uphill, studying the gap in the ridge. Chuck eyed the gently sloping ramp between the rock faces with her. Somewhere in the notch, Thorpe's flight had gone horribly awry.

Janelle turned a slow circle. "The same forces that brought his leg here—" she pointed at the battered limb in the tree above them "—should have propelled the rest of his body in roughly the same direction." She pointed at the far cliff wall. "There. See?"

He looked where she pointed. "I don't see anything."

"More blood."

He squinted. She was right. A streak of dark cherry shone in the sunlight, splashed across the quartz crystals that spotted the granite face.

She aimed a finger down the slope, where Sentinel Gap opened to the forested lower ridge. "And there," she said, her voice breaking.

"Oh, my God," Ponch moaned from behind Chuck.

A piece of red fabric was tucked at the bottom of a head-high boulder resting on the forested slope below the opening of the gap.

Janelle side-hilled to the boulder ahead of Chuck and Ponch. She put a hand to the stone and leaned around it. "He's here," she said, her voice controlled. "The rest of him."

Chuck looked over her shoulder along with Ponch. The

piece of fabric visible from above was the corner of Thorpe's wingsuit airfoil. Thorpe lay facedown on the far side of the boulder, his arms and remaining leg splayed. Blood was gathered in a small depression beyond and below his head.

Janelle dropped her medical pack to the ground. Donning a pair of latex gloves from an outside pocket of the pack, she knelt and turned Thorpe's head to her. Thorpe's black helmet encased his skull. Somehow, his camera remained affixed to the helmet's crown. His goggles were smashed, his eyes, nose, and cheeks pulverized.

Janelle pressed two fingers to the side of Thorpe's neck below his jawline, then rocked back on her heels. "No pulse, of course. But we're always supposed to check." Her gloved hands, cupped around one another, hung between her legs, her forearms resting on her thighs. "He must have died instantly."

Ponch turned away and vomited down the slope. Wiping his mouth with the back of his hand, he returned to studying Thorpe's body with Chuck and Janelle.

"What's this?" Janelle asked. She touched the suit's lower airfoil, two swaths of fabric held a few inches apart by stays that lay on the ground between Thorpe's left leg and where his right leg should have been. One of the swaths of fabric had separated along a seam in the airfoil, resulting in a V that extended several inches into the wing from the foil's bottom hem. The separation had exposed one of the stays that held the fabric swaths apart to form the airfoil.

The stay, a plastic rod half the thickness of a drinking straw, stuck out from the fabric. The rod was white to its final inch, which was red, like the wingsuit.

Janelle ran her gloved finger along the last inch of the stay. Her fingertip came away smudged. "It's blood."

"The suit must have torn," Chuck said, "when he . . . when his . . ."

"It doesn't look like a tear to me. It separated. It came apart."

Chuck leaned around Janelle for a closer look. A length of nylon thread extended from the top of the V'ed separation and lay crumpled on the ground below the loosed plastic stay. "No wonder it came apart, considering the forces involved."

Janelle cleaned the blood from her covered finger with an antiseptic wipe from her kit. She continued to eye the airfoil and Thorpe's corpse along with Ponch, but Chuck stepped away. He'd seen enough. The stench of Ponch's vomit mixed in the air with the rank odor emanating from Thorpe's mangled body. Chuck swallowed, his stomach heaving.

"I'm tempted to grab the camera from his helmet and smash it to bits," Ponch said, "even though I know the investigators will want it."

"You think the footage will reach the internet?"

"I bet it'll go viral. The whole world will watch him die, over and over and over again."

"The investigators should keep it private. That's their job."

"Huh," Ponch scoffed. "Everything reaches the internet these days." He lifted his phone. "It's time," he said grimly.

Chuck took out his phone, too. "From way up here, it shouldn't take long for one of us to get through."

"As twisted as this may sound," Chuck said to Ponch as they walked down Four Mile Trail, "I'm not sure how much Thorpe would mind if the footage of his death made it to the internet."

They'd left Thorpe's body thirty minutes ago. After getting through to a 911 operator, they had waited until an advance team of half a dozen YOSAR team members arrived before leaving the scene.

"He lived his life in the public eye," Chuck continued. "He made his living putting himself on display."

Ponch spun and walked backward, facing Chuck. "Him and all the babes he hung out with." He turned forward and continued down the trail.

"Hey," Janelle warned from the front of the line. "That's the second time you've used that word."

"Young ladies," Ponch corrected himself.

"Some of us 'young ladies'—" she made air quotes with her fingers as she hiked a step ahead of Ponch "—don't have a problem hanging out with older guys."

"Thanks," Chuck said. "I think."

"Janelle's right," Ponch said over his shoulder to Chuck. "It's no secret that Thorpe's success as an older guy was the result, to a significant extent, of the young ladies who hung out with him."

"Success?" Janelle asked, an edge to her voice.

"Remember," Chuck told Ponch, "she's the mother of two little girls."

"Who," Janelle added, "are growing up way too fast."

"She's already on her guard for them," Chuck said to Ponch. "So am I."

"Thorpe figured out what you two already know," Ponch said, "which is that boys like girls—a lot. He realized right away that nine out of ten extreme-sport viewers online are males between the ages of eighteen and thirty-four. The best way to increase his viewership numbers, he figured, was to give those young males what they wanted."

"Babes," Janelle said, biting off the word.

"Young ladies," Ponch agreed. "Thorpe made sure he included a scantily clad female in every one of his videos—hanging out with him in the back of his van, zipping him into his wingsuit on the edge of a cliff before he flew, cracking open a can of beer for him after he landed."

"How professional," Janelle deadpanned.

"If by professional you mean building a solid, money-making profession, you'd be right."

"He was that successful?"

"He and Jimmy were pioneers in the whole idea of outdoor athletes making a living through sponsorships. At their peak, they had lots of sponsors—High Summit energy bars, Rinson ropes, Trongia harnesses, their backpacks, and all their clothes, from their long underwear to their hats to their rain jackets. They'd take anything that came their way. They even accepted a stake in MoJuice, the energy drink, when the company was just getting started. You know the one: *For Renegades Only.* The MoJuice people didn't have any money, so they gave Jimmy and Thorpe some stock in the company to sell after it went public. Of course, MoJuice has stayed private while talking about holding its initial public offering year after year all the way through to this year." Ponch shrugged. "What are you going to do? When Thorpe went off on his own, he got sponsorships as a flier— his wingsuit manufacturer and parachute company, even the maker of his landing shoes. He sold advertising on his website and YouTube channel, too."

"How do you know all this?" Janelle asked.

"I'm an adjuster for State Farm in L.A., so I'm online all the time. It was easy for me to keep tabs on his new videos—featuring his latest, um, young ladies. He plugged his sponsors every chance he got."

Janelle glanced up, taking in the ridge above, as she continued along the trail. "You're making me less and less upset about what happened to him up there."

"There's never a lot of public grief for wingsuit fliers when they get killed. Most of them are estranged from their families. That was true of Thorpe, from what I gathered. I heard he'd gotten himself a girlfriend of late, but he never married. I can't imagine the women he featured in his videos will spend too much time mourning his passing, either."

"Bad timing for this to happen, though," Chuck said. "At the start of the reunion."

"Or suspiciously good timing," said Ponch.

"What do you mean by that?"

"If you'd watched Thorpe's most recent videos, you'd know what I'm talking about. There was a certain melancholy to his latest postings. Fewer babes and more scenic shots while he talked about how great his years of flying had been—in the past tense."

"You're suggesting he might have killed himself?"

"His last video really made me wonder what was going on with him. He was alone in his van, at night, talking to the camera. He started out defending the fact that he'd turned away from Sentinel Gap three times in a row, and he claimed wing-suit flying had become a cult of death. But then, in his very next breath, he swore he would shoot the gap the next time he jumped off Glacier Point. He said everybody should keep an eye out for his next video because it would be incredible."

The trail snaked through the trees, descending toward the valley floor. Chuck tripped on a rock protruding from the path and jogged a few steps forward, catching his balance.

"And then I dealt the cards," Ponch continued. "The message was so clear when I laid them out. By the end of the hand, there was no question. I planned to tell him when I met up with him this morning. After the tone of his last video, I figured I could for sure get him to stop. But he wasn't at all like what I was expecting. He joked around, seemed perfectly happy. He was so jazzed to make his big entrance to the reunion and to see everyone again. I kept thinking, who was I to say anything? He'd been flying all these years. He knew what he was doing. I couldn't bring myself to mention the hand I'd dealt." Ponch's breathing was in check now that he was walking down the path rather than trudging up it. "If I'd had any sense whatsoever he wanted me to talk him out of his flight, I would have. But he was stoked. He talked about how excited he was to shoot the gap and post the footage online right away, to kick off the weekend."

Chuck frowned. "So you don't think he was suicidal, or you do?"

Ponch glanced back at Chuck. "Based on the video he posted when he was alone in his van, I'd say yes. But based on how he acted this morning, I'd say no way."

"There's that thing about people being really happy, almost euphoric, right before they kill themselves."

"Which is why, to be perfectly honest, I just don't know."

Janelle said to Ponch, "I overheard you telling Chuck about your tarot cards when you first got to the campground this morning. You said they told you more than just that something bad was going to happen to Thorpe. You said the bad thing was going to happen to him at the hands of someone else."

"That's right," Ponch replied, subdued. "Me. I'm the 'someone else.' I didn't tell Thorpe about my reading, and now he's dead."

"I'm not convinced the cards were referring to you."

From the back of the line, Chuck waved his hands in exasperation. "One crazy card person is enough," he said to Janelle. "There's no need for two of you."

She stopped and turned to Ponch and Chuck. They halted on the trail. She circled her thumbs around the shoulder straps of her pack. "This isn't necessarily about the cards. It's about the loose thread and the separation in the wingsuit."

Chuck frowned. "That was from when he hit the cliff. It had to be."

"I might agree with you—if it weren't for the cut in his ankle."

Chuck's frown deepened.

"You saw it," Janelle said. "On his leg, in the tree."

57

"I don't really want to think about what I saw up there."

"You owe it to him to think about it. There was a clean cut in his ankle, remember? It was deep and straight, and his sock and shoe were soaked with blood. The end of the plastic rod, sticking out of the bottom of his flying suit, had blood on it, too. I understand that the forces involved could have torn his suit and ripped the rod free. But the cut in his ankle and his blood-soaked sock and shoe tell a different story. Think about it. We all agree Thorpe's death was instantaneous. He died upon impact in the gap."

"That's obvious," Chuck said.

"Stay with me here," said Janelle. "The definition of death is the cessation of bodily functions—brain, lungs, and muscles, including the heart."

"So?"

"So that's what is critical in this case. If, as we all agree, Thorpe died the instant he hit the cliff in the gap, then that's the instant his heart would have stopped pumping blood through his circulatory system. That means the blood soaking his sock and shoe couldn't possibly have pumped out of the cut in his ankle after he died, which tells us the injury to his ankle wasn't the result of the blunt force trauma from his hitting the cliff."

Ponch asked Janelle, "That kind of injury would be rough and bruising, wouldn't it?"

"Yes. Like his leg being torn off. Whereas the cut on his ankle, up in the tree, was a clean slice, like from a knife. No way was it the result of blunt force. Much more important, though, is the fact that his sock and shoe were soaked with blood. That's what proves the cut had to have happened before he hit the cliff."

Chuck began, "I don't see—"

Janelle broke in. "There's something about the cut and the separation in Thorpe's suit that, together, don't add up. One of the things they stressed in every one of my classes is that part of a paramedic's job is to be observant. An ambulance call may not necessarily be for the reason given. Plenty of times, the patient is a victim of a crime. It's up to us, as first responders, to be aware of that and bring in the police if necessary."

"You honestly believe Thorpe was the victim of foul play?" Chuck asked. "With Ponch up there filming him when he jumped?"

"My classes were all about following particular protocols. If patient A is suffering from medical condition B, then we provide medical care C."

"Which is to say, you don't believe what a hand of tarot cards might say."

"Except that my teachers always said there's still a place for intuition, for what your gut tells you."

"I don't think I like where this is headed."

Janelle turned to Ponch. "The cut in your friend's ankle was caused by something in advance of his striking the ground. That's the only way that much blood could have pumped from the laceration before his instantaneous death and equally instantaneous cessation of heart activity. The only thing I saw that could have caused the cut on his ankle is the rod sticking out of the bottom of his wingsuit, with blood on it."

"Which," said Chuck, "could have happened accidentally."

Ponch said, "Except for what the cards told me."

Chuck held up one palm to Janelle and the other to Ponch. "That's enough, you two. I'm willing to accept the notion that the seam in Thorpe's suit could have come unraveled and the rod may have cut his ankle, and maybe even caused him to lose control and contributed to his death. But that's as far as I'm willing to take it. He was participating in a dangerous sport. He had an accident, like lots of fliers before him. And that's all."

Janelle aimed her chin at Chuck. "You can think what you want. As for me, I think somebody may have cut his suit. What are the odds it would have come apart on its own?"

"I'd go a step further," Ponch said with a firm nod to Janelle. "I'm not sure my cards were referring to me anymore."

6

Dale Bowles raised one of the bottles from the several cases of craft beer he'd brought to the reunion. "To Thorpe," he said.

The others raised their drinks along with him. "To Thorpe," they echoed.

They sat in camp chairs, circled in the reunion campsite, the tall trees of the campground shading them from the afternoon sun. Chuck stood at the edge of the circle, having just returned from Sentinel Ridge.

The final three reunion attendees, Dale, Caleb Holt, and Mark Sansoni, had arrived at Camp 4 while Chuck, Janelle, and Ponch were away on the ridge. Dale had driven up from San Luis Obispo, Caleb had made the shorter drive south from Lake Tahoe, and Mark had flown from Seattle to Modesto and driven to the valley from there.

Dale was head sommelier for Zanstar, the famous mid-coast eatery overlooking the Pacific on its own windswept knoll halfway between San Francisco and Los Angeles. He wore flip-flops and cargo shorts. A Cal Poly Half Marathon T-shirt hugged his lean torso. His face and legs were bronzed, his hair sun-bleached.

Three beer-filled coolers were stacked next to the picnic table, but no wine was in evidence; twenty years on, Dale still knew his crowd.

Caleb sat forward, a can of MoJuice in hand. Despite the fact that Jimmy and Thorpe had to date received no payoff from the company, their names remained closely associated with the popular energy drink. Caleb lifted his can, displaying it to the others, who held bottles of beer. "This is what we ought to be toasting Thorpe with," he said. "But I guess me and Jimmy are the only renegades left these days."

While Chuck and the others had dedicated themselves to climbing during their summers in Yosemite two decades ago, Caleb had devoted himself to the social side of the Camp 4 lifestyle. He'd made no secret of the fact that he preferred hanging out with climbers in Yosemite Valley far more than the act of climbing itself.

Generally, groupies like Caleb were shunned by the tight valley climbing community. But Caleb had offered something other groupies had not—a steady supply of pharmaceuticals. Access to the prescription pad of his father, a Bay Area surgeon, had enabled him to supply valley climbers with all manner of painkillers. He also had served as a ready conduit to recreational drugs through connections in the Tahoe area, where his family had a second home.

Caleb had liberally sampled his own wares during his summers in Yosemite, leaving him in a near-constant state of contented befuddlement. Unsure what Caleb did for a living these days, Chuck had trouble picturing him doing anything besides sitting cross-legged on the dusty ground of a campsite rolling the tight joints for which he'd been well known.

Caleb plopped his can of MoJuice behind him on the picnic table's bench seat with a *thump*, causing liquid to splash from the can's top. Despite his drug-addled past, he appeared healthy enough, seated across from Chuck in jeans and a T-shirt, his eyes the same washed-out blue, his hair still dark and curly. "Thorpe sure figured out how to make an exit, I'll give him that."

"Sounds like you saw his last video," Ponch said.

Caleb shook energy drink from his fingers. "I'm hurting for him, that's for sure. And this whole thing with Jimmy, too." He turned to Chuck. "What's the latest on our broken leader?"

"It looked to be just his foot and ankle."

"Bernard's with him?"

Chuck nodded. "He'll get a call through to one of us at some point."

"That is, he'll call if he manages to take a break from counting how many times the nurse comes through the door to Jimmy's room, or how often the air conditioning turns on and off."

The others chuckled.

"Is he still as nutty as always?" Caleb asked Chuck.

"I barely got to talk to him."

Mark leaned back, his beer resting on his belly. "People don't change."

Caleb picked up his can and tilted it at Mark's bulbous stomach. "You sure did."

More laughter crackled around the circle.

Mark managed a string of cafeterias that served organic fare to high-tech workers on corporate campuses in the Northwest. Thin when Chuck last had seen him, Mark these days carried more extra weight around his midsection than the extra pounds of Bernard and Clarence combined. Mark's short-sleeved shirt blanketed his large belly, which cascaded over the waistline of his baggy jeans. A bushy blond beard covered his face, and wraparound sunglasses hid his eyes.

From the stream of pre-reunion emails, Chuck knew Dale had been assigned by Jimmy to provide drinks for the weekend. Mark, in charge of food preparation, already had grumbled to the group about his lengthy stop at a Modesto grocery store on his way from the airport to the valley.

"I meant, inside," Mark said, leaning forward in his seat to hide his paunch. "People don't change who they really are inside."

"Talk about things changing," Caleb said. "Jimmy and Thorpe, the safest of the safe, both in one day." He looked at Chuck. "The guy in the campground office told me the rangers grilled you about Jimmy's fall."

"Just one ranger," Chuck said. "Owen Hutchins, Jr. Old Ranger Hutchins' kid. He's convinced I tampered with the auto-belay. It was in the release position when Jimmy fell."

Mark chortled. "Sure. Straight-arrow Chuck tried to kill Jimmy. What's that guy thinking?"

The corner of Caleb's mouth turned down. "He's thinking like his dad. How many times did Hutchins, Sr., kick me out of the park? And he took my stash every single time."

"But you kept coming back," Mark said. "We couldn't get rid of you."

"You didn't want to get rid of me." Caleb pulled a thin case made of shiny silver metal from his back pocket. "On account of this." He flipped the case open to display a row of half a dozen marijuana cigarettes, the paper at each end twisted closed. "I still have a connection or two, even with it all legalized these days."

Dale crossed the circle for a closer look. "Are those machine-rolled?"

"You think my fingers don't have it anymore?"

Dale reached for the case. "It's been a long time since I've done any toking."

"Your crowd isn't into pot?"

"You mean, my gay crowd?"

Dale had been closeted during his summers at Yosemite, but he had let it be known in his emails to the group that he was out and proud these days.

"Actually, I was thinking of your wine-sipping crowd. If they're anything like—"

Caleb stopped in mid-sentence when the deep-throated *chuff-chuff-chuff* of an approaching helicopter sounded from down the valley. As the sound grew louder, Chuck hurried with the others out of the campground to the edge of the trees next to the road. Janelle joined Chuck from the campground. A rescue helicopter, blue against the green trees and gray granite cliffs of the far valley wall, flew toward Sentinel Ridge.

Opposite the campground, an ambulance pulled off the road and parked next to a bladed landing zone. The vehicle's uniformed attendants hopped out and craned their heads as the chopper proceeded up the valley high above them.

The rescue helicopter slowed to a hover above the ridge. Dangling on a line from the chopper's open side door, an empty wire-cage stretcher descended toward the ground. The stretcher disappeared from view, hidden by ponderosas growing on the mountainside. After less than a minute, the helicopter rose from the ridge, its engine growling as it climbed. The stretcher reappeared out of the trees below the chopper, a black body bag now strapped inside the wire cage.

The ambulance attendants pulled a gurney from the back of their vehicle as the rescue helicopter turned toward them. The chopper descended across the valley and came to a hovering standstill fifty feet above the waiting ambulance, the roar of its engine deafening.

The wash of the chopper's rotor blades flattened the meadow grass around the landing zone as the ambulance attendants grasped the dangling stretcher, suspended from its guy line a few feet off the ground, and guided it to the wheeled gurney. They settled the stretcher on the gurney, unhooked the line, and directed a pair of raised thumbs at the chopper overhead. The helicopter rose and departed back down the valley, the line retracting as it flew, while the attendants loaded the gurney into the back of the ambulance and climbed in front.

The ambulance stopped traffic with its flashing lights, turned onto the road, and headed west, trailing the helicopter out of the valley.

"They sure are efficient," Caleb remarked, his eyes on the receding helicopter, a dark speck in the western sky.

"They ought to be," Janelle said. "I read that YOSAR conducts more than two hundred missions a year in the park, forty involving helicopter assistance."

"That's almost one helicopter operation a week," Chuck said. "Hard to believe they—"

He stopped at a tap on his shoulder. Turning, he came face to face with Owen Hutchins, Jr.

"I've got more questions for you," Owen said.

"I was as clear with you this morning as I could be," Chuck told him.

The ranger pointed at Janelle. "And for her."

"She had nothing to do with Jimmy's accident."

"It's not about that. It's about the wingsuit death," the ranger said. "Thorpe Alstad."

7

Chuck stiffened. "What about Thorpe's death?"

"I understand from the ranger team on the ridge that you located the body. The team is securing the scene and collecting evidence in advance of the SAIT being selected and assigned," Owen said.

"You mean a Serious Accident Investigation Team, like you talked about for Jimmy's fall from the climbing tower."

"Correct. The incident involving Jimmy was a maybe. But they're already assembling a team for the Alstad incident. The team will generate an FIR, a Fatality Investigation Report. But all that takes time. For now, I've been assigned to conduct initial interviews. I'm using the campground office building. I need to take statements from the two of you. It's standard operating procedure in advance of the SAIT's formation."

"Now?" Chuck asked. He waved in the direction of their campsite. "We've got to—"

"Yes," Owen interrupted. "Now. We prefer to take statements ASAP." He swiveled and indicated the front of the campground with an open hand.

"What about me?" Ponch asked.

"You are . . . ?"

"Ponch Stilwell. My given name is Henry. That's probably what you've got on your list."

Owen consulted his clipboard. "Right. Stilwell, Henry. You were with the vic this morning, too, weren't you?"

"The 'vic'?"

"Alstad."

Ponch nodded.

"I was going to find you next." Extending an elbow at Chuck and Janelle, Owen said to Ponch, "Why don't you come to the office after I'm finished with these two?" Without waiting for a response, he marched toward the front of the campground, his clipboard clamped beneath his arm.

A worried frown scored Janelle's face when she turned to Chuck.

"We didn't do anything wrong," Chuck assured her.

"That's not what he makes it sound like, with all of his 'SAIT' this and 'ASAP' that." She looked into the campground, where Clarence sat with the girls at their campsite picnic table. "Okay," she said with a sigh. She mimicked Owen's officious tone: "I guess it's just 'standard operating procedure.'"

Ponch tagged along as they made their way through the campground toward the small A-frame office.

"This should be pretty straightforward," Chuck said to Janelle and Ponch, "provided the two of you don't say anything about your conspiracy theory."

"It's not a theory," Janelle said. "There's very clear evidence pointing to potential wrongdoing."

Chuck groaned. "The rangers securing the scene on the ridge will see what you saw. They'll pass it on to the accident investigation team. The team members will follow up on their own to the extent they want, regardless what we say or don't say." He looked to Ponch for support.

"I don't know," Ponch equivocated.

"You, too?"

"This is Thorpe we're talking about. I was with him this morning. He was alive, stoked, excited for the reunion."

"As near as you could tell."

"Right. As near as I could tell. And he was the safest flier ever. For years, no mistakes, no accidents. But now he's dead. I don't care how much grief you give me about my cards, there's nothing wrong with giving them their due. If I want to be suspicious on Thorpe's behalf, I'll be suspicious. And if I want to tell Owen, Jr., about my suspicions, I'll do that, too."

Chuck raised his hands in surrender. "Tell him whatever you want."

"That's better."

Ponch peeled away, heading for the reunion campsite. Chuck continued with Janelle toward the A-frame.

After a few steps, she said, "I have to say, though, the more I think about it, the more Ponch's suicide theory makes sense. One of my final lectures was by a psychologist who talked about how easy it is for people to make bad choices in their lives. It was aimed at paramedics—how important it is to recognize when job stress is getting to be too much."

"But you think it might apply to Thorpe? You think his happiness with Ponch this morning was fake?"

"I just wish we had some way of knowing."

"Sit," Owen said, waving Chuck and Janelle to a narrow bench along the front wall of the tiny, one-room building that served as the Camp 4 office.

The ranger sat in a worn chair behind a compact oak desk in the middle of the small room. The chair squeaked as he rolled it across the plywood floor until his stomach met the desktop.

Behind him, loose papers and bound manuals covered a folding table set against the triangular rear wall of the building. A handheld radio in a recharger tray occupied one end of the table, while an ancient, drip coffeemaker took up the other. Dust motes hung in the air, lit by a shaft of sunlight streaming through the building's sole window, a smudged pane of glass set in the front wall. The room smelled of stale coffee.

Owen removed the sheath of papers bound in his clipboard.

After arranging the papers into three tidy piles on the scarred desktop in front of him, he took a pen from his shirt pocket, clicked it several times beside his ear, and lowered it to the sheet atop the center stack of papers.

He requested and jotted Janelle's personal information on the sheet as she recited it. When he finished writing, he looked up at her, his pen poised above the piece of paper. "I understand from speaking with the YOSAR team that you were the first to encounter the vic." He cleared his throat. "The victim."

"Yes."

"You didn't feel it was the officials' job to conduct a search? That's what YOSAR is for, after all."

Chuck broke in. "Who knows how long the park service would have waited? We knew where he'd headed. We were worried he might be injured."

Owen kept his eyes on Janelle. "The YOSAR team leader said you told her you touched the body. You moved it."

Janelle squared her shoulders. "I'm a paramedic. I completed my coursework in Colorado a few weeks ago; I'm waiting for my certification to come through. All I did was follow my training. I assessed the patient."

"Wasn't it obvious to you that your patient, as you're calling him, was deceased?"

"I was taught never to make such an assumption. I wanted to be absolutely sure, which resulted in my handling the patient."

Owen peered down his long nose at Janelle. "What, exactly, did you do?"

Remaining composed, Janelle told Owen how she'd turned Thorpe's head and checked his jugular for a pulse, determining within seconds that he'd likely died upon impact with the cliff somewhere above, and that he was certainly dead where he lay.

"You told the YOSAR team leader you were the first to spot the severed leg, too," Owen said.

Janelle inclined her head. "It was what led us to the body." She described the leg's location in the tree and the condition of the appendage itself. If she was at all squeamish, it wasn't apparent to Chuck. She mentioned the laceration on the ankle of Thorpe's severed leg, describing it as deep and straight. She told the ranger about the separated wingsuit foil and exposed plastic stay, and her concerns about its potential correlation with the cut in Thorpe's ankle.

"I'll make a note of it," Owen said, though his tone was dismissive and he wrote nothing down. "Is there anything else you'd like to add?"

Janelle pressed her lips together. "No."

The ranger shifted his attention to Chuck, his gaze penetrating. "What about you?"

Chuck tipped his head toward Janelle. "I followed her lead up there. She covered things pretty well with you just now, I'd say. Exceptionally well, in fact."

Janelle straightened beside him on the bench.

Owen requested Chuck's personal information and ran him through the same questions as Janelle. Chuck kept his responses short, mirroring Janelle's answers.

With his questions completed, Owen dismissed them without thanks, his head down as he studied his notes on the desk.

"Finding Thorpe's body didn't really bother you, did it?" Chuck said to Janelle as they walked back through the campground together.

"If you'd seen what I saw growing up . . ." She let her comment dangle.

"You don't really talk about it."

"*Mamá* and *Papá* could only do so much to shield Clarence and me."

Not long after their arrival in the United States from Mexico, Janelle's parents had purchased a cheap, barren lot south of downtown Albuquerque. On it they'd built a modest, single-story home, stacking concrete blocks by hand and troweling the blocks with stucco. They created a sanctuary within their walled lot that included a small rectangle of grass, a handful of pecan trees, and a productive vegetable garden. But they couldn't do much about the war zone outside their front door.

"The sound of gunshots started up as soon as it got dark," Janelle said. "Squealing tires. Screaming, yelling. I saw my share of dead bodies."

"But you escaped."

She put her arm around Chuck's waist. "It took me a while, but I found my knight in shining armor."

He pulled her to his side. "It took me a long time to find my princess, too."

"I just wish I could convince them to get out of the South Valley and move to Durango with us."

"It's only a matter of time. They miss the girls enough, that's for sure."

They neared the side-by-side campsites at the west end of the campground. Ahead, the reunion attendees sat in their circle of camp chairs, bottles of beer in hand.

"Speaking of the girls," Chuck continued, "I'd like to get them away from all the talk about Thorpe. And I wouldn't mind getting away myself."

"It's almost dinner time."

"We'll grab some snack food. We still have two hours of daylight. Plenty of time to check things out."

"The contract?"

Chuck nodded. "Clarence and I have a lot to get done this week. The sooner we get started, the better. It'd be great to have your and the girls' help on the front end."

"We're not exactly professional archaeologists."

"The first thing on the to-do list is a recon mission to get a sense of what we're up against. For that, the more sets of eyes the better, trained or untrained."

"Does the IRS know you use child laborers to fulfill your projects?"

"I won't say anything if you don't."

"What's the guy's name again, the one you're supposed to study?"

"Stephen Grover. He came to Yosemite Valley in 1852 with a group of gold prospectors. Researchers working for the Indigenous Tribespeople Foundation were going through the Yosemite Museum archives. They ran across Grover's account of the killings of two members of his group, supposedly by hostile tribespeople."

"Supposedly?"

"That's the reason the foundation decided to put the contract out to bid—Grover's account raises quite a few questions about that conclusion."

8

From "A Reminiscence" (Part One) by prospector Stephen F. Grover:

*O*n the 27th of April, 1852, a party of miners, consist-ing of [myself and] Messrs. Babcock, Peabody, Tudor, Sherburn, Rose, Aich, and an Englishman whose name I cannot now recall, left Coarse Gold Gulch in Mariposa County on an expedition prospecting for gold in the wilds of the Sierra Nevada Mountains.

We followed up Coarse Gold Gulch into the Sierras, traveling five days, and took the Indian trail through the Mariposa [Sequoia] Tree Grove, and were the first white men to enter there. Then we followed the South Fork of the Merced River, traveling on Indian trails the entire time.

On reaching the hills above Yosemite Valley, our party camped for the night and questioned the expediency of descending into the Valley at all. Our party were all op-posed to the project except Sherburn, Tudor, and Rose. They over-persuaded the rest and fairly forced us against our will, and we finally followed the old Mariposa Indian trail on the morning of the 2nd of May. Entering the Valley on the East side of the Merced River, [we] camped on a little opening, near a bend in the River free from any brush whatever, and staked out our pack mules by the river.

I, being the youngest of the party, a mere boy of twenty-two years, and not feeling usually well that morning, re-mained in camp with Aich and the Englishman to prepare

dinner, while the others went up the Valley, some prospecting, and others hunting for game. We had no fear of
the Indians, as they had been peaceable, and no outbreaks
having occurred, the whites traveled fearlessly wherever
they wished to go. Thus, we had no apprehension of trouble.

To my astonishment and horror, I heard our men
attacked, and amid firing, screams, and confusion, here
came Peabody. [He] reached camp first, wounded by an
arrow in his arm and another in the back of his neck, and
one through his clothes, just grazing the skin of his stomach, wetting his rifle and ammunition in crossing the river
as he ran to reach camp. Babcock soon followed, and as
both men had plunged through the stream that flows from
the Bridal Veil Falls in making their escape, they were
drenched to the skin.

On reaching us, Aich immediately began picking the
wet powder from Babcock's rifle, while I with my rifle
stood guard and kept the savages at bay the best I could.
The other men, with the exception of Sherburn, Tudor,
and Rose, came rushing into camp in wild excitement.

Rose, a Frenchman, was the first to fall, and from the
opposite side of the stream where he fell, apparently with
his death wound, he screamed to us, "'Tis no use to try to
save ourselves. We have all got to die." He was the only one
of our company that could speak Indian and we depended
on him for an interpreter.

Sherburn and Tudor were killed in this first encounter,
Tudor being killed with an ax in the hands of a savage,
which was taken along with the party for cutting wood.

The Indians gathered around as near as they dared to
come, whooping and yelling, and constantly firing arrows
at us. We feared they would pick up the rifles dropped by
our companions in their flight, and turn them against us,

but they did not know how to use them.

As we were very hard pressed, and as the number of Indians steadily increased, we tried to escape by the old Mariposa Trail, the one by which we entered the Valley, one of our number catching up a sack of a few pounds of flour and another a tin cup and some of our outer clothing, and fled as best we could with the savages in hot pursuit.

We had proceeded but a short distance when we were attacked in front by the savages who had cut off our retreat. Death staring at us on almost every hand, and seeing no means of escape, we fled to the bluff, I losing my pistol as I ran. We were in a shower of arrows all the while, and the Indians were closing in upon us very fast; the valley seemed alive with them—on rocks, and behind trees, bristling like Demons, shrieking their war whoops, and exulting in our apparently easy capture.

We fired back at them to keep them off while we tried to make our way forward, hugging the bluff as closely as possible. Our way was soon blocked by the Indians, who headed us off with a shower of arrows, two going through my clothing, one through my hat, which I lost. From above, the rocks began to fall on us, and in our despair we clung to the face of the bluff.

Scrambling up, we found a little place in the turn of the wall, a shelf-like projection, where we succeeded in gathering ourselves, secure from the falling rocks, at least, which were being thrown by Indians under the orders from their Chief.

The arrows whistled among us thick and fast, and I fully believe—could I visit that spot even now after the lapse of all these years—I could still pick up some of those flint arrow points in the shelf of the rock and in the face of the bluff where we were huddled together.

We could see the old Chief Tenieya in the Valley in an open space with fully one hundred and fifty Indians around him, to whom he gave his orders which were passed to another Chief just below us, and these two directed those around them and shouted orders to those on the top of the bluff, who were rolling the rocks over on us. Fully believing ourselves doomed men, we never relaxed our vigilance, but with the two rifles we still kept them at bay, determined to sell our lives as dearly as possible. I recall, with wonder, how every event of my life up to that time passed through my mind, incident after incident, with lightning rapidity, and with wonderful precision.

We were crowded together beneath this projecting rock (two rifles were fortunately retained in our little party, one in the hands of Aich and one in my own), every nerve strung to its highest tension, and being wounded myself with an arrow through my sleeve that cut my arm and another through my hat, when all of a sudden the Chief just below us, about fifty yards distant, threw up his hands and with a terrible yell fell over backwards with a bullet through his body [from one of our guns].

Immediately, the firing of arrows ceased and the savages were thrown into confusion, while notes of alarm were sounded and answered far up the Valley and from the high bluffs above us. They began to withdraw and we could hear the twigs crackle as they crept away.

It was now getting dusk and we had been since early morning without food or rest. Not knowing what to expect, we remained where we were, suffering from our wounds and tortured with fear till the moon went down about midnight. Then, trembling in every limb, we ventured to creep forth. Not daring to attempt the old trail again, we crept along and around the course of the bluff and worked our way up through the snow, from point to point. Often feeling the utter impossibility of climbing farther, but with an energy born of despair, we would try again, helping the wounded more helpless than ourselves, and by daylight we reached the top of the bluff.

A wonderful hope of escape animated us though surrounded as we were, and we could but realize how small our chances were for evading the savages who were sure to be sent on our trail. Having had nothing to eat since the morning before, we breakfasted by stirring some of our flour in the tin cup, with snow, and passing it around among us, in full sight of the smoke of the Indian camps and signal fires all over the Valley.

Our feelings toward the "Noble Red Man" at this time can better be imagined than described.

Starting out warily and carefully, expecting at every step to feel the stings of the whizzing arrows of our deadly foes, we kept near and in the most dense underbrush, creeping slowly and painfully along as best we could, those who were best able carrying the extra garments of the wounded and helping them along, fully realizing the probability of the arrow tips with which we were wounded having been dipped in poison before being sent on their message of death. In this manner we toiled on, a suffering and saddened band of once hopeful prospectors.

9

"Time for a history quiz," Chuck told Carmelita and Rosie, seeking to get their minds, and his own, off Thorpe's death and Jimmy's accident.

Their footsteps echoed on the hikers' bridge over the Merced River as they crossed it, following the same route to the south side of the valley Chuck, Janelle, and Ponch had taken on their way to Sentinel Ridge earlier in the day. They stopped in the middle of the bridge to check out the dozens of swimsuit-clad park visitors floating down the calm river on inner tubes and paddle boards. Gusts of wind swept in waves across the grassy field on the far side of the river. The meadow stretched to the south wall of the valley, which rose to dizzying heights ahead in a series of ridges, bluffs, and broken cliff faces lit by the early evening sun.

"On the first day of the Battle of the Somme in World War I," Chuck told the girls, "the Allied forces—the good guys—lost more troops than in any single day of battle ever before or since in the history of modern warfare. Can you guess why?"

"What's a world war?" Rosie asked.

Carmelita told her sister, "It's where everybody fights everybody else."

"Like where we're going right now," Rosie said with a serious nod.

"Not quite," Chuck said, turning forward. "We're looking into a small battle that happened here 150 years ago between a few gold prospectors and the tribespeople who lived in the valley back then."

"You told us people were shooting at each other," Rosie said.

She stuck out a forefinger and blasted across the river at imaginary foes, making popping noises with her lips, before blowing on the end of her finger and sticking it in the waistband of her shorts.

"You're right," Chuck said. "People were shooting at each other here in the valley. It's the way they were shooting at each other that's similar to what happened in the Battle of the Somme. It's the main reason we're here, in fact. Any ideas?"

When the girls shook their heads, Clarence said, "Asymmetrical firepower, is that it?"

"That's right," said Chuck. "Shortly after machine guns were invented, the Germans recognized how advantageous they were and set up thousands of them along the Western Front in France. When the Allied forces attacked, the Germans mowed them down with the machine guns."

"The tribespeople wouldn't have had any machine guns," Carmelita said, tapping her chin, "but there was still something asym . . . asymmet . . ."

"Asymmetrical," Chuck finished for her. "Yes. The miners had rifles, while the tribespeople only had—" He paused, giving her the chance to fill in the blank.

"Bows and arrows," Carmelita said.

"Right you are," Chuck commended her.

Rosie pretended to draw back a bowstring and release it, shooting an imaginary arrow at the sky. "Got 'em!" she crowed.

Chuck explained, "Rifles vs. bows and arrows is what resulted in the genocide of indigenous tribespeople—Indians—all across the country in the 1800s, including here in California."

"What's 'genocide' mean?" Carmelita asked.

"It's when a whole group of people are wiped out, killed, because of their religion or the color of their skin—just because they're considered different than other people for some reason. But the miners weren't coming here to kill the tribespeople who lived in the valley. They were looking for gold, and in their case, their rifles are what saved their lives."

"Except the two dead ones you told us about," Carmelita said.

"Their deaths are what Clarence and I have been hired to investigate."

"You're not the police, though."

"This all happened too long ago for the police to be involved. Indigenous tribespeople who live in the West nowadays are the ones who are interested."

"Why?"

"There's been renewed interest in recent years about battles and crimes that happened in the Old West. People want to make sure the historical accounts of what took place are as accurate as possible—the Mountain Meadows massacre in Utah for one, the Sand Creek massacre in Colorado for another. The Indigenous Tribespeople Foundation looks into old crimes said to have been committed by tribespeople that, in fact, might have been committed by others."

"You mean, might have been part of the genocide you were talking about?"

"That's the big question." Chuck rested his hand on Carmelita's skinny shoulder. "The whole story started with the discovery of gold in the Sierra Nevada Mountains, which resulted in the California gold rush of 1849."

"And," Clarence added, "the name of the San Francisco 49ers football team."

"Prospectors kept going deeper into the mountains looking for gold," Chuck continued. "One of the places they eventually came to was right here, Yosemite Valley."

Rosie's eyes widened. "They went looking for gold in a national park?"

"It wasn't a national park back then. It was just a beautiful valley where the Yosemite tribespeople lived."

Carmelita said, "I bet they didn't like it when the gold miners showed up."

Chuck squeezed her shoulder in agreement. "This was the only home they'd ever known. It was their special place. Most of the tribespeople in the area had already been killed or taken as slaves or kicked off their lands and forced to live on reservations. Remote valleys like this were the last places indigenous tribespeople in California were still living on their ancestral lands. They were ready to defend themselves."

"But they only had bows and arrows," Rosie noted.

"And the gold prospectors had guns," said Carmelita.

"Asymmetrical firepower," Chuck agreed. "The miners made their camp somewhere in the meadow near here after coming in on a trail from the southeast." He pointed down the valley through the welded lattice of steel support beams rising ten feet above the walkway on either side of the bridge.

"I think I can see the trail going up through the trees," Carmelita said, peering through the latticework. She grasped two of the beams and hoisted herself off the deck of the bridge, climbing the support structure.

"Whoa, whoa, whoa!" Chuck cried, reaching for her.

She stopped a couple feet off the deck of the bridge, balanced on the metal beams. "I'm just getting a better look," she told Chuck over her shoulder.

"Sure, but—"

Janelle laid a hand on Chuck's arm. "She's fine." Janelle looked at her daughter. "Aren't you, Carm?"

Carmelita's gaze flicked between Janelle and Chuck.

Chuck shrugged, less than certain. "I guess if your *mamá* thinks it's okay."

Rosie urged, "Go for it, Carm."

Clarence added, "Yeah, baby cakes. Let's see what you can do."

Carmelita resumed climbing. She reached the top of the support structure, ten feet above the bridge deck, in seconds.

Rosie asked, "What's it look like from up there, Carm?"

"It's really cool." Carmelita rested her arms over the top of the uppermost steel bar, her feet even with Chuck's head. The afternoon sun lit her dark hair, blown back from her head in wavy tendrils by the breeze coursing up the river. "I can see forever."

Chuck wrapped his arm around Janelle's waist. "Good for you, letting Carm go up there. She takes after you. She's fearless."

Rosie poked herself in the chest with her thumb. "So am I. I'm fearless, too." She pointed at her sister, perched on the metal latticework above. "I just don't want to climb way up there."

"You're fearless, too, all right," Chuck said.

Leaning against Chuck, Janelle told Rosie, "You're beyond fearless. Which is what keeps me up at night."

Chuck looked up at Carmelita. "She's the one who ought to be keeping you up at night."

"Remember," Janelle said to Chuck, "it's you who started her on this whole climbing thing." She followed his raised gaze to Carmelita. "Like you keep saying, she's good at it."

Carmelita climbed back down, rejoining the others on the bridge deck. They crossed the remainder of the bridge and continued on the wide walking trail through the meadow toward Southside Drive.

Rosie spun in a circle. "Are you going to dig up all the grass?" she asked Chuck.

"No," he replied. "This area has been excavated over and over again. Each time an artifact works its way to the surface, park service archaeologists conduct a surrounding excavation to learn more about it. There's not much left to be discovered down here in the valley bottom." He pointed past Southside Drive at the bluffs and cliffs that made up the valley's south wall. "But there might still be something to learn up there."

He took the girls' hands and crossed the road, stopping at the foot of the valley wall. Unlike the unbroken granite faces lining the north side of the valley, the south side consisted of granite outcrops and knobs broken by ledges and overhangs. Where water courses plunged between the granite promontories, ponderosas grew above an understory of whiteleaf manzanita.

"The group of prospectors consisted of eight men," Chuck told the girls. "The morning after they made camp, five of them headed up the valley looking for gold. The other three stayed behind. After a while, the three men in camp heard screaming and shouting. The five prospectors who'd headed up the valley were under attack. Two of the five crossed the river and reached camp despite being wounded by warriors' arrows. But the three other men were trapped on the far side of the river. Those three all happened to own a gold mine together outside the valley. One of the three—his last name was Rose—yelled that he and the other two were done for, and that the rest of the prospectors should make a run for it." Chuck looked at Rosie. "Can you guess which way they ran?"

Rosie's eyes went to the granite bluffs and outcrops looming above. "I'd go up there. It would be like a fort for them."

"Good thinking," Chuck praised her. "That's exactly what they did. They grabbed their guns and ammunition and hightailed it up into the cliffs. One of the survivors, Stephen Grover, told the story of how they ran up there with the warriors' arrows flying all around them." Chuck crouched between the girls and lowered his voice to a conspiratorial whisper. "And that's where the real mystery begins."

10

Chuck straightened from his crouch between Carmelita and Rosie and took folded sheets of paper from his pocket. He held them low, so the girls could look at the printout of Grover's account with him.

"Here's how Grover described what happened," he said. "Listen for the clues, okay?"

"'We tried to escape by the old Mariposa Trail,'" Chuck read from the account. "'We had proceeded but a short distance when we were attacked in front by the savages who had cut off our retreat.'" He broke from his recitation to tell the girls, "That's what they used to call indigenous tribespeople back then." He went back to reading. "'Death staring at us on almost every hand, and seeing no means of escape, we fled to the bluff.'"

Rosie stared wide-eyed at Chuck. "Whoa. That really happened?"

"Yep," Chuck said. "A long time ago."

Carmelita looked around her. "They got chased right across this field," she said, her voice filled with wonder.

"Somewhere near here," Chuck agreed. He lifted a finger to the bluffs. "And on up into those cliffs, just like Rosie figured they would."

"Where'd they go up there?" Carmelita asked.

"That's one of the questions Clarence and I have been hired to answer."

"You don't know?"

"No one does. Our job is to see if we can figure it out."

"Someone's paying you? Why?"

Chuck again dropped his voice to a furtive whisper. "Because of the mystery."

"The clues," Janelle said. "Read them again, would you?"

Rosie clung to Chuck's arm as he studied the sheets in his hand. "First, they tried to escape via the Mariposa Trail, their original route into the valley from the south the day before." He continued to paraphrase from the sheets. "They 'proceeded but a short distance' before they were cut off and 'fled to the bluff.' Notice he uses the singular term, 'bluff,' not bluffs."

He peered with Carmelita and Rosie up at the valley wall. A prominent nose of rock pressed out from a cliff face two hundred yards east of where they stood. To the left of the granite nose, a tight chute served as a channel, draining rainwater and snowmelt around the outcrop. Higher up, the chute opened onto a forested slope, speckled with boulders, that rose to the southern skyline.

Chuck looked back at the sheets of paper and continued quoting Grover. "'From above, the rocks began to fall on us, and in our despair we clung to the face of the bluff. Scrambling up, we found a little place in the turn of the wall, a shelf-like projection, where we succeeded in gathering ourselves, secure from the falling rocks, at least, which were being thrown by Indians under the orders of their Chief.'"

He lowered the sheets and studied the cliff face once more.

Beside him, Clarence quoted from memory. "A 'little place in the turn of the wall, a shelf-like projection.'"

Chuck aimed a finger at a protected, cavern-like space beneath the prominent nose of rock. "There. See where it's shadowed? That's the place I spotted on my computer, using satellite data, that looks most promising to me."

"Could that be it?" Janelle asked.

"It fits Grover's description. It's the most protected place all along this section of the valley."

"Since they were cut off from the Mariposa Trail," Janelle

said, "it makes sense that they'd have headed for the drainage on the far side of the rock because it leads all the way out of the valley."

Clarence extended his lower lip. "Then, when the warriors tumbled rocks down the drainage at them from above, they'd have been forced to fall back to avoid being hit."

Rosie yanked on Chuck's forearm. "Let's go up there."

Chuck tensed his arm muscles and lifted her off the ground. "I told the foundation people that's where I thought we would start." He lowered her back to the meadow grass. "Race you."

He slid Grover's account back in his pocket and set off at a jog with Rosie at his side. They angled across the last of the valley floor to the foot of the hillside below the granite outcrop. They slowed as they made their way up the steep slope toward the base of the outthrust nose of granite, climbing through breaks in the manzanita understory. Rosie matched Chuck's pace while the others trailed behind.

They left the brush covering the lower slope and entered a grove of ponderosa pines, growing tall where moisture from the Sierra's pounding winter storms saturated the slope below the cliffs.

Chuck paused to lift his cap and wipe sweat from his brow. He looked up the steep slope through the tree branches to where the granite bluff reared into the sky. A lower cliff, hidden from distant view by the ponderosas but visible through the tree trunks from where Chuck stood, rose straight up out of the slope. A narrow ramp ran up to the lower cliff face. The ramp ended at a bench of level ground that extended several feet from the base of the imposing prow of granite towering above the treetops. He resettled his cap and resumed the upward climb, slowing to allow Rosie to surge ahead of him.

She made her way up the ramp to the dirt bench, three feet wide, beneath the prominent granite nose. She leapt up and down at the base of the outcrop, dust rising around her hiking boots. "I'm the winner!" she cried, her arms lifted in triumph.

Reaching the bench, Chuck picked her up and gave her a congratulatory cheer. He set her down and together they surveyed the valley floor, visible through breaks in the trees. The Merced River described a winding S across the meadow in the center of the valley. An open area half a mile to the east, where the meadow ended at a thick stretch of forest next to the river, marked the place the prospectors likely had pitched their camp. If true, the bluff beneath which Chuck stood with Rosie would have been the most logical destination for the prospectors when the warriors cut off their down-valley retreat.

Rosie extended a hand, helping Carmelita up the last of the sloping ramp to the level bench at the base of the granite nose. Janelle and Clarence followed.

"Is this where they ran to?" Carmelita asked Chuck.

"It certainly fits Grover's description," Chuck answered. "The prospectors would have 'hugged the bluff' as they made their way up the ramp to this 'shelf-like projection' in the 'turn of the wall.' We've reached the shadowed alcove we spotted from below." He pointed around the face of the cliff, beneath the overhanging nose of granite. "After holding off the warriors until dark, they most likely would have made their escape that way."

"But it's straight up," Carmelita said, craning her head to study the nose of rock.

"I bet you could do it, Carm," Rosie told her sister. "You can climb anything."

Carmelita blushed.

Chuck told Rosie, "Even if Carm could climb up from here, the prospectors couldn't, not with the guns and ammunition they were carrying." He leaned outward from the bluff and aimed his finger farther left, where the bench continued around the base of the outcrop toward the brush-choked water drainage visible from below. "They'd have gone up the chute, working their way through the bushes. Want to see if it's possible?"

At Rosie's energetic nod, Chuck led the way along the base of the cliff to where the dirt bench gave way to the water channel, dry this time of year. He grasped small oaks and manzanitas that grew alongside the granite outcrop to hoist himself as he led the others up the steep chute.

"You really think they could have climbed this?" Clarence called up to Chuck from his place at the end of the line, below Janelle and the girls.

"They were desperate," Chuck called back down. He pointed farther up the valley wall, where the channel tightened to a series of ladder-like stone ledges, then opened to a forested slope. "They were looking for any way out, and that may well have been it, straight up there."

Clinging to brush with both hands to maintain his place in the chute, Clarence jutted his chin at the drainage above Chuck. "Which means that's where the tribespeople would have rolled rocks down from above, keeping the prospectors trapped on the ledge."

Chuck said to the girls, who stood on the slope between him and Janelle and Clarence, "Imagine what it must have been like for them. They were surrounded, trapped from above and below. But they had one key advantage."

"Their guns," Carmelita said without hesitation.

"Blam, blam, blam!" Rosie shouted.

"Right," Chuck said. "The five prospectors who escaped from the camp used their rifles to hold off the attackers until they could escape after dark."

"Geezo majeezco," Rosie said.

"But Clarence and I are here on account of the prospectors who were trapped on the far side of the river. The three of them were left for dead—" Chuck paused and raised his eyebrows "—but only two actually died."

"You mean, one of them escaped?" Carmelita asked.

"One of them survived, let's put it that way. How and why he survived are the questions your uncle and I have been contracted to look into."

"But why are we way up here if you're studying the ones who were trapped down in the bottom of the valley?"

"Because no one has ever done any excavating above the valley floor."

"What are we looking for up here?"

"Confirmation of Grover's story. If we can find proof that the prospectors really were trapped here on the side of the valley like he says, that will add veracity—truth—to the rest of Grover's account, including the questions he raises about who really was responsible for the deaths of the two prospectors down below, on the far side of the river."

Perched in the drainage, Chuck again took out the sheets of paper. "In his account, Grover said the chief, Tenaya, was relaying instructions to a sub-chief, who directed the warriors shooting arrows from below and tumbling boulders from above. Grover reported something very important about that point in the attack." He read from the prospector's account. "'The arrows whistled among us thick and fast, and I fully believe—could I visit that spot even now after the lapse of all these years—I could still pick up some of those flint arrow points in the shelf of the rock and in the face of the bluff where we were huddled together.'" He paused, eyeing Rosie and Carmelita. "If Grover could just 'visit that spot' where he and the other prospectors were trapped," he hinted as he replaced the printout of Grover's account in his pocket.

"Oh, oh, oh," Rosie exclaimed, thrusting her hand in the air. "We're the ones who are coming back for a visit. We're going to look for the arrowheads."

"Right you are," Chuck said. "In fact—"

A loud *crack* sounded from the drainage above, followed by a deep rumbling sound.

"Run!" he screamed.

PART TWO

*"The captives declared that the valley was their home,
and that white men had no right to come there
without their consent."*

—Early California explorer Lafayette Bunnell

11

"Rock!" Chuck yelled. "Everyone, run! Back to the shelf!"

The rumbling grew louder. Clarence led the way back down the drainage, grabbing branches as he plunged lower. Janelle and the girls bounded downward behind him. They, too, grasped branches for balance, gaining on him with each running stride.

From above, the rumbling noise built to a roar as Chuck charged down the drainage after the others, the sound signaling the approach of a dislodged boulder tumbling toward them from higher in the chute.

When Clarence reached the flat bench of soil at the base of the bluff, he skidded to a halt and, holding out his hand, tugged the girls and Janelle past him to safety. Rosie, Carmelita, and Janelle sprinted along the dirt bench and out of sight around the base of the rock outcrop.

Clarence looked up the drainage past Chuck, his eyes widening in horror. Chuck glanced over his shoulder. A rounded hunk of granite the size of a small car hurtled down the drainage toward him, smashing undergrowth as it came. The rolling boulder struck the trunk of a stout ponderosa. The trunk bent at the force of the blow but did not break. Instead, the boulder caromed off the tree trunk and bounded straight for Chuck, less than ten feet away. He spun and leapt for Clarence's outstretched hand. Clarence grabbed his wrist and they tumbled backward onto the dirt bench at the same instant the boulder slammed into the place where Chuck had just stood.

The granite outcrop shuddered when the boulder struck it a solid blow before bouncing away and tumbling on down the mountainside. The rumbling noise diminished as the rock crashed through a thicket of manzanita where the drainage opened and the steepness of the slope lessened near the bottom of the valley. The boulder slowed, then came to rest in the thicket at the base of the slope. On the two-lane road a hundred yards beyond, traffic continued unabated.

Janelle reappeared from around the base of the cliff with the girls, who huddled behind her.

"Oh . . . my . . . God," she breathed, her hand to her chest.

Chuck climbed to his feet and swept dirt from his pant legs, avoiding Janelle's gaze.

"What . . . ?" she asked. "How . . . ?"

"Gravity's a bitch," Clarence joked, but his face was pale and his hands trembled at his sides.

Rosie tugged Janelle's arm. "What's a bitch, *Mamá*?"

Spots of cherry bloomed on Janelle's cheeks. "It's a word your uncle shouldn't say in front of you."

"Sorry, sis," said Clarence.

Chuck directed a thumb behind him, where the boulder had struck the cliff wall and careened on down the drainage. "That, right there," he said, "was a perfect example of the difference between sport climbing and big-wall climbing." He looked at Carmelita, his heart rate gradually returning to normal. "And why, as talented as you were on the sport wall this morning, I'm not sure I like the idea of you ever climbing any big cliffs."

"Isn't that what you used to do?"

"Yep. Which is why I know what I'm talking about. Sport climbing is safe and controlled—Jimmy's accident this morning notwithstanding." He touched the rock wall beside him. "But anything can happen on cliffs and mountains out here in the natural world. That boulder was probably sitting there, ready to let loose, for decades."

"You really think," Janelle said, "the rock happened to

choose right now, this minute, to fall—just when we were climbing toward it?"

Chuck turned away, his insides thrumming.

Always the truth between them, he and Janelle had promised one another when they'd first become a couple. Always.

Over the last three years, he'd worked hard to maintain that pledge. But how to do so now?

He turned back to her. "The small vibrations through the ground from the five of us working our way up the drainage *could* have set it off," he offered in halfhearted defense of his earlier comment.

He pointed east, where a dozen boulders the size of houses rested haphazardly at the foot of the next drainage up the valley. Cars filled a parking lot on the valley floor between the gathered boulders and Southside Drive. "That's Cathedral Bouldering Area, where climbers attempt short routes on rocks that have tumbled into the valley," he said. "In geologic time, Yosemite Valley is a newborn baby. That's why its walls are so vertical, and why chunks still break off and roll down to the valley floor. There's even a name for it; it's called spalling."

Janelle pulled Rosie close. "I've had enough spalling for one day." She reached for Carmelita's hand. "I say we get out of here."

Chuck breathed a silent sigh of relief. His half-version of the truth had worked.

"Awww," Rosie moaned. "I want to go back up where the prospectors went."

She aimed a frustrated kick at the loose dirt of the bench, then stopped, looking down. She stooped and plucked a small object from the ground at her feet.

"What's this?" she asked Chuck, holding it out to him.

Chuck placed the object in his palm. It was a black sliver of obsidian shaped like an isosceles triangle, no larger than a quarter.

"This is incredible," Chuck cheered Rosie, intent on putting the close call with the boulder behind her and the others. He tousled her thick hair. "You've done it!"

"What have I done?"

"You've taken a huge first step for us."

Rosie's eyes lit. "It's an arrowhead, isn't it?" she asked, shoving out her chest.

"A projectile point," Chuck agreed, using the academic term. "You're an official archaeologist now."

She took the sliver of glass-like stone from Chuck and laid it in her open hand. "What should I do with it?" she asked.

"Put it back where you found it."

She frowned at Chuck.

"I know it sounds weird," he said, "but a lot of what we archaeologists learn comes not just from what we find, but where we find it, too. An archaeological excavation is like a three-dimensional jigsaw puzzle. We uncover pieces one by one and try to understand, from what we uncover, what was going on in a particular place at a particular time. For the preliminary survey Clarence and I are conducting, we'll be leaving any objects we discover in situ—that is, in place—where we find them."

Rosie closed her fingers over the projectile point and twisted back and forth, her face aglow. "I'm an archaeologist. A real, live archaeologist."

She stopped and opened her hand again, revealing the sliver of obsidian. "Do I really have to leave it here?"

"I'm afraid so," Chuck said. "If everybody picked up all the artifacts they found, pretty soon there wouldn't be anything left to study, and archaeologists wouldn't be able to learn about what happened in the past."

"Well, dingle-dongle-dingle berries," she declared.

She squatted and placed the arrowhead back in the divot created when she'd kicked the dirt with her boot. Chuck held out a hand to stop her before she scooped soil back over it.

"No need to re-bury it," he said. "It's an important find. Clarence and I will want to catalog its location and photograph it with our camera when we come back up here."

"Okay," she said, brushing her hands against one another. She rose and looked at Janelle. "Can we go now? I'm starving."

Rosie and Carmelita left the dirt bench together, descending toward the valley floor. Before Janelle followed them, she stared at the place where the boulder had struck the rock wall. "The girls are not coming back up here," she said to Chuck. "Ever."

"Understood."

She stepped off the bench and trailed the girls down the slope.

Using his phone, Chuck snapped initial pictures of the projectile point and its location on the shelf. He crouched with Clarence, studying Rosie's discovery. Tiny scallops marked the projectile point's two sides and shorter base, where it had been worked with a fletching tool.

"That's some pretty good knapping," Clarence observed. "Any idea where the obsidian would have come from?"

"East of the mountains near Mono Lake, most likely. There was a big quarry on that side of the Sierra, and lots of intertribal trading."

Picking up the point, Clarence held it to the sky between his thumb and forefinger. "It's discolored in the center. See?"

Chuck leaned closer. Rays of sunlight passed easily through the fluted edges of the triangular point, but the center of the piece of obsidian was smudged, nearly obscuring the light. He touched the smoky middle of the sliver with a fingertip. "It was heated before it was knapped. California tribes were known for that. They thought heating obsidian over a fire made it easier to work with—that it flaked more uniformly, enabling them to create finer work. But studies have shown it didn't make any difference."

"You mean, preheated or not, the quality of the knapping was the same?"

"The preheating was all peer pressure. Everyone was doing it, so everyone else kept doing it, too."

Clarence replaced the arrowhead in the divot and went to the edge of the shelf, ready to head down the dirt ramp and into the trees after Janelle and the girls. Chuck straightened but didn't join Clarence.

"I take it," Clarence said, "you're not coming along, are you?"

Chuck gave a slow shake of his head.

"I figured you were feeding us a line."

"It could have happened like I said."

"But the odds that it did . . ."

". . . are infinitesimal at best," Chuck admitted.

"Which means somebody tried to kill us a few minutes ago."

Chuck rocked his lower jaw back and forth in indecision. "I don't think so. I think, instead, somebody was sending us a message."

"Like what? You think the ghosts of the tribespeople were trying to scare us, from 150 years ago?"

"I think somebody from right now, today, doesn't like the fact that we're up here. They're not happy with what we're doing and they want us to stop doing it."

"Who would want that?"

"Maybe somebody from the foundation. Or someone in charge of the archives. Or somebody with the park service. There's no shortage of people who know why you and I are in Yosemite."

"But how could anyone have known we were coming up here this afternoon?"

"The foundation put our plans on their website, complete with the expectation that we would start our search right here, below the outcrop."

"Still," Clarence said with a disbelieving shake of his head.

"I agree. Long odds. But the odds that the boulder chose right then to fall? Much, much longer."

Clarence's eyes darted around him. "We should get the hell out of here, then."

Chuck looked at Clarence, unblinking.

Clarence exhaled. "Do you want me to come with you?"

"No. I want you to stay close to Janelle and the girls."

"If I thought it would do any good, I'd try to talk you out of this."

Chuck summoned a thin smile. "I know."

Clarence headed down the mountainside.

Leaving the dirt shelf, Chuck climbed back up the drainage, grabbing bushes and the trunks of small trees for support. He followed the tumbling boulder's path of destruction—snapped branches, crushed brush, deep cuts in the soil—until he reached the place, two hundred feet up the chute from the ledge, where the car-sized boulder had begun its downhill plunge. Among low outcrops of rock eroding out of the mountainside in the middle of the drainage, a shallow depression marked the boulder's former resting place. Uphill from the depression, discarded on the ground, lay an eight-foot length of ponderosa branch as big around as Chuck's forearm. He hefted it. One end of the stout branch was crushed, as if it had been used as a lever to dislodge the rock and send it down the drainage.

He squatted, studying the ground directly uphill from the depression. Shoe-sized gouges in the dry soil marked the places where feet had dug into the earth as someone had shoved the end of the branch beneath the rock, working to topple it. Shallower gouges revealed where the person had approached the boulder and retreated from it, side-hilling into and out of the steep chute.

Chuck snapped pictures with his phone of the depression and branch, then followed the gouges in the dirt as they led east from the drainage. In the dry, crumbly soil, the gouges showed no revelatory indentations of shoe or boot sole. Beyond the drainage, the tracks led into a stand of ponderosa. There, the gouges disappeared where the soil firmed up beneath the trees.

He spotted no signs of movement through the trees ahead—not that he expected to see anything. Whoever had rolled the boulder down the drainage would be well away from here by now.

He returned from beneath the trees to the edge of the chute and looked east, where the south wall of the valley met the valley floor at the foot of the next drainage over. There, the Cathedral boulders speckled an area half a mile across. Dozens of climbers, tiny specks from Chuck's distant vantage point, made their way from the parking lot to the scattered boulders and from boulder to boulder along the foot of the slope. Above the boulders, the valley wall was heavily forested.

Whoever had toppled the rock no doubt had approached from the bouldering area and would easily mix in with the Cathedral climbers upon returning there.

Chuck eyed the far-off climbers, rage burning inside him. Someone, very possibly one of those distant specks, had just tried to intimidate him and his family—with deadly intent.

12

Chuck caught up with his family as they crossed the valley floor, nearing Camp 4. Janelle fell back with Chuck, out of earshot of the girls and Clarence.

"What really happened up there?" she asked, her voice tight.

"I didn't want to admit to anything until I was sure."

"And?"

"I'm sure now. The boulder was no accident." He described what he'd found—the depression, the tree branch used as a lever. "We need to get out of here," he concluded. "It's not safe."

"No," Janelle said. There was no give in her voice. "If somebody had wanted to kill us up there, they'd have killed us. It would have been easy with a gun. But they didn't do that."

"They tried."

"Wrong. They tried to scare us. And they *did* scare us. Enough that you want to leave."

"On account of you and the girls. I—"

"Don't you see?" she broke in. "The whole point of the boulder was to get you to do exactly what you're about to do. For some reason, somebody wants you, us, to leave the valley."

"But who could possibly want that?"

She shrugged. "That's what we're going to find out. We'll be safe from any more scare tactics as long as we stay out in public. If we leave, I know you'll just come back later, by yourself. That's when you'll be in real danger." She stopped and turned to him. "All of us are staying here, together, until we get to the bottom of this."

"And just how do you propose we go about doing that?"

"We keep our eyes and ears open."

"That's it? That's all you've got?"

"Do you have something better?"

Chuck clamped his mouth shut.

"Listen to me," Janelle said to his silence. "We're Ortegas. The girls, me, Clarence—and you, too, now. When my parents came to the U.S., the only choice they had was the South Valley. They could have run back to their families in Mexico from there many, many times. But they didn't. They never have." She looked at Chuck, her eyes dark as steel. "We're Ortegas," she repeated. "We're not going anywhere."

The campground sat in deepening evening shade upon their return.

Chuck angled away to check in with the guys in the reunion campsite while Janelle led the girls to their campsite with Clarence. Janelle bent close to her brother, speaking into his ear as they walked. Clarence's back went straight. He shot a questioning look at Chuck. When Chuck nodded, Clarence went back to listening to Janelle, the tendons at the back of his neck stiff as iron rods. She spoke while making a levering motion with her hands, illustrating the toppling of the boulder from its resting place in the drainage.

The guys sat slumped in their chairs in the reunion campsite, their feet crossed before them and their latest beers balanced in their laps. A line of empty beer bottles snaked across the top of the picnic table.

"Chuck," Caleb intoned, lifting his bottle in greeting. He burped.

More tents ringed the perimeter of the reunion site. A pot bubbled on a cookstove at the end of the picnic table, filling the air with the tangy scent of onions, tomatoes, and oregano.

Dale drew in his feet and sat up. "We were just talking about you," he said to Chuck.

Mark added, "We decided it's your call whether to continue this charade."

Dale said of Mark, "No secret where he stands."

"I'll hear him out," said Mark, sitting forward in his seat. "As we all agreed."

Caleb and Ponch sat up, too. Chuck stopped at the edge of the circle of chairs.

"You always were the levelheaded one," Dale said to him. "Whenever we got one or another of our wild-hair ideas, it was up to you to inject a little logic into things."

In acknowledgment of Dale's assessment, Chuck raised and lowered his chin. His levelheadedness had come at a price. As a child, he'd had no choice but to assume the role of the mature one in his two-person family, shopping for groceries, paying the electric bill, negotiating a rent extension with the landlord while his mother was off on a bender with another of her feckless boyfriends. He knew his early, hard-earned maturity had played a significant role in the success of Bender Archaeological right out of college. His maturity had shown itself during his summers in Camp 4 as a young man, too.

Caleb belched again. "Remember the time we wanted to carry a yule log up Half Dome and set it on fire and toss it off the north face?"

Dale snapped his fingers. "I'd forgotten about that. Christmas in July, that was our plan. We were going to do the same thing the rangers used to do on Christmas Eve in the old days— chuck a burning log off the top of the dome to give the folks watching from down in the valley a big show."

Caleb chuckled ruefully. "I chopped down a tree and hid it at the trailhead, ready for us to carry up there that night. We probably would have torched the whole valley if we'd have gone through with it in the middle of the summer like that. What were we thinking?"

"We weren't thinking," Dale said. "That was the whole point. We were just stupid kids doing stupid stuff."

"*Almost* doing stupid stuff," Caleb said. He looked up at Chuck from his seat. "Lucky for us we had you around to tear into us and tell us not to do it. You used the term 'idiots' about ten times, from what I remember."

"It worked, didn't it?" Chuck said.

"Which is why we're turning to you again."

"You're thinking of calling off the reunion?"

Caleb's eyes went to his beer bottle.

Dale spoke for the group. "We're thinking maybe it's best just to pull the plug, call it good after tonight and get out of here in the morning."

Chuck glanced around the circle. "I can't really blame you— us—for thinking like that," he said, his own mind on the safety of his family. "Maybe you're right. Maybe this whole get-together wasn't meant to be."

He looked from the campground to the meadow stretching across the valley floor, aglow in the evening light. Ortegas didn't run, Janelle had just said. They weren't quitters. And he was an Ortega now.

He turned to Ponch, who sat next to Caleb with his head bowed. "You were with Thorpe this morning. What do you think?"

Ponch raised his head, revealing a pallid face and hollow eyes. He set his bottle in the netted holder in the arm of his chair. "I've listened to you guys talk about Thorpe all after-noon—whether he had a death wish, if what happened today was his plan to go out in a big burst of glory. If you'd have been with him before his flight today, though, you'd know how wrong you are."

He put his hands on his knees.

"People joked about Thorpe—how old he was, how he was a Peter Pan who never grew up. And that's exactly what he was, as near as I could tell. But the thing is, he knew it. While he was suiting up this morning, he told me he understood his place in the world. This was it, he said—the valley, the cliffs, the sunsets, the dawns. He said he knew people thought he was past his prime, and that his turning away from Sentinel Gap over and over this summer proved he didn't have it anymore. Whatever *it* is."

Chuck held his breath. Would Ponch mention the hand of tarot cards, and the suspicions the cards had raised in his mind regarding Thorpe's death? And what of the bloody plastic rod from the airfoil and the cut on Thorpe's ankle?

Ponch's voice gained strength as he continued. "I'm here to tell you Thorpe still had it this morning. He was calm, steady, assured, ready to go."

Ponch took in the group with steady eyes.

"I don't know what went wrong in the gap this morning, but I do know Thorpe didn't kill himself. He was happy we were all getting together again after all these years. He couldn't wait to see everyone. Whatever happened in the gap, it just happened. The last thing Thorpe would want is for us to cancel the reunion and go home because of him. What he would want, instead, is for us to celebrate his life and to celebrate our own lives, too, like this was our last weekend on Earth—because, really, who knows? Maybe it is."

He clasped his hands and sat back in his seat.

Chuck looked around the group. "I think Ponch just gave us our answer," he said, noting Janelle listening in at the edge of the campsite. "Who's in charge of dinner?"

Mark lifted a finger from the neck of his bottle. "That would be me."

"Smells good," Chuck said.

Ponch pushed himself from his chair. "I'll get a campfire going."

Caleb rose beside him. "I'll help."

Janelle cocked a finger at Chuck. He followed her away from the group.

"I heard Ponch just now," she said when they were out of earshot. "What he told your buddies was different than what he said to us. He went hard against the idea that Thorpe might have committed suicide."

"No mention of the cards, either," Chuck said, his voice low. "It sounded like he was fed up with what the others had been saying about Thorpe all afternoon, so he decided to stick up for him."

"Either way, mixed messages."

"Chances are we'll never know for sure what happened to Thorpe. When it comes to wingsuit flying, if something goes wrong at the wrong time, whenever that wrong time comes along, you're dead."

"Like a separated airfoil seam."

"Maybe that was the thing that went wrong at the wrong time this morning."

"Or the thing that someone *made* go wrong."

Chuck turned to her. She released his arm and met his gaze.

"You did exactly right," he said. "You told Owen what you saw up there. You mentioned the cut on Thorpe's ankle. He didn't ask you any more questions about it. Not one."

"He should have followed up, though. In my classes, we learned the two types of lacerations. There are clean lacs—cuts from knives, razors, broken glass—and blunt-force wounds, like a bomb going off, from car wrecks, objects, falls from height." She set her jaw. "The lac in Thorpe's leg wasn't anything like what a blunt-force laceration should look like. Something stiff and cutting caused it—like a wind-whipped plastic rod sticking out of a separated airfoil."

"Fine. Okay," Chuck said. "Let's say you're right. In which case, so what? The airfoil came apart and the stay cut him and maybe had something to do with his death or maybe not. Which gets us, basically, nowhere. It's no different than Jimmy's accident this morning. Bad things happen in life."

"The boulder didn't just happen."

"Which is why that's where we should keep our focus. As far as Thorpe's loss of control in the gap is concerned, if the investigative team comes up with some theory based on the separated airfoil, I'll listen. In the meantime, I'm sticking with the obvious. Thorpe was participating in the most dangerous sport there is. He'd been doing it longer than anyone else still alive. The odds finally caught—"

A loud cry from Clarence sounded from the edge of the campground. Chuck spun with Janelle to see a tiny human form—Carmelita—clinging to Columbia Boulder's overhanging south side, twenty feet off the ground.

Chuck took a running step toward her just as she lost her grip and plummeted toward the rocky earth below.

13

Chuck charged toward Carmelita as she fell. Janelle ran beside him. Ahead, Carmelita disappeared into the upraised hands of onlookers gathered at the base of Columbia Boulder.

Upon breaking her fall with their grouped hands—the appropriate technique for safely catching unroped climbers after falls from bouldering routes—the spectators lowered Carmelita to a standing position on the ground. Cheering, they stepped back and raised their arms, their hands clenched in her honor. Several slapped her back in congratulations as she stood among them, looking down at her climbing shoes. When Chuck neared the boulder, still running, she lifted her head to reveal a look of glowing pride on her heart-shaped face.

Clarence stood among the onlookers with Rosie. He turned to Chuck and Janelle as they slid to a halt at the edge of the group. "Incredible," he said, grinning.

His smile faded when Janelle demanded, "What in God's name are you doing with her over here?"

Uncertainty replaced the pride in Carmelita's eyes. Janelle reached to caress her arm. "Not you, Carm. This has nothing to do with you."

Chuck surveyed the spectators, more than a dozen in all. Several were members of the YOSAR team, returned from Sentinel Ridge. The remainder were park workers and their families from the campground—men and children along with several women in long skirts, their dark hair gathered in loose buns at the backs of their necks.

"Incredible is right," a male YOSAR team member said to Clarence, ignoring Janelle's outburst. He rubbed his forehead beneath the brim of his cap, looking up at the spot where Carmelita had fallen from the boulder. He turned to Chuck and Janelle. "She just on-sighted Midnight Lightning, all the way to the final move."

"'On-sighted'?" Janelle asked.

"That means," the team member explained, "she'd never attempted the route or received any beta about it. This is Midnight Lightning we're talking about. V8 on the Vermin scale. Ron Kauk's impossible dream from, like, the 1970s. Kauk was the first person to send it, but only after he worked on it every day for two months straight." The team member patted Carmelita's shoulder. "This little one here, she shot the spider monkey swing—" he pointed up at the rock "—from the undercling up and over the mini-roof without even hesitating, like she'd been doing it her whole life. She was one move from the top when she came off. One little move."

Carmelita went back to studying her feet, her face growing red.

The YOSAR team member, in his mid-twenties, his hair escaping from beneath his cap in blond waves, gaped at Chuck and Janelle. "Are you her parents?"

Chuck nodded.

"I've been stationed here the last two summers," the young man said, pointing at the ring of YOSAR tents west of the campground. "People attempt Midnight all the time, but nobody—and I mean nobody—ever gets more than a few feet off the ground, much less sending the monkey up at the top." He gawked at Carmelita, his admiration obvious, then said to Chuck and Janelle, "You've got a phenomenon on your hands." He paused. "Wait a minute," he said, turning again to Carmelita. "Now I get it. You're here for the Slam, aren't you? You really are one of those climber-kid phenomenons. Is there somewhere I can read about you? Has *Rock and Ice* or *Climbing* done a

SCOTT GRAHAM

feature on you yet?"

Chuck cleared his throat. "I'm afraid you don't get it. She's not like that. The first time she ever climbed was this morning, over on the climbing wall."

The tower, in sight through the trees at the front of the campground, was now back in use. A line of climbers waited behind the boulders at the edge of the parking lot in the waning light while a woman made her way upward, roped to what presumably was the swapped-out auto-belay device.

"Seriously?" the team member said to Chuck. He gawked at Carmelita again. "You're really something, you know that? You climb like a cat."

"Hear that, Carm?" Rosie said. "That should be your nickname—Cat Girl." She scratched the air in front of her with her fingers. "Meow, meow!" she yowled, arching her back, her face to the sky.

Janelle wrapped her arm around Carmelita's shoulders. "What in the world made you go up there?"

The onlookers waited with Janelle for Carmelita's response.

"I . . . I . . ." Carmelita began, her voice barely audible. "I asked Uncle Clarence if we could come over because there was another kid climbing on the rock."

Among the spectators, a boy of no more than fourteen, as slight as Carmelita, glanced her way. A lock of black hair swooped low over his forehead, covering one eye.

"You were talking," Carmelita said to her mother, "so I grabbed my shoes."

"The three of us came over together," Clarence said, his hand on Rosie's shoulder. "When Carm kept going higher, I got people to come help, to make sure we could catch her." He pointed at the two nearest campsites, empty of people. Laundry lines, hanging low with worn jeans, flannel shirts, and white housekeeper aprons, ran from tree trunk to tree trunk along the

112

edges of the sites.

The YOSAR team member said, "We hustled over, too. Man, am I glad we did. That was so freakin' cool."

A rush of pride surged through Chuck. He asked Carmelita, "How'd you do it, anyway?"

She lifted one of her bony shoulders. "I . . . I just kept going."

"The overhang didn't scare you?"

"A little. But everybody started coming."

"We tell her, 'Go, go, go,'" a stout woman said. Streaks of gray highlighted her charcoal hair. She pointed at the boy. "My grandson, he get only a little bit off the ground. But the girl? *¡Dios mío!*"

Janelle pressed Carmelita to her side. "*Gracias,*" she said to the woman.

"*Por nada,*" the woman replied. "*Tienes una muchacha talentosa.*"

Janelle lowered her head in acknowledgment. "I agree. She's pretty talented."

"*Pero,*" the woman continued, a twinkle in her eyes, "*es porque ella no tiene bastante peso.*"

"You think Carmelita's too skinny?"

The woman aimed a stubby finger at her grandson. "*Él, tambien.*" Her wrinkled face cracked open in a smile, revealing a row of stained teeth. "*Y tú, lo mismo,*" she said to Janelle.

The woman left the group and headed for the unattended campsites. "*Plátanos,*" she said over her shoulder to those gathered at the base of the boulder. "*¡Plátanos para todos!*"

Chuck turned to Janelle. "Did she just offer plantains to everybody?"

"That's what it sounded like." Janelle looked down at Carmelita, still pressed to her side. "Like your *abuela* makes."

The onlookers followed the woman, but Carmelita drew in her shoulders, looking up at her mother. "I'm sorry I came over here. I didn't mean for you to get mad at Uncle Clarence."

"You don't need to apologize," Janelle told her. "It's just, I want us to stick close to one another."

Clarence aimed his head toward the park worker campsites and said to Carmelita, "You're a rock star now. You need to put in an appearance with your fans." He looked at Janelle. "We'll all go together. *Juntos.*"

"Yeah," Rosie told Carmelita. "Come on, Cat Girl. Let's go eat some bananas."

"Plantains are different, remember?" Janelle said to Rosie. "They have to be cooked. They're not as sweet."

Rosie rubbed her belly. "As long as they have lots of honey, like Grandma puts on them, they'll be grrrreat!"

Taking the girls' hands, Clarence walked with them toward the park worker campsites.

"Don't eat too many *plátanos,*" Chuck called after Carmelita. "You don't want to overdo it before the Slam tomorrow."

Janelle gripped his wrist. "How well she does tomorrow doesn't matter."

Chuck shifted his weight from one foot to the other. "It might matter to her."

"Or to you." Janelle's gaze was penetrating.

"As long as we're staying in the valley, I see nothing wrong with Carm's taking advantage of the opportunity to be success-ful tomorrow."

"How well somebody climbs or doesn't climb up a fake cliff isn't exactly my idea of success."

Chuck aimed his chin at the group now gathering in the nearer of the two campsites, where the grandmother fired up a campstove and centered a skillet over one of its burners. "Those folks would beg to differ. You heard that YOSAR guy refer to Ron Kauk like he was some sort of a god. To a lot of people in Yosemite, that's exactly what he was, along with others, like

Jimmy and Thorpe, who sent routes on El Cap and Half Dome and all the other faces in the valley that, until they climbed them, people had thought were impossible."

Janelle's mouth turned downward. "They climbed rocks. Not exactly earth-shattering stuff."

"Not to you, maybe." Chuck eyed Kauk's pioneering route up the overhanging face of the boulder. "Most people have no idea what draws climbers like me to Yosemite to spend weeks or months or, in the case of Jimmy and Thorpe, their entire lives climbing cliffs around the valley. A few years ago, two of the best climbers in the world, Tommy Caldwell and Kevin Jorgeson, sent the Dawn Wall route on El Capitan for the first time ever without any aid—that is, without using nuts or cams or pitons to help their ascent. They spent an entire month on the wall, working their way upward little by little, while supporters resupplied them from below. They ripped their fingertips to shreds, hung out in their portaledges until their fingers healed, then inched higher. The media got hold of the story and reported on their progress day after day. The coverage drew all sorts of criticism from people who thought what they were doing was a total waste of time."

"Which it was, as far as I'm concerned."

Chuck closed one eye as he looked at Janelle. "You're right that there's no obvious value in rock climbing per se. But what Caldwell and Jorgeson were attempting on Dawn Wall is what the valley is all about. Places like Yosemite let people challenge themselves in the outdoors to whatever degree they want. Caldwell and Jorgeson did exactly what Jimmy and Thorpe and the rest of us did twenty years ago, and what climbers and hikers and backpackers have been doing here in the park for more than a century—they challenged themselves to the furthest extent of their abilities. That's not necessarily a bad thing, in my opinion."

Janelle's eyes went from Carmelita's route on Columbia

Boulder to the high cliff faces of the valley, visible through breaks in the trees, then back to Chuck. "I don't want to let you off so easy, but . . ."

"But I'm right, aren't I?"

"Every now and then," she admitted. She slid her fingers from his wrist to his hand. "Come on. Let's go keep an eye on the girls."

"And eat some fried bananas."

Half a dozen children, Rosie among them, chased each other through the campsites. The grandmother tied an apron over her skirt and flipped sliced plantains in a cast iron skillet in front of her. The sweet, smoky smell of the sizzling fruit filled the air. Clarence, other campers, and YOSAR team members piled paper plates with grilled chicken, potato salad, and cookies laid out on the picnic table in front of the camp stove.

The woman set down her spatula next to the skillet and stood with her hands behind her back as everyone dove into the food. Janelle approached the woman, who resumed flipping the plantains on the stove. The two fell into conversation, speaking Spanish.

Chuck wandered over to where Clarence and Carmelita stood with several middle-aged men in worn jeans and denim work shirts. The men's caramel-toned faces were weathered and wrinkled, like that of Janelle's father.

"*Hola, jefe,*" Clarence said to Chuck, lifting a drumstick in greeting, his loaded plate balanced in his free hand. "*La gente aquí* know what they're doing when it comes to food."

Carmelita scooped a strip of fried plantain from her plate and took a big bite. "Mmmm," she said. Then she looked at Chuck and froze, her cheeks bulging.

Chuck raised a hand to her in apology. "Eat as much as you

want. You'll do fine tomorrow no matter what."

Clarence said to her, "Food this good is magical, *niña*. It'll help you fly up the tower tomorrow."

She smiled and took another bite, then closed her eyes and moaned in delight as she chewed.

"It's that good?" Chuck asked her.

"It reminds me of Grandma."

One of the campers held out a calloused hand, indicating the food-laden picnic table to Chuck. "*Por favor, señor.* Help yourself."

"*Gracias*," Chuck said. "But I have to save myself for dinner over there." He pointed at the reunion campsite, where Mark moved between the stew pot, still bubbling on the stove, and steaks, sizzling on a freestanding grill.

"Ah," the man said, nodding. "Your friend here—" he pointed at Clarence, who gnawed on his drumstick "—he say you come here much times."

"Every summer for five years or so," Chuck said. "A long time ago."

"Is my third summer here."

"Do you always stay in Camp 4?"

"Some of the time. We take turns standing in the line to get our fourteen days *máximo* for each of us. We stay here much of the summer that way. There is no place else to stay in the valley, and apartments outside the park are far away and cost much money. The camping is very cheap." He grinned as the youngsters ran by. "And good for the children."

From the reunion campsite, Caleb waved a beer bottle at Chuck. "If you'll excuse me," Chuck said to the man and Clarence, leaving them.

"Not so fast," Clarence said, hurrying after Chuck.

They stopped at the edge of the campsite, alone together.

"I need to know what's going on here," Clarence said.

"Janelle tells me you found clear evidence somebody knocked that boulder down on us, but here we are, hanging around like nothing happened."

"It's not me. It's your sister."

"You mean your wife."

"That makes her both your problem and mine. She said she won't run. More specifically, she said Ortegas don't run. But maybe you can talk some sense into her."

"Not me. You know good and well by now, Ortegas don't run from nobody or nothing."

Chuck rolled his eyes. "You, too?"

"Look around us. We're in the middle of the valley with millions of other people. Ain't nobody gonna be able to do anything more to us."

Chuck groaned. "That's exactly what Janelle said."

"She's right. We just gotta figure out who it is that tried to scare us off."

"That's what she said, too."

Clarence grinned. "*Mi hermana*, she's one smart cookie, ain't she?"

Chuck couldn't find it in himself to return Clarence's smile. "I'll need your help. Anything you see, any ideas you have."

"Sure. But you're the one who signed the contract. You know the players involved. I'm just here for the chicken and *plátanos*."

Clarence headed back to the park worker campsite. Chuck walked toward the reunion site, asking himself who possibly could have something against looking into what had happened to the prospectors 150 years after the fact. Had the person who toppled the boulder been waiting, expecting Chuck and Clarence to show up based on the posting of their plans on the Indigenous Tribespeople Foundation website? Or had the person watched them from the campground, setting off to the drainage only after Chuck and Clarence set out across the valley with Janelle and the girls?

Chuck studied the campsites around him. If the latter was the case, then someone around here was keeping a close eye on him and Clarence. Who might that someone be?

Caleb waved again from the reunion campsite. Chuck continued toward him, lifting a hand in response.

"We should tie one on," Caleb urged after dinner. "Get hammered and go for a midnight swim in the river, like the old days. That's what Thorpe would want us to do. Jimmy, too."

Despite Caleb's suggestion, however, the evening's somber mood prevailed. The guys drifted off to their tents one by one, their stomachs full of Mark's New York strip and Italian pasta, until Chuck sat alone in the dark in front of the glowing red coals of the dying campfire.

He upended his bottle, finishing his beer, and rose from his seat. Snores from the tents in the reunion campsite filled the night air as he made his way through the darkness to the campsite next door, where Janelle and the girls were already in their two-room family tent.

He slipped inside and found his way to his portable cot using his cell phone light. The narrow bed creaked as he sat down on it. He set his cell phone on the floor, its light shining up, and leaned forward to unlace his boots.

Janelle rose on an elbow on the cot beside him, her face lit by his phone.

"Long day," she whispered. She rested a hand on his knee. "How are you doing?"

"Better than I'd have thought," he whispered back, "thanks to having you and the girls here. I'm worried, though, for the same reason."

"The boulder was meant to send a message to you and

Clarence. All we have to do is figure out who's trying to scare you off and why, and stay away from the survey site in the meantime."

"The boulder was only part of it today. You saw some pretty grim stuff up on the ridge."

"We both did."

"Not to mention being questioned by Owen."

She flicked her fingers as if shooing a fly. "He's nothing. As for what we saw on the ridge, I just kept trying to imagine it as pictures in the books for my classes."

"That doesn't make it any less gruesome."

"If I get on with Durango Fire and Rescue—"

"*When* you get on," Chuck broke in. "You *will* get on with them, and when you do, you'll do great."

"Okay," Janelle assented. "*When* I get on with Durango Fire and Rescue, I'll be seeing a lot more of that sort of thing."

"And . . . ?"

"After today, I know I'm going to be okay with it."

"That's my babe."

"Hey," she warned, a teasing lilt to her voice. "I'm nobody's babe."

"Sure you are," he said with a smile. "You're all mine, mine, mine."

He thumbed off his phone light, lay back, and ran through the day's events in his mind—Thorpe's death, Jimmy's accident, and, over and over again, the boulder rumbling down the drainage. Eventually, he fell asleep to the reassuring memory of Clarence's outstretched hand pulling him to safety, with Janelle and the girls already shielded by the nose of granite.

He awoke when his phone beeped. Janelle rolled to face him, her eyes questioning, as he peered over the edge of his cot at the phone, alight with an incoming text.

First, he checked the time. Four in the morning.

Then he checked the text. *We need you*, it read.

14

Chuck drove out of the valley in response to Bernard's text, after Janelle insisted she and the girls would be safe staying in camp with Clarence.

Chuck followed the snaking highway westward along the Merced River, descending out of the mountains. Two hours later, he turned the pickup into the drive leading to the front entrance of Mercy Medical Center in north Merced. He braked to a stop, the crew cab's headlights shining on Jimmy and Bernard. Jimmy balanced on crutches outside the hospital, the left leg of his jeans scissored to his knee. Bernard gripped one of Jimmy's elbows, supporting him.

Teaming with Bernard, Chuck helped Jimmy slide sideways across the truck's rear bench seat until his left leg, encased in a soft, velcro-strapped cast to the top of his shin, rested lengthwise on the seat.

"Go, go, go," Bernard said to Chuck, slamming the back door and hopping into the front passenger seat.

Chuck climbed behind the wheel, threw the truck into gear, and accelerated. Visible in the rearview mirror, Jimmy leaned the back of his head against the side window and said, "It's not a prison, B."

"We're going AWOL," Bernard countered. "What do they call it? Leaving against medical advice." He tapped his fingertips on the dashboard and counted the taps beneath his breath in varying beats, like a jazz drummer. "One, two . . . three, four, five . . . six, seven . . . eight, nine, ten—"

"I'll be back after the weekend," Jimmy said over Bernard's

whispered count. "I'll ask for their forgiveness then." He closed his eyes.

The truck lurched as Chuck negotiated a gutter between the hospital parking lot and street, provoking a groan from Jimmy.

Bernard withdrew his hands from the dashboard and turned in his seat to face Chuck. "I know we shouldn't be doing this, but he insisted."

From the back, Jimmy said, "You haven't changed a bit, B, you know that? I swear to God, you're more of a chicken-shit now than you ever were."

Bernard squeezed his hands together in his lap, stilling his fingers. "You just got out of the operating room a few hours ago."

"They didn't even do any surgery. No pins or screws or anything. They just put me under long enough to pop my foot back into place. There's a non-displaced fracture at the base of my ankle, but nothing else. They said I'll be good as new in a few weeks. Besides, I'm not about to miss the Slam. I want to start it off with a memorial to Thorpe first thing, while everybody's there."

Bernard said, "He's been on the phone nonstop, with the rangers, YOSAR, the whole world."

Jimmy caught Chuck's eye in the mirror. "I keep thinking I should have done something. Anything."

"If it helps, everyone else feels the same way," Chuck replied.

He piloted the truck through Merced's quiet streets. Above the crest of the Sierra range to the east, the horizon was gray with the coming dawn.

"We hadn't seen much of each other lately," Jimmy said.

"He got himself a woman in Fresno," said Bernard. "That's what he posted, anyway."

"He'd come up to the park every week or two. He'd hang around with the other fliers out at Wawona on the way to Glacier

Point, do his flights, and head right back down to her."

Bernard faced forward in his seat. Unclasping his hands, he rat-a-tapped his thighs with his fingers. "What about his van?"

Chuck glanced at Bernard. "The one with the shag carpeting and the fuzzy dice hanging from the rearview mirror? He still had that thing?"

"He got a new one a little while ago. He posted all kinds of pictures of it online. It was one of those fancy camper vans with a high roof and polished wood finishes inside. It even had a bathroom, which he made a big deal about, like indoor plumbing was this new thing in the world. I bet it's still parked up at the point."

"I'm sure it's been towed by now," Jimmy said from the rear seat. "The rangers wouldn't let it sit there for long."

Chuck steered the truck onto the interstate at the edge of the city. Ahead, pink and orange mixed with the gray on the eastern skyline. "The Slam's supposed to start at nine, right? We won't get there much before that."

"I talked to Alden after I came out of the OR. He'll have everything ready to go."

Chuck raised his elbows, widening his shoulders, his hands still on the wheel. "That guy?"

Jimmy chuckled. "That's him. He works for Sacramento Rock Gym, hauls the tower up to the valley for me every year. He's helped with the Slam since the start. He checks everyone in, keeps the brackets updated, frees me to do the announcing. Not sure how much of that I'll be able to do this year, though."

"You think you'll be able to pull off the memorial for Thorpe, at least?"

"That's non-negotiable."

"People were climbing on the tower again yesterday, not long after they hauled you away. Alden said he was going to replace the auto-belay."

"He told me he couldn't find anything wrong with the one that let me fall."

"Either the ratchet's broken or the switch is faulty or it got turned off. Something."

"He said he changed it out regardless."

"The ranger was all over it—Owen Hutchins, Jr. Old Ranger Hutchins' son, did you know that?"

"Of course. He's had it in for me since the first day he put on his badge."

"He picked up right where his dad left off, seems like."

"He's pretty much alone with his hard-ass routine at this point. Things have really calmed down between the rangers and climbers these days. The Sunday morning coffee at Columbia Boulder has helped. Plus, lots of the current rangers are climbers themselves. Several were YOSARians before they joined the ranger ranks. There are more and more women rangers, too. By and large, the rangers nowadays are good people. But with Owen, Jr., it's as if nothing's changed. Everything is still us vs. them. It's like he's still in the trenches and the war never ended. The first few years after he rangered up weren't so bad. They had him stationed on the outskirts, in Wawona or Tuolumne Meadows, with the other rookies. Now that he's built up some seniority, though, he's worked his way into the valley. This year, he got Camp 4 as part of his beat."

"He raked me through the coals yesterday. Twice. Once because of your accident. Then on account of Thorpe."

"You and Ponch found him, didn't you?"

"Along with my wife. When we got up there, he was hard to miss."

"You did a good thing, finding him. Better to know right away."

Chuck set the cruise control. The truck sped across the pan-flat expanse of California's Central Valley. The highway was quiet.

Farmhouse lights speckled the landscape in the gloom of the fading night. The mountains rose where the farmland ended thirty miles ahead.

"Junior didn't think so," Chuck said. "He claimed we should have let YOSAR take care of it."

"That's Owen for you. Just like his dad. He thinks every park visitor should stay on the roads and buses and never leave the pavement. I've noticed the other rangers tend to keep their distance from him."

"He seems to get along pretty well with your tower attendant, Alden."

"Everybody gets along with Alden. Thorpe liked him, too." Jimmy paused. "Thorpe," he said softly. "All these years, no accidents for either of us." In the rearview mirror, he shook his head, his braided beard sweeping back and forth. "I just wish he could've been with everybody this weekend—finally, all of us together." He sighed. "How does everyone look?"

Chuck hooked his thumbs over the bottom of the steering wheel. "About what you'd expect. Receding hairlines. Some gray hair, including mine. Plenty of pudginess, but Mark's the only one who's really gone overboard. Dale's in good shape. He was wearing a marathon T-shirt."

"Those gay guys," Jimmy said. "They're all about their bodies."

"I don't think he's as fit as you, though. The way you were climbing before you fell, it was like you hadn't aged a bit."

"I just work hard not to show it. Thorpe, though? He ran his butt off, never stopped doing sit-ups and push-ups and pull-ups. It was all I could do to hang in there with him all those years." Jimmy stroked his beard. "You're looking pretty good yourself, Chuck."

"I spend a lot of time with a shovel in my hands. Keeps the pounds off."

"I checked out your website. You've done all right for yourself,

I'll say that. All your discoveries—man, you're big time. I remember when you rattled into the valley in your beater car every summer, living on peanut butter and jelly sandwiches."

"It took a while to break in, but I'm doing all right now."

"Good for you, seeing's how you've got those extra mouths to feed these days. Your wife, what's her name?"

"Janelle."

"Yeah. Janelle." Jimmy whistled, low and ribbing. "I'd work pretty hard to keep her fed if I was you—not that she eats much, from the looks of her."

Morning sunlight flooded the Camp 4 parking lot as Jimmy crutched his way to the foot of the climbing tower. He turned to face the several dozen climbers and spectators gathered behind the waist-high boulders lined at the front of the campground.

Chuck stood with Janelle, the girls in front of them. Carmelita rolled her shoulders and swung her arms, her eyes on other climbers doing the same to loosen up among the onlookers in advance of the competition.

Ponch, Bernard, Dale, Mark, and Caleb stood together in the crowd. Bernard drummed his legs with his fingertips, keeping time with a beat only he could hear. Ponch's shoulders sagged. Dale stood straight beside him. Mark's stomach was corralled by a large, plaid shirt tucked into equally voluminous shorts. Next to Mark, Caleb studied the tower with eyes that were bright with either curiosity or some form of artificial stimulation, Chuck couldn't tell which.

Alden made notes on a clipboard as he stood in the crowd with several of the fit, twenty-something climbing contestants. The competitors were discernible by their brightly colored nylon shirts and tights, which hugged their lean, muscular bodies, and the bottles of water in their hands. Non-contestants in jeans and T-shirts rubbed the necks and shoulders of a number of competitors, who bowed their heads and closed their eyes as if they were prizefighters preparing to enter the ring.

Among the spectators, Chuck spotted the *platano*-serving grandmother and several other campground-resident park workers from the previous day. The park workers shot supportive glances Carmelita's direction.

Owen Hutchins, Jr., looked on from one side. He was dressed the same as yesterday, in dark green ranger slacks and a crisply pressed uniform shirt.

A sheet of billowy gray nylon draped the climbing tower. The length of fabric hung a few feet out from the wall on aluminum stanchions, hiding the tower and its holds from view.

Alden lowered his clipboard and spoke into the ear of the female climber who'd commanded his attention the day before. This morning, the climber wore black tights and a form-fitting tank top in bright magenta with spaghetti straps strung over her tanned shoulders. Twice as he spoke into the woman's ear, Alden's eyes strayed to the sheet-draped tower.

Jimmy began his remarks by thanking the climbers for their participation in the Slam. Then he pushed himself upright on his crutches. "Yesterday, we lost one of our own," he told the gathered crowd. "Thorpe Alstad was a fixture here in the valley, a one-man institution. I'm proud to have shared a rope with him for many, many years."

Jimmy briefed the spectators and climbers on Thorpe's history in the valley, from his early climbs and run-ins with park authorities to his later arrests as a wingsuit flier.

"For far too long, Yosemite Valley was a place of contention, of threats and counter-threats," Jimmy said. "I'm glad we've moved beyond those days. In fact, I don't think it's too much to say that Thorpe's death yesterday represents the end of an era—and the beginning of a new and better one."

Jimmy lowered his head. A few onlookers clapped uncertainly. When Jimmy said nothing else, Alden walked to his side and faced the crowd, clipboard in hand. He wore a seat harness over khaki slacks. His cotton, button-up shirt, though heavily wrinkled, lent him an air of officialdom.

"I believe all of you know the rules," he said to the competitors, his voice raised, "but I'll run through them just to be sure. First and foremost, at the beginning of each round, all contestants will wait in the parking lot, behind the tower, so no one sees the route until it's their turn to climb. I set the route last night, in Jimmy's absence, so any complaints are on me."

Jimmy said to Alden, beside him, "I'm sure you put up a solid first-round route."

"We're about to find out," Alden responded. He again addressed the climbers, scattered in the crowd: "This is an on-sight competition. You'll be allowed five seconds to study the route before you begin climbing. After your climb, you, of course, will not be allowed to go back around to the far side of the tower, to avoid sharing any beta with those still waiting their turn."

"This is a top-out tourney, right?" a climber asked from the crowd.

"Yes, it is," Alden answered. "Only those who reach the top of the tower will move on to the next round of the competition. I'll reconfigure the route after each round, increasing the degree of difficulty. We'll hold three rounds this morning, then finish up tomorrow morning with as many more rounds as necessary to crown a winner in each division."

Another climber raised a hand. "Any word as to why the auto-belay failed yesterday?"

"Nothing yet. But I changed out the device that failed with a new one, and we used it yesterday with no problems. Just to be absolutely safe, our one and only super lightweight climber will be belayed by her father." Alden's eyes came to rest on

Carmelita for a moment. "Okay, I think that's everything," he announced to the crowd. He popped his hand against his clipboard. "Climbers, please move to the back of the tower, and we'll do the unveiling."

The brightly clad competitors trooped past the climbing wall and gathered amid the parked cars in the gravel lot.

In front of Chuck and Janelle, Carmelita didn't move. She looked up at her mother with pleading eyes. "I have to go back there by myself?" she asked, her voice quavering.

"Looks that way."

Chuck explained. "It's so you can't see the route when they take down the sheet."

"But . . . but . . ."

"I'll go with her," Rosie offered.

"Afraid not," Chuck told her. "It's climbers only back there."

Carmelita's chin trembled and tears built in her eyes.

"You don't have to climb if you don't want to," Janelle told her.

"I *do* want to," Carmelita said. "I just thought . . ."

"I know the other climbers are a lot older than you," Chuck said. "But they're nice people."

"Remember," said Janelle, "this is all just for fun. It's about raising money to support the campground."

"It's about winning, too," Chuck said.

"It's about fun," Janelle insisted, shooting Chuck a look.

"It *is* a competition, after all."

Carmelita looked from Chuck to Janelle and back. "I want to win," she said resolutely. "Or, at least, I want to try." She left them and wormed her way through the crowd.

"Carm!" Rosie cried. She ran after her sister, bouncing off spectators, and caught up with her at the base of the shrouded tower. "Good luck," Rosie said. Her deep, raspy voice carried through the crowd, eliciting grins from the onlookers.

With a grave look on her face, Rosie held out her fist. Carmelita mirrored her. In rapid succession, the girls ran through a choreographed series of fist bumps, elbow knocks, palm slaps, and finger points that ended when they turned sideways and bounced their hips off each other.

Smiling, Carmelita disappeared around the back of the tower, while Rosie skipped back to Chuck and Janelle.

"What on Earth was that?" Chuck asked her.

"We practiced it yesterday," she reported, breathless, "but I almost forgot to do it with her. I made it up all by myself. It's for luck—not that Carm needs any. She's the best!"

When Alden called Carmelita's name during the initial round, Chuck tied her into his seat harness and belayed her as she moved with ease from hold to hold to the top of the tower. Every other competitor mastered the initial route, too.

After the first round, Alden drew a rope attached to the aluminum stanchions at the top of the tower, lifting the nylon sheet back into place to enshroud the climbing wall once more. He disappeared behind the fabric. A crisp, metallic *click* sounded as he clipped the carabiner attached to his harness into the climbing rope to ascend the tower and prepare the route for round two.

"They always make the first round easy," Chuck reported to Carmelita, Janelle, and Rosie as they stood together in the crowd. "Alden will pull holds now and things'll get interesting."

Carmelita rolled her shoulders. "I'm ready."

Alden reemerged from behind the sheet a few minutes later. "All set," he announced.

He again directed the climbers to the back of the tower. Like the other competitors among whom she walked, Carmelita's hands were white to her wrists with powdered, sweat-absorbing chalk from the drawstring bag hanging from her narrow waist.

When the climbers were gathered behind the tower, Alden dropped the sheet once more. Far fewer holds remained for round two, with a significant gap, free of holds, fifteen feet off the ground, and a second gap ten feet higher.

The two blank spaces on the wall proved too much for a number of climbers, who fell away from the tower and were lowered to the ground by the auto-belay device. Still, more than three-quarters of the climbers made it past the gaps and topped out.

When Carmelita came to each of the gaps during her turn, Chuck held his breath while he belayed her from below. He needn't have worried, however; she hoisted herself past each blank spot without difficulty and reached the top within a minute of beginning her climb.

After again resetting the route beneath the shroud, Alden announced to the remaining climbers as they trooped past him to the parking lot, "This will be our third and final round of the day. Good luck to all of you."

He offered a subtle tilt of his head to the female climber in the skin-tight tank top as she passed him. In response, she glanced away from him and straightened the spaghetti strap at her shoulder with a hooked finger, a quick, nervous gesture.

15

The spectators gasped when Alden lowered the sheet for the start of round three. In addition to the two previous gaps on the route, he had removed a number of holds to create an even larger blank space near the top of the tower. The distance from the hold at the bottom of the new gap to the nearest hold at its top was nearly three feet, and the hold at the top of the gap consisted of only a tiny nubbin of molded resin.

"Whoa," a YOSAR team member muttered, looking up at the route.

"No way, dude," breathed another.

Alden tensed and looked to Jimmy questioningly. Leaning on his crutches amid the onlookers, Jimmy raised a thumb to him in reassurance.

At the foot of the tower, Alden raised and lowered his broad shoulders, loosening his muscles. "Okay, then," he said. He cleared his throat and, referring to his clipboard, addressed the spectators with a raised voice. "First up for round three: Thomas Reynolds, Oxnard, California."

A male climber rounded the tower. He locked his eyes on the blank space near the top of the wall as he powdered his hands with chalk from his waist bag, then began to climb.

Chuck leaned forward, anxious to see how the initial third-round competitor would cope with the tough, new route. The Oxnard climber had lifted himself past the two smaller blank spots on the wall with no apparent trouble during his second-round climb. He did so again this time. But when he came to the newly added gap near the top of the tower, he stopped, his fingers and toes perched on small holds beneath the bare section of wall. He leaned his head back, eyeing the tiny hold at the top of the blank space.

"You can do it, Tommy," a woman's voice called from among the onlookers.

The climber launched himself upward from the holds below the gap. He stretched his right hand high above his head, his fingers straining to reach the small hold, but his upward momentum stalled with his fingers an inch below the nubbin. He hung suspended in midair for a millisecond, then fell away from the wall. The auto-belay device caught him, halting his downward trajectory, and the automatic brake on the mechanism kicked in, lowering him down the face of the tower as he hung limply from the rope, his head down and his arms at his sides.

As the third round progressed, a handful of climbers, all of them male, managed the powerful move required to overcome the uppermost blank space on the wall and secure a grip on the tiny hold above it. Each of the successful climbers continued onward after that, reaching the top of the tower to remain in the competition.

Thirty minutes into round three, with only a few climbers still waiting their turn, Alden called out, "And now, our teeniest, tiniest contestant, coming to us all the way from Durango, Colorado. Please join me in giving a warm welcome to little Miss Carmelita Ortega!"

"¡Ándale, Carmelita!" one of the park workers from the campground cried out.

"¡Arriba, arriba, arriba!" hollered another.

Chuck wormed his way out of the crowd as Carmelita emerged from behind the tower. She dipped each of her hands into her chalk bag while Alden snapped the end of the climbing rope into her nylon harness.

As he had the first two rounds, Chuck removed the other end of the rope from the auto-belay mechanism at the base of the tower and ran it through the alloy belay device attached by a D-ring carabiner to the harness at his waist. He backed away from the wall to take up the slack in the line.

Carmelita smacked her chalked hands against the sides of her legs, leaving two white handprints on her navy tights. She looked up at the route for no more than a second and began her climb without any sign of having noticed the new, large blank space high on the tower.

She again overcame the first two blank spaces on the wall without difficulty. Chuck took in the rope as she continued higher. He made sure the rope drooped slightly toward the ground before it ran up to the top of the tower and back down to her, assuring he added no upward tension to the belay line that would aid her ascent.

Carmelita reached the blank space near the top of the tower in less than a minute. She leaned back from the small holds below the gap, her fingers crimped, her hair dangling in a ponytail from beneath the back of her helmet.

Chuck bit down on his lower lip. When faced for the first time with a difficult climbing problem, whether on a cliff or a sport wall, a climber's initial instinct—particularly that of a new climber like Carmelita—was to take a moment to assess the situation. During a competitive climb, however, every second mattered; energy expended clinging to the wall was no longer available to help overcome the problems above.

But Carmelita proved herself unlike most rookie climbers. She took no more than a cursory glance at the blank space and the nubbin above it before she sank low on the holds to which she clung, her nose to the tower and her knees pressed out to either side so that her center of gravity remained close to the wall.

The spectators fell silent. Only the whoosh of passing traffic on Northside Drive outside the campground disturbed the otherwise quiet morning.

Chuck eyed her intently. Perhaps it was simply the fact that, without a frame of reference, Carmelita didn't know how distant the tiny hold was from where she clung to the tower below it. Whatever the reason, her body remained loose as she reached the bottom of her downward crouch and instantly propelled herself upward, uncoiling her bent legs like a pair of springs.

Chuck relaxed as she shot straight up, inches from the wall, her right hand stretched high above her head. Most new climbers tended to tip their heads back when reaching for holds, their eyes fixed on the objects of their desire, unaware that the weight of a backward-tipped head shifts a climber's center of gravity appreciably outward. Even when rookie climbers reached overhead holds at the top of demanding moves, their back-tilted heads often created enough weight imbalance to peel their fingers from the holds, resulting in falls.

But Carmelita's senses were true. She kept her head straight and reached blindly overhead. So powerful was her upward launch that her fingers extended above the nubbin at the top of the blank space and her palm first made contact with the hold. Thanks to her vertical posture, she fell straight back down the face of the wall, closing her hand around the nubbin as it slid past her palm and into her curled fingers.

She clung to the hold like a trapeze artist, her body penduluming across the blank space. Using the momentum generated by her swing, she grasped the next hold higher on the wall with her left hand. Gaining what purchase she could on the blank fiberglass panel below her with the sticky rubber toes of her shoes, she climbed the remaining holds up the wall and gave the top of the tower a triumphant tap.

The onlookers roared. Rosie leapt skyward, cheering with everyone else. Standing among several of the park workers from the campground, Clarence jabbed the air in front of him with his fists, shimmying his ample backside. Jimmy smiled and leaned forward on his crutches, freeing his hands to clap.

Chuck basked in the acclaim for his stepdaughter, who had just proved herself extraordinarily talented at his—*his!*—favorite sport.

Only when the cheers died away did he loosen his brake hand and lower Carmelita to the ground. Alden unclipped her from the climbing rope and she hurried over to Janelle for a hug.

One by one, the remaining climbers followed Carmelita on the tower until Alden announced, "It's time now for our final climber of the day—Berkeley, California's own Tara Rogan, women's division champion at last month's Joshua Tree Open."

The woman in the magenta tank top appeared from behind the tower.

Chuck leaned down and said in Carmelita's ear, "You're the only female climber who has topped out this round." He aimed a forefinger at the climber, Tara, as she chalked her hands at the base of the tower, her eyes locked on the gap near the top. "If she falls, you'll win the female division right here and now, without even having to compete tomorrow."

Carmelita's mouth fell open. "I will?"

"I think Alden made the round-three route a little too hard," Chuck said. "One of the primary goals of every two-day climbing competition is to make sure at least some competitors from every division make it to the second day. But that might not happen with this year's Slam."

Tara set off up the tower. Like Carmelita, she climbed smoothly past the two lower blank spaces on the wall. Chuck found himself hoping she would hesitate for a long time upon reaching the large blank space near the top of the tower, weakening in advance of attempting the strength move necessary to overcome it.

Instead, she surprised him.

16

When she reached the bottom of the large blank spot on the wall, without a glance at the nubbin above it, the champion climber, Tara, performed a quick hand switch. Upon trading her left hand for her right on the hold just below the blank space, she crouched and lunged, her body close to the wall. But rather than leap straight up past the blank space with the same cannon-like action as Carmelita and the successful male climbers, Tara leapt to her left, reaching with her outstretched hand around the side of the bowed wall. At the farthest extent of her lunge, she grasped a hold made of resin dyed the same color as the gray, rock-like panels that comprised the fiberglass tower itself. The hold, all but invisible against the wall, featured a jug-handled top that provided a sure grip for Tara's fingers.

Tara transferred her right hand to the jugged top of the hold and performed a simple pull up, lifting her body until her head was above the hold, her feet splayed on the fiberglass wall below her. She reached back around the tower with her right hand and easily grasped the nubbin at the top of the large blank spot. From there, she swung across the space and scrambled on up the wall to the top of the tower.

As they had with Carmelita, the spectators broke into a raucous cheer for Tara's unorthodox move and successful ascent.

"Hmm," Chuck said, his eyes on the tower, as the auto-belay mechanism lowered Tara to the ground. He explained to Janelle and Carmelita, "That's called an out move. Every now and then, a route setter will place a hold on the farthest edge of a route. Given how quickly competitors must climb to conserve their energy, most never notice the out hold. That's especially true if—" he pointed at the gray hold "—it's the same color as the wall itself."

"She didn't even slow down," Janelle said. She gazed at the hold, barely visible where it was bolted to the wall on the far side of the tower. "It's almost as if she knew it was there, waiting for her."

Chuck sat with Janelle in their campsite. They were alone after round three of the Slam, Clarence having taken the girls for what he called an "uncle treat," hopping one of the free park-service buses circulating the valley to visit the ice cream shop in Yosemite Village in celebration of Carmelita's successful ascents.

The reunion campsite next door was empty. Jimmy and the others had headed west on the paved trail out of the campground for an old-times'-sake look at El Capitan from the foot of its three-thousand-foot face, Jimmy crutching along the path while Bernard hovered at his side.

"I'll catch up with you for happy hour," Chuck had told his fellow attendees, begging off going with them as the glow of Carmelita's success in the Slam wore off and his thoughts turned increasingly troubled. The rumbling sound of the boulder crashing down the drainage wouldn't leave him, the noise serving as a foreboding soundtrack to ominous visions parading through his mind.

Those visions included Thorpe's leg, wedged in the tree, and the deep ankle laceration, along with the plastic stay poking from the wingsuit airfoil.

And Jimmy's flailing arms as he plummeted from the tower, the sharp crack of fracturing bone when he hit the ground. What if that had been Carmelita?

Plus, Owen's harsh interrogations, first concerning Jimmy's

accident, then Thorpe's death.

There also was Alden's apparent cheating on Tara's behalf during round three of the Slam.

And, finally and most frightening, the fact that someone had sent the boulder down the drainage, aiming for Chuck and his family.

He clasped his hands between his legs. Questions, questions, questions, but no clear answers.

Best for now, he decided, to go with what he knew.

"The more I think about it, the more convinced I am we found the right spot," he said to Janelle.

"It seems pretty unlikely to have found it on the first try," she said, waving a circling fly away from her face.

"Not as unlikely as you might think." He directed a finger through the trees. "See the bend in the river?"

Across the road outside the campground, water rippled in the midday sun where the Merced River meandered beneath the pedestrian bridge.

Her eyes went to the river's glittering surface. "*Sí.*"

"A Yale dig in the 1950s on the far side, across from where the forest starts up, uncovered an old fire pit. Unlike tribal fire pits, which would have been lined with lots of large stones and filled with ashes, the pit contained just a day's worth of ashes backed by only a couple of stones. If what the Yale team found was the gold prospectors' overnight camp, then the prospectors' retreat from the attackers, based on Grover's description, would have taken them a short distance down the valley. From there, after being cut off from the west, they'd have headed up into bluffs."

"To where Rosie found the projectile point."

"That's what I'm thinking."

"And where the boulder came from."

"Like I said before, the Indigenous Tribespeople Foundation

posted our plans for the survey on their website a couple of weeks ago, including the expectation we would start below the granite prow."

"That would explain how someone could have been waiting up there ahead of us yesterday."

"In order to scare us," Chuck agreed. "I think you're right, that the boulder was a one-off."

"You're singing my tune right back at me."

"Ortegas don't run. That's what you said."

Her eyes constricted. "You want to go back up there, don't you?"

"That's why I didn't head for El Cap with the guys. Somebody doesn't want us up there for a reason."

"And you want me to come with you."

"Two sets of eyes are always better than one."

She shook herself, the feet of her camp chair rocking in the dirt. Then she straightened in her seat. "Promise me no more boulders will fall on us."

"I promise no more boulders will fall on us."

"You're a lousy liar," she said. Still, she rose from her chair. "What more are we looking for?"

"Anything that will lend credence to Grover's story—particularly, the suspicions he raises at the end of his account about the murdered prospectors."

"The ones who were attacked on the opposite side of the river from their camp?"

"Right. As the sun came up the morning after the assault, smoke from the tribe's fires rose all over the valley floor, proving to the five prospectors who'd escaped to the rim of the valley that they were totally outnumbered. Plus, all five of them had suffered wounds of some sort in the battle the day before. They were extremely lucky to have made it to the top of the valley alive themselves, and couldn't risk going back down after the other three members of their party. They had no choice but to head south, off-trail, back the way they'd come."

"So they left without knowing for sure what had happened to the others."

"They didn't learn that until two weeks later."

17

From "A Reminiscence" (Part Two) by prospector Stephen F. Grover:

Suddenly a deer bounded in sight. Some objected to our shooting as the report of our rifle might betray us, but said I, "As well die by our foes as by starvation," and dropping on one knee with never a steadier nerve or truer aim, the first crack of my rifle brought him down.

Hope revived in our hearts, and quickly skinning our prize, we roasted pieces of venison on long sticks thrust in the flame and smoke, and with no seasoning whatever it was the sweetest morsel I ever tasted. Hastily stripping the flesh from the hind quarters of the deer, Aich and myself, being the only ones able to carry the extra burden, shouldered the meat and we again took up our line of travel.

In this manner we toiled on and crossed the Mariposa Trail, and passed down the south fork of the Merced River, constantly fearing pursuit.

As night came on, we prepared camp by cutting crotched stakes which we drove in the ground and, putting a pole across, enclosed it with brush, making a pretty secure hiding place for the night, where we crept under and lay close together. Although expecting an attack, we were so exhausted and tired that we soon slept.

An incident of the night occurs to me: One of the men, on reaching out his foot quickly, struck one of the poles, and down came the whole structure upon us. Thinking that our foes were upon us, our frightened crowd sprang out and made for the more dense brush, but as quiet followed, we realized our mistake and, gathering together again, we passed the remainder of the night in sleepless apprehension.

When morning came we started again, following up the river, and passed one of our camping places. We traveled as far as we could in that direction, and prepared for our next night to camp and slept in a big hollow tree, still fearing pursuit. We passed the night undisturbed and in the morning started again on our journey, keeping in the shelter of the brush, and crossed the foot of the Falls, a little above Crane Flat—so named by us, as one of our party shot a large crane there while going over, but it is now known as Wawona.

We still traveled in the back ground, passing through Big Tree Grove again, but not until we gained the ridge above Chowchilla did we feel any surety of ever seeing our friends again.

Traveling on thus for five days, we at last reached Coarse Gold Gulch once more, barefooted and ragged but more glad than I can express. An excited crowd soon gathered around us, and while listening to our hair-breadth escapes, our sufferings and perils, and while vowing vengeance on the treacherous savages, an Indian was seen quickly coming down the mountain trail, gaily dressed in war paint and feathers, evidently a spy on our track, and not three hours behind us. A party of miners watched him as he passed by the settlement. E. Whitney Grover, my brother, and a German cautiously followed him. The haughty Red Man was made to bite the dust before many minutes had passed.

My brother Whitney Grover quickly formed a company

of twenty-five men, who were piloted by Aich, and started for the Valley to bury our unfortunate companions. They found only Sherburn and Tudor, after a five days march, and met with no hostility from the Indians. They buried them where they lay, with such land marks as were at hand at that time.

I have often called to mind the fact that the two men, Sherburn and Tudor, the only ones of our party who were killed on that eventful morning, were seen reading their Bibles while in camp the morning before starting into the Valley. They were both good men and we mourned their loss sincerely.

After we had been home six days, Rose, who was a partner of Sherburn and Tudor in a mine about five miles west of Coarse Gold Gulch, where there was a mining camp, appeared in the neighborhood and reported the attack and said the whole party was killed, and that he alone escaped. On being questioned, he said he hid behind the Waterfall and lived by chewing the leather strap which held his rifle across his shoulders. This sounded strange to us as he had his rifle and plenty of ammunition and game was abundant.

After hearing of our return to Coarse Gold Gulch camp, he never came to see us as would have been natural, but shortly disappeared. We thought his actions and words very strange and we remembered how he urged us to enter the Valley, and at the time of the attack was the first one to fall, right amongst the savages, apparently with his death wound—and now he appears without a scratch, telling his version of the affair and disappearing without seeing any of us.

We all believed he was not the honest man and friend we took him to be. He took possession of the gold mine *in which he held a one-third interest with Sherburn and Tudor, and sold it.*

Here ends the account of Stephen F. Grover

18

Chuck held the sheets containing Grover's account in his hand as he walked with Janelle across the pedestrian bridge over the river, having just read the conclusion of the account to her.

"The end of Grover's story is what has the Indigenous Tribespeople Foundation so interested," he explained. "The part when the guy named Rose shows up back in Coarse Gold Gulch."

"He was one of the three prospectors trapped on the far side of the river from the camp, right?" Janelle asked.

Chuck nodded. "The five surviving prospectors figured the three others were goners. According to Grover, Rose even hollered as much to them, telling them to get out of there and save themselves."

"But then, miraculously, he survived."

"Not only did he survive, he prospered. With the deaths of Sherburn and Tudor, he took sole possession of the gold mine the three of them had owned together, and, according to Grover, sold it and disappeared."

A group of hikers in heavy leather boots passed Chuck and Janelle, crossing the valley the opposite direction. The hikers spoke German to one another as they tromped across the span, led by a guide flying a red, black, and yellow flag on an aluminum staff above her head.

When the clomping of the hikers' boots on the bridge receded, Chuck flipped to the last page of Grover's account and paraphrased Rose's return to the gold camp, his avoidance of the other surviving prospectors, and his sale of the gold mine he'd co-owned with Sherburn and Tudor.

"In his account," Chuck explained to Janelle as they made their way through the meadow on the far side of the river, "Grover points to a very clear motive for Rose to have either murdered his fellow mine owners or arranged for their murders. Grover even indicates that Rose might have encouraged the warriors' attack. That's what the people from the Indigenous Tribespeople Foundation are wondering. After leaving camp and crossing the river, Rose could have killed his two partners himself—one of the two was killed with a blow from an ax of one of the prospectors, after all. Then, with his partners dead, he could have shot at the warriors, who would have retaliated while he slipped safely away on his own. Or he might simply have paid the tribespeople to initiate the attack on the prospectors while ensuring his own safety. Remember, according to Grover, Rose was the only one among the prospectors who spoke the tribal language."

Taking the printed sheets from Chuck, Janelle studied them as they walked across the valley floor. "Who figured this out?"

"An ITF researcher, fulfilling the foundation's mission. Tribespeople were accused of all sorts of atrocities during the settling of the Old West. For the most part, the accusations were true. The settlers and the Army and local militias committed genocide as they came west. They slaughtered the indigenous tribespeople and took the tribes' lands by force. It was only natural for the tribespeople to respond with savagery of their own. In addition, though, the absence of the rule of law in the Old West presented opportunities for settlers to falsely accuse tribespeople of having committed crimes the settlers actually committed among themselves. The Indigenous Tribespeople Foundation works to right those false accusations—or, at least, call them into question."

Janelle handed the sheets back to Chuck. "I don't see what

you or anyone else can do to prove something like this after so many years."

Chuck folded the papers and slipped them into his pocket. "When it comes to archaeology, one-hundred-percent proof is virtually impossible to come by, whether thousands of years or, as in this case, 150 years later. Instead, Clarence and I are looking into whether we can add validity to Grover's account. Any additional evidence we find will be used in the foundation's case regarding Rose's motivation in the deaths of his business partners."

"Wouldn't the best evidence be the record of the sale of the mine?"

"If anything like that existed, yes. But hardly any financial records were created during the California gold rush. ITF researchers haven't found a deed or any other recordings of the mine sale referenced by Grover in his account."

"Sounds pretty hopeless."

"Archaeology is all about playing long odds. But it's also about looking into history with the possibility of revealing the past in a new, clearer light. In this case, based on the uncertainties exposed in Grover's account, there's a lot to be said for digging into the past with an eye toward uncovering a wrong and making it right—or, at the very least, raising questions, in this particular case, about the accepted indigenous-people-as-savages narrative that runs through so much of the history of the Old West."

"I'm beginning to understand why you were so excited when Rosie found the projectile point yesterday."

"And why so I'm anxious to get back up there."

"Despite the boulder."

"Almost, if I'm being truly honest, *because* of the boulder and what it says about how interested others might be in what else could be up there."

"The arrowhead isn't enough?"

"It's a great start. But we didn't get to check things out very much before we had to get out of there. The shallow burial depth of the projectile point tells me no one else has conducted a formal search beneath the bluff. If they had, the point Rosie kicked up would have been long gone."

"Which means . . . ?"

Chuck's cheeks grew warm as his face flushed with excitement. ". . . anything else dating back to Grover's time is still up there, waiting to be found."

They reached the dirt shelf beneath the overhanging granite nose thirty minutes later.

"I can't believe we're up here again," Janelle said, her eyes darting around her as she caught her breath.

Chuck stood on the ledge beside her. "The boulder came at us from way around the corner."

"Don't remind me."

"We'll be fine here, just like the prospectors, under the nose of rock."

He faced the bluff, the outcrop directly above him. At his feet, the projectile point rested in the divot created by Rosie's boot. The dirt ledge at the foot of the granite bluff ran fifty feet from the projectile point in each direction, giving way to trees and brush at both ends. To the east, the shelf narrowed to nothing at the steep drainage down which the boulder had tumbled yesterday. A hundred yards beyond the west side of the ledge, a tree-studded, brush-choked hillside came up against another section of vertical granite looming above the valley floor.

Chuck turned from the outcrop and pointed through the trees at the meadow in the valley below. "They camped down there somewhere, on the near side of the river. The tribespeople were on the far side." He angled his finger to the southwest. "There's where they would have retreated, trying to get to the Mariposa Trail. But they were cut off, at which point—" he swung his finger up the steep slope to the dirt ledge upon which they stood "—they made their way here, per Grover's description. Or, at least, that's what Rosie's find appears to indicate."

He pointed west along the bluff. "How about if you have a look that way? I'll head the other direction, toward the drainage. Then we can trade, so we'll both have examined the entire ledge."

"Can I kick at the dirt, like Rosie?" Janelle asked.

"It's fine to use your hands. That's what I'm going to do. We just can't do any full-on digging with shovels and trowels, per our contract."

Janelle set off west along the ledge. Chuck took a moment to absorb the scene, casting his mind back a century and a half. He envisioned Stephen Grover and the other prospectors huddled together here, beneath the granite prow, injured and bleeding and convinced they were about to die.

As Grover reported in his account, the prospectors had held off the tribespeople with their two rifles, determined to "sell their lives only at great expense." They'd probably made their stand until dark right where Chuck stood on the ledge, directly below the outthrust granite nose. That would have put them far back beneath the rock outcrop, out of range of tumbling boulders—and right where Rosie had uncovered the projectile point.

Chuck knelt next to the sliver of obsidian and raked his fingers through the dirt. He worked his way east along the shelf in methodical fashion, gouging shallow, overlapping finger tracks through the dusty soil as if contouring the grounds of a Japanese bonsai garden with a round-toothed rake.

Moving sideways as he worked, he furrowed the dirt with his fingers from the base of the sheer face of the bluff outward to the edge of the four-foot-wide ledge. He'd moved along the dirt shelf less than ten feet when his gouging fingers turned up a second projectile point buried in half an inch of soil.

He held the point up to the afternoon sunlight flooding the ledge. This one, twice the size of the one uncovered by Rosie, was smoky gray at its center; it, too, had been scorched before it was flaked.

Chuck exhaled in elation. A single projectile point could, conceivably, have been from an indigenous hunter firing at an animal on the ledge. But no animal would have waited around for a hunter to take a second shot at it. Rather, the second projectile point indicated some sort of greater conflict had occurred here.

Grover's words came back to Chuck: "I fully believe—could I visit that spot even now after the lapse of all these years—I could still pick up some of those flint arrow points in the shelf of the rock and in the face of the bluff where we were huddled together."

"Yowza," Chuck muttered to himself. He'd barely begun his contracted work for the ITF, and already he'd justified the foundation's decision to examine the prospectors' movements in the valley.

He sat back on his haunches. If someone knew what was waiting here to be found, that could explain why they'd rolled the boulder down from above yesterday, trying to scare Chuck and Clarence away from their contracted work.

But that idea didn't make sense. If anyone knew what was up here, they'd have absconded with the finds long before now.

He twisted his mouth, perplexed. Something else was at play here, something he couldn't quite figure out. Not yet, anyway.

He set the projectile point atop the dirt where he'd uncovered it and continued sideways on his knees, sifting the soil with his fingers. Ten minutes later, he found a third projectile point.

A minute after that, near the end of the ledge, he uncovered a fourth.

He met Janelle back in the middle of the dirt shelf.

"I found three more points," he crowed. "Can you believe it?"

"I heard you cheering yourself on. I figured it was good news."

"Any luck at your end?"

She dusted her palms against one another. "Not a thing."

Chuck eyed the west end of the ledge, where the bluff fell back from the dirt shelf. "They must have huddled from the middle of the ledge to its eastern end, toward the drainage, where they were more protected by the overhang."

He used his phone to snap preliminary pictures of the three newly uncovered projectile points and their locations, then he and Janelle swapped sides. Kneeling, Chuck raked his fingers through dirt already tracked by Janelle's fingers as he worked his way westward. He uncovered no projectile points until, nearing the west end of the dirt ledge, he heard Janelle draw a sharp breath at the far east end of the shelf.

He spun on his knees to see Janelle standing before the granite bluff at the back of the ledge. She reached a hand into a crevice in the bluff, her eyes locked on the rock wall in front of her.

19

"What's this?" Janelle asked, her voice filled with wonder. Chuck shot to his feet and hurried along the dirt shelf to her side, stepping around the four uncovered projectile points along the way.

He expected to see yet another arrowhead in her fingers when she removed her hand from the crevice in the rock wall. But she withdrew from the cleft an object too shiny to be a projectile point. When Chuck reached her, she centered the object in her palm, holding out for their mutual inspection a circle of gold metal sparkling in the afternoon sun.

"It's a ring," she murmured.

Chuck extended a finger and gave the golden band a reverent touch. "I didn't think to check the rock face," he told her admiringly.

Janelle stared at the gold ring. "The prospectors were surrounded up here, outnumbered. They thought they were done for."

"That's what the ring proves. I'm sure of it," Chuck said. "The settlers and militiamen were extremely savage to the tribespeople they killed—scalping them and, awful as it sounds, even cutting off their genitals and parading them as war prizes. The tribespeople scalped and mutilated settlers they killed, too. They also took anything they could use from their victims, particularly anything made of metal, which they often refashioned for body decoration."

Chuck plucked the ring from Janelle's palm and held it up between his thumb and forefinger. "The owner of this ring was cornered here, arrows flying at him from below, boulders rolling

SCOTT GRAHAM

down from above. He couldn't stand the idea of his ring falling into the hands of the warriors, or, worse, the idea of a warrior slicing off his finger—maybe even while he was still alive—to get at it. So he shoved it in the crevice instead." He held the ring higher. "In the 1800s, the most common form of ornamentation among male settlers in the Old West was rings made of brass. See the—?" He stopped.

"Huh," he said.

He turned the ring, studying it. "This has been exposed to air—to oxygen—for more than a century. It should be stained green on its edges from oxidization, but it's not."

"What does that mean?" Janelle asked.

"That means it's not brass." Chuck stared at the ring, fascinated. "The only other thing it could be is gold."

His stomach churned with excitement. He rotated the ring, catching the sun and revealing faint etching inside the band. He brought the ring close to his eyes but couldn't make out the inscription. "What does it say on the inside?" he asked, handing the ring to Janelle.

She held it up and squinted. "Initials. Two capital letters, a G and a P. And a date." She looked at Chuck. "1849."

"This is unbelievable!" he rejoiced. He wrapped his arm around her. "*You're* unbelievable. You found the golden ticket. The P stands for Peabody. It has to. He was one of the prospectors. His first name must have started with a G—George or Gregory or something. According to Grover's account, Peabody was wounded in the neck and arm at the start of the attack. Trapped here on the shelf, he must have been convinced he was as good as dead."

Chuck kissed Janelle on the cheek, a quick, celebratory peck, the ring in her hand pressed between them.

"I have to believe G. Peabody was one of *the* Peabodys," he said. "If I'm right . . ." He stopped, gulped, started over. "This is . . . this is absolutely incredible."

He kissed her again, on the lips this time, soaking in the moment.

He stepped back, took a breath, and explained. "You've probably heard of the Peabody coal mining empire. They're known for their strip mines and for lots of other mining around the world. They've been around since the 1800s as a big corporation, mostly digging coal out of the ground in West Virginia, Kentucky, places like that. But they got their start out West. The first time I read Grover's list of the prospectors who came into Yosemite Valley looking for gold with him, the Peabody name stuck out to me. I did some checking online and learned the Peabody name was connected to some early Sierra mining, right at the start of the gold rush in 1849. It makes sense that a Peabody might well have been among the prospectors exploring the last valleys of the Sierra three years later, in 1852."

"That would be a big deal?"

Chuck turned the ring over in his hand. "It would be a huge deal. If this ring really is pure gold, and it was owned by a member of the Peabody family, then it's worth a fortune."

Janelle stared at the ring, her eyes wide. "Really?"

"Yep. Something like this, if it can be traced back to its origin with a strong degree of certainty, tells the kind of story collectors go wild over. It's like finding a shipwreck at the bottom of the ocean. People love that sort of thing. And the involvement of a company like Peabody adds that much more value to it."

"Why's that?"

"The value of any archaeological discovery—a shipwreck, King Tut's tomb, whatever—is the value society places on it." He proffered the ring. "A company like Peabody and all the wealthy Peabody heirs almost certainly will see this as valuable to their namesake and their corporate history. They'll be willing to throw big bucks at it, which will make other collectors want to throw even bigger bucks at it, just to try to snatch it away from them. Which might well make this thing—" he raised the ring in the palm of his hand like a chalice "—worth millions."

"Millions?" Janelle's mouth fell open. "Of dollars?"

"At least one million, anyway. Maybe two. Depends on how big a play the Peabody family decides to make for it—assuming, that is, its provenance turns out to be ascertainable, which I fully expect it will be."

"Provenance?"

"A quick look at the ring under an electron microscope will prove, first, whether it's pure gold, and second, if so, its precise mineral composition. That composition will be traceable, within a few miles, to a specific place on the globe—that is, most likely, to a specific part of the Sierra Nevada Mountains, probably where a Peabody-owned gold mine was located. That wouldn't entirely prove true G. Peabody ownership, but it would be more than enough to set off a bidding war."

"Won't the Peabody heirs simply be able to claim it's theirs, since it belonged to their great-great-grandfather or whoever?"

"Not without something in writing. It's like all the art-work looted by the Nazis during World War II. After the war, the paintings and sculptures that had clear trails of ownership went back to their rightful owners or their heirs. But everything else went up for auction. Not exactly fair, but that's the way the world works."

"Who would get the money for the ring?"

"It'd probably be split between the park service and the Indigenous Tribespeople Foundation. Or maybe the park service will find a way to hold onto the ring, with funding from the Smithsonian or some other deep-pocketed organization. Regardless, everybody's going to love you."

"Me?"

"Of course. Even though Grover mentions in his account

the idea that projectile points might have ended up lodged in the cliff wall, I don't know how long it would have taken me and Clarence to search there, if ever. We'd have been too focused on what was in the dirt underfoot. You saved us from our archaeologist selves."

The same pink color as the gemstone in the side of Janelle's nose rose in her cheeks as Chuck continued. "It's even better than that, actually. Clarence and I will, of course, go ahead with the full site survey here next week, but your discovery of the ring is as close to validation of Grover's account as we possibly could hope to find. It tells us his account of the prospectors' escape from the valley is legit. Not even Sherlock Holmes could definitively solve the Case of the Murdered Gold Prospectors more than a century after the fact. But the ring lends credence to the suspicions about Rose, as suggested by Grover at the end of his account—when Rose shows up in Coarse Gold Gulch and announces that the other prospectors are dead, after which he sells the mine he'd owned with the two dead prospectors and disappears with the money."

Janelle took the ring from Chuck's hand and turned it in her fingers. "So, legitimizing Grover's overall account adds legitimacy, in turn, to Grover's suspicion that Rose may have murdered his business partners."

"Or paid the tribespeople to kill them for him."

"When you put it all together, Rose looks pretty guilty, doesn't he?"

"He makes an awfully good suspect." Chuck bent his fingers back one by one, counting off. "He had motive. He had opportunity. And he clearly profited from the murders."

Janelle lowered the ring. "But no one will ever know for sure, will they?"

"At this point, the only thing we know for certain is who, ultimately, paid the price for the two murders."

"I'm guessing you're about to tell me it wasn't Rose."

"Given the history of the Old West, you can probably guess who it was instead." Chuck reached for the printed pages, folded in his pocket, of a second account of the prospectors' murders he'd studied in preparation for fulfilling the Indigenous Tribespeople Foundation contract.

20

From *Discovery of the Yosemite and Ensuing Years* by early California explorer Lafayette H. Bunnell:

*E*arly in May 1852, a small party of miners from *Coarse Gold Gulch started out on a prospecting tour with the intention of making a visit to the Yosemite Valley. The curiosity of some of these men had been excited by descriptions of it.*

This party spent some little time prospecting on their way. Commencing on the south fork of the Merced, they tested the mineral resources of streams tributary to it; and then, passing over the divide on the old trail, camped for the purpose of testing the branches leading into the main Merced. While at this camp, they were visited by begging Indians; a frequent occurrence in the mining camps of some localities.

The Indians appeared friendly, and gave no indications of hostile intentions. They gave the party to understand, however, that the territory they were then in belonged to them, although no tribute was demanded. The miners comprehended their intimations, but paid no attention to their claim, being aware that this whole region had been ceded to the Government by treaty during the year before.

Having ascertained that [the Indians] were a part of the Yosemite Band, the miners, by signs, interrogated them as to the location of the valley, but this they refused to answer or pretended not to understand. The valley, however, was known to be near, and no difficulty was anticipated when the party were ready to visit it, as an outline map, furnished them before starting, had thus far proved reliable.

Unsuspicious of danger from an attack, they reached the valley, and were ambushed by the Indians. Two of the party were instantly killed. Another was seriously wounded, but finally succeeded in making his escape. The names of the men were Rose, Sherburn, and Tudor.

The reports of these murders alarmed many of the citizens. The officer in command at Fort Miller was notified of these murders, and a detachment of regular soldiers under Lt. Moore, U.S.A., was at once dispatched to capture or punish the red-skins. Beside the detachment of troops, scouts and guides and a few of the friends of the murdered men accompanied the expedition.

Among the volunteer scouts was A. A. Gray, usually called "Gus" Gray. His knowledge of the valley and its vicinity made his services valuable to Lt. Moore, as special guide and scout for that locality. The particulars of this expedition I obtained from Gray.

Under the guidance of Gray, Lt. Moore entered the valley in the night, and was successful in surprising and capturing a party of five savages; but an alarm was given, and Chief Ten-ie-ya and his people fled from their huts and escaped. On examination of the prisoners in the morning, it was discovered that each of them had some article of clothing that had belonged to the murdered men.

The naked bodies of the murdered men were found and buried. The captives declared that the valley was their home, and that white men had no right to come there without their consent.

Lt. Moore told them, through his interpreter, that they

had sold their lands to the Government, that it belonged to the white men now; that the Indians had no right there. They had signed a treaty of peace with the whites, and had agreed to live on the reservations provided for them. To this they replied that Ten-ie-ya had never consented to the sale of their valley, and had never received pay for it. The other chiefs, they said, had no right to sell their territory.

Lt. Moore became fully satisfied that he had captured the real murderers, and the abstract questions of title and jurisdiction were not considered debatable in this case. He promptly pronounced judgment, and sentenced them to be shot. They were at once placed in line, and by his order a volley of musketry from the soldiers announced that the spirits of five Indians were liberated to occupy ethereal space.

This may seem summary justice for a single individual, in a republic, to mete out to fellow beings on his own judgment. This prompt disposition of the captured murderers was witnessed by a scout sent out by Ten-ie-ya to watch the movements of Lt. Moore and his command, and was immediately reported to the old chief, who with his people at once made a precipitate retreat from their hiding places, and crossed the mountains to their allies, the Paiutes and Monos.

Here ends the account of Lafayette H. Bunnell

21

After reading Bunnell's account aloud to Janelle, Chuck folded the sheets of paper and slid them into his back pocket against the folded pages of Stephen Grover's account.

"I almost have the two accounts of the murders memorized by now," he told her. He looked east along the ledge at the four uncovered projectile points lying atop the dirt. "Both Grover's and Bunnell's descriptions match perfectly with what we've found." He touched the ring in Janelle's palm. "Especially with what you found."

She made a sweeping gesture, the ring cupped in her hand, taking in the vehicles passing on Southside Drive at the foot of the slope, the dozens of hikers on trails crisscrossing the valley floor, and, a mile upriver amid the trees, the valley's commercial center, Yosemite Village, with its restaurants, gift shops, galleries, visitor center, and museum. "I can't believe history from a century ago can be so present in the middle of all this. We just walked up the hill and—" she held out her hand "—*voilà.*"

He grinned. "You sound like a gung-ho rookie archaeologist."

The ring sparkled in the sun. "Finding something like this will do that to a person."

"As it should."

"But . . ." She hesitated.

Chuck suspected she was thinking the same thing he was.

". . . if someone knew we would find this," she continued, "they'd have taken it themselves rather than try to scare us away by rolling a boulder down at us. It's not like it was that hard to find."

Chuck nodded. "I'm as confused as you are. They might not

have found the ring in the cliff face right away, but they'd have uncovered the projectile points in a matter of minutes, just like we did."

"What if they left the arrowheads for us to find?"

"You mean, could they have planted them up here?"

"Something like that. I don't know."

"I can't figure it out, either."

He took the ring from Janelle's palm. "No way did they plant this," he said. He used his cell phone to snap a couple of preliminary pictures of the ring, then sealed it in a clear plastic bag from his daypack.

He held up the bag with the ring inside. "I bet the foundation people will see this as all the evidence they need for the circumstantial case they're building against Rose, and against Lt. Moore for his summary executions of the five Yosemite tribespeople, too. It's definitely more than they ever could have hoped we'd find for them."

"Don't forget Grover's description of the scout who was killed in revenge after the surviving prospectors made it back to the mining camp."

"Him, too," Chuck agreed. "That's six dead tribespeople, all told, who may well be exonerated in the court of public opinion by your find—not to mention the money the foundation and park service might make off it. Good work."

She smiled, her teeth flashing.

He tucked the bagged ring in his pack. "We don't dare risk leaving it up here." He indicated the route back down the slope with an open hand. "Shall we?"

She looked over her shoulder, where the boulder had crashed down the drainage past them the day before. "I'll be more than happy to be long gone from here."

* * *

The reunion attendees sat in a loose circle in their campsite after their return from the base of El Capitan. Jimmy slunk low in his webbed seat with his eyes closed. His crutches lay on the ground at his side, his soft-splinted lower leg stretched out in front of him.

Chuck carried a chair from the Bender Archaeological camp to the reunion camp and unfolded it. Sitting forward in the chair, he displayed the gold ring in its clear plastic bag and told the story of its discovery. He heaped credit on Janelle and described what her find would mean to the Indigenous Tribespeople Foundation.

Leaving his seat, Dale crossed the circle to Chuck and fingered the ring through the layer of plastic. "It's like Bilbo's ring, from *The Hobbit*," he marveled.

"Hopefully it's not quite that evil," Chuck said. "But it's worth a fortune, that's for sure."

He recounted the prospectors' actions as chronicled by Grover, pointing through the trees at the south face of the valley up which the prospectors had escaped. He described the executions of the tribespeople, as reported by Bunnell, too.

"You get paid to check out things like that?" Dale asked, returning to his chair.

Chuck passed the ring to Mark, seated beside him. "I usually study ancient history—societies more than five hundred years old. From an archaeological perspective, looking into something that happened only 150 years ago is fairly unusual."

Mark studied the bagged ring. "These Indians you're talking about seem pretty fired up."

"'Indigenous tribespeople' is the preferred term these days."

"What about 'Native American'?"

"That's mostly okay. Some people don't like the word 'native,' though. It's considered demeaning. And lots of people still like the term 'American Indian' as well."

"Sounds political."

"It is. People fight over the various names all the time these days. As for the Yosemite tribespeople, they were fighting for their ancestral lands here in the valley 150 years ago." Chuck glanced at the meadow, shimmering in the afternoon sunlight across the road from the campground. "I think we'd all agree this place is worth fighting for."

"I wasn't talking about the Yosemites," Mark said. "I was asking about the, uh, tribespeople who hired you. Why are they so interested in this stuff after all these years?"

Chuck leaned forward, addressing Mark and the rest of the group. "Millions of people pass through Yosemite Valley every summer. They're interested in the natural world, in the outdoors, and—to your question, Mark—in what happened here in the valley before it became a national park. The average visitor spends less than twenty-four hours in Yosemite Valley. In the short time they're here, they're fed a quick story by the park service about the park and its history. Right now, the shorthand narrative is that the white man drove the Yosemites out of the valley after killings by both sides. But what if a significant piece of that narrative is wrong? Reading between the lines of Stephen Grover's account, it's entirely possible that the prospector named Rose murdered his business partners, Tudor and Sherburn, by his own hand, or somehow bribed or incited the tribespeople to kill them, so he could gain full control of the gold mine he co-owned with them."

Mark handed back the ring. "I still don't see what that does for the foundation you're talking about."

Chuck hung the bag from his fingers. "In telling the human histories of the national parks, the park service creates clean, simple narratives that are easy for tourists to digest during their short visits. But when you factor in the never-ending propensity for people to give in to the most powerful of human emotions—

greed—there's never a clean, simple history of any particular place or any particular national park, Yosemite included."

"So," Mark said, "the Indigenous Tribespeople Foundation is trying to set the record straight."

Chuck rocked his head from side to side. "Yes and no. The foundation has an agenda, and it's looking for evidence to support that agenda. The foundation's researchers go through historical records at museums, universities, and research centers looking for clues that might change the existing narrative of the settlement of the West."

"In the case of Yosemite," Mark noted, "they found Grover's account."

Chuck inclined his head. "Upon close reading, his account appears to tell a different story than the general understanding of what happened to the prospectors, and what subsequently happened to the tribe."

"Which is why they hired you to follow up."

Chuck lifted the plastic bag. "And, man, will they be stoked to see what Janelle found for them."

"But the ring doesn't necessarily prove anything, does it?"

"Ultimately, that's not the idea. The most basic goal of the foundation is to instill a sense of pride in modern tribal peoples' lives. You've probably heard of the Innocence Project, dedicated to freeing innocent death-row inmates from prison. The work of the Indigenous Tribespeople Foundation is similar. The ITF can't entirely prove the innocence of tribespeople a century or more ago, but it *can* call into question their killings and executions by settlers or militiamen in the Old West. The case I'm looking into for the foundation here in the valley is a perfect example. The five Yosemite warriors I told you about were executed within minutes of their capture, without trial or any legal recourse whatsoever, for the supposed murders of the two white prospectors a week earlier."

Mark frowned. "But you're saying whatever you find won't necessarily solve anything."

"The goal is to raise questions. Who was responsible for the murders of the prospectors? Most likely, no one will ever know for sure. But a discovery like this—" Chuck turned the bag, showing off the ring "—once it's released for the world to see, proves the reports of what happened are basically valid. That, in turn, proves the questions raised by the accounts of Grover and Bunnell are basically valid, too. In this case, no matter what Rose may or may not have gotten away with, the killings of his two business partners led directly to the summary executions by government-paid militiamen of five Yosemite tribespeople, in complete contravention of America's laws, right here in this valley. The discovery of the ring helps make clear that the Yosemites were executed without due process for a crime they may well not have committed."

"You're involved in some pretty esoteric stuff, you know that?" Mark said.

"Everything archaeologists do is esoteric—digging up old stuff and trying to attach meaning to it." Chuck pressed the gold ring, in its bag, between his palms. "But this ring isn't esoteric at all. It's the real deal. I couldn't even begin to think how much it would bring on the black market."

"Seriously? That thing?"

"Absolutely." He described the ring's probable connection to the Peabody family and its potential million-plus-dollar value, given the likelihood of its traceability to a Peabody mine.

"But who'd be interested in buying it on the black market?" Mark asked.

"The same people who are buying all the antiquities illegally flowing out of the Middle East and South and Central America these days. There's a huge, global black market for archaeological discoveries. The Chinese, mostly. Rich Malaysians and

Singaporeans are big buyers, too. Antiquities from the U.S. are particularly popular—and, therefore, particularly valuable."

"All I know is, you're making my head hurt." Mark pushed himself from his seat. "I could use another beer." He made his way to the cooler and turned to the others. "Can I get one for anybody else while I'm up?"

Hands shot into the air. Chuck tucked the bagged ring into his pocket and raised his hand, too.

"It was Jimmy's idea," Dale whispered to Chuck a few hours later, after Dale popped his hand on the outside of Chuck's tent to wake him up. Better, Dale explained on Jimmy's behalf, for the group to do something other than just sit around and mope after Thorpe's death.

"We decided not to tell you," Dale said with an accompanying chuckle, his voice low, when Chuck had dressed and they stood together in the middle-of-the-night darkness outside the tent.

Chuck checked his phone. Just past midnight, a few hours after the second reunion dinner in camp and another early bedtime by the reunion attendees.

Dale's teeth shone white with a grin in the dim light filtering to the campsite from the central bathroom. "We figured you'd try to talk us out of it."

"Where is it you're going?" Chuck asked, his voice also low.

"You mean, 'Where are *we* going?'"

22

"Where?" Chuck insisted.

"You'll find out soon enough," Dale said.

Chuck groaned. "If I come with you."

Clearly, Jimmy, Dale, and the others hadn't tired of their mischief-making ways—which wasn't necessarily a bad thing. Perhaps a little mischief was what they all needed to move beyond, or at least come to grips with, Thorpe's death. Besides, the times Chuck had allowed himself to be talked into participating in one or another of the group's high jinks in the past, he'd enjoyed the escapades as much as the rest of them—midnight skinny dips in the Majestic Yosemite Hotel pool; loading one another's climbing packs with hidden, heavy cans of beer, then revealing and drinking the golden nectar upon topping out on climbs; singing love songs as a group chorus, drunk and a cappella, in the wee hours outside the tents of the few female climbers who had made Camp 4 their temporary home twenty years ago.

"What's going on?" Janelle asked from inside their family tent, her voice husky with sleep.

"The guys are up to something," Chuck whispered to her through the tent wall. "I have to keep them from doing anything too stupid."

Janelle muttered to herself. Then she warned Chuck, "Promise me you won't get yourself arrested. We didn't bring enough cash to bail you out."

He smiled. "I don't think we'll be gone for long. Are you and the girls okay here, with Clarence next to you?"

"I guess," she said grudgingly. Then, after a pause, "We'll be fine, Chuck."

She pressed her hand to the tent wall. He pressed his hand to hers in response.

The reunion attendees gathered in the middle of their campsite in the dark with extinguished headlamps strapped to their foreheads. Chuck made out Jimmy on his crutches, exchanging quiet banter with the other members of the group.

Next to Chuck, Bernard tapped his legs with his hands in a quick, steady beat. "Glad to see you're coming," he said in Chuck's ear.

"I'd like to know what we're doing."

"You and me both. Jimmy said I should come along, that it would be fun, fun, fun. He said there's nothing to be worried about."

"That was all he told you?"

Bernard continued to drum his legs with his hands. "I couldn't get anything more out of him. He said I was too much of a chicken, chicken, chicken-shit, and that you were too sensible for your own good."

Chuck's reply was thick with sarcasm. "Nothing to be worried about, huh?"

"You're coming?"

Chuck grunted. "To start with, I guess."

Dale distributed provisions of a sort impossible to determine in the darkness. He finished by handing Chuck a pair of one-pound tin cans, their labels invisible in the shadowy light.

"These are crucial," Dale said as he placed the cans in Chuck's palms. "You'll have to come all the way with us."

"I can always give them back," Chuck said, dropping the cans in his pack.

"If you manage to keep up with us."

Dale led Chuck and the others across the road and onto a trail to the head of the valley, leaving Jimmy in the campground. They walked single file along the deserted trail in the moonlight, Dale setting a brisk pace at the front of the line. From his position at the rear of the group, Chuck counted five shadowy figures ahead of him in addition to Dale—Caleb, Mark, Ponch, Bernard, and one unknown other.

Dale raised a hand when they reached the head of the valley, bringing the group to a halt where the flat pedestrian trail ended and the renowned John Muir Trail began its tortuous, 276-mile route south through the High Sierra to the 14,505-foot summit of Mount Whitney, the highest point in the Lower 48.

Catching his breath, Chuck checked his watch. Not yet one o'clock. They'd covered the two miles across the flat valley floor to the trailhead in forty minutes. Three miles per hour. Not bad for a bunch of old guys.

Dale clicked on his headlamp. The others, standing in a circle, followed suit. Their bright LED beams shone on one another. In the sudden light, Chuck identified the grinning faces of his old friends and that of Alden, the climbing tower attendant.

"What are you doing here?" Chuck asked him.

"Jimmy sent me in his place. He said I should carry the packs for anyone who got tired."

"We'll see about that," Caleb said with a huff.

But Mark, gulping air, his hands clasping his bulging stomach, said to Alden, "I might just take you up on that."

Dale reached across the circle and gave Mark's round belly a solid *whap*. "That's why I didn't give you anything extra to carry when I was divvying things up."

Dale led the group up the steep, rocky trail. Dappled by beams of moonlight breaking through the trees overhead, the group members climbed alongside the upper Merced River, which tumbled from the mountains to the valley floor in a series of roaring cataracts. They switchbacked out of the tight canyon alongside towering Vernal Falls as the moon settled in the west behind them.

At the back of the line, Chuck took deep breaths, perspiration building on his forehead despite the coolness of the night. So much for not being away from camp for long—though, he assured himself, Janelle and the girls and Clarence were safe together in the campground.

Where the canyon opened at the top of the falls, Dale, still in the lead, left the river and climbed alongside the rounded hump of Half Dome.

By now, Chuck knew where they were headed. During his summers in the valley twenty years ago, he'd participated several times in the annual, highly unofficial, full-moon climbers' race to the summit of the massive granite dome. The informal race, hosted each summer by Jimmy and Thorpe, started at the head of the valley and followed the famed Cable Route up the south flank of the bare rock peak.

Participants left the valley in the middle of the night, competing to see who would reach the top of Half Dome first. The contest became interesting where the racers climbed the final four hundred feet up the south side of the dome, ascending the steeply sloped granite face between parallel lengths of wound steel attached to iron posts drilled into the stone every few feet.

The waist-high steel strands lining the last stretch to the summit should have made the last portion of the ascent to the top of Half Dome safe. Every year, however, a handful of the hundreds of unseasoned climbers who attempted the route during daylight hours managed to lose their grip on the cables and plummet off the peak, some to their deaths.

Though no one died during the years Jimmy and Thorpe hosted their under-the-radar nighttime race to the top of the dome, it wasn't from lack of effort by the competitors. So coveted was the unofficial title of first full-moon Half Domer that those at the head of the pack elbowed and jostled one another up the cabled stretch to the summit. In several cases, scuffles broke out at the top of the Cable Route as Jimmy and Thorpe, waiting at the top, attempted to determine the year's winner in the pre-dawn darkness.

As he had when he'd participated in the full-moon races up Half Dome twenty years ago, Chuck hung back while the others climbed through the night ahead of him. Soon, his position at the back of the line meant he fell farther and farther behind the rest of the group as Mark slowed a step ahead of him, then slowed still more.

The former climber turned overweight restaurateur gasped for air, placing one wobbly foot in front of the other. Finally, he collapsed to a sitting position where the trail angled out of the forest and onto the expanse of granite that rose steadily to the start of the Cable Route.

The gray rock gleamed in the light of the half moon sitting just above the horizon in the western sky. Three hundred yards ahead, the bare granite steepened and the parallel steel strands of the Cable Route marked the way to the summit up the nearly vertical south face of the dome.

Mark sat forward, his hands hanging from his knees and his shoulders heaving. In the light of Chuck's headlamp, his face was ashen. Sweat streamed down his cheeks and dripped from his blond beard and mustache.

"That's all I got," he said, wheezing.

He closed his eyes and keeled over on his side.

At Chuck's cry for help, the others scrambled back down the sloped granite. Alden arrived first, with Dale on his heels, followed by Caleb, Ponch, and Bernard.

"I'm finished," Mark moaned, struggling back to a sitting position.

"Jesus," Alden muttered, his voice filled with disgust.

Bernard, breathing hard, drummed his own sizable girth with his fingers. "I'm feeling the climb, too," he assured Mark.

Alden said to Bernard, "At least you're still upright."

Mark swallowed, corralling his wheezes. "Just because you're still a kid," he accused Alden, looking up from his seated position on the rock.

"Wrong." Alden, looming over Mark, put a hand to his own flat stomach. "Just because I know how to control my appetite."

Mark's eyes constricted to an angry pinch in the lights of the group members' headlamps.

"Hey, now," Ponch said, stepping forward. "Tonight's supposed to be fun."

Alden turned away, his hands on his hips.

"It'd be great to have somebody filming from down below, at the foot of the cables," Dale suggested to Mark. "Can you make it that far?"

Mark looked at where the parallel cables rose to the starry night sky a few hundred yards away. "Yeah," he said, pushing himself to his feet. "I can do that."

He teetered on the smooth stone surface. Chuck grabbed his elbow, steadying him.

Alden slid Mark's daypack off his back. "I thought Jimmy was joking."

"Thanks," Mark said, looking at his feet.

Alden slung Mark's backpack over his own pack and headed up the granite slope. The others followed. Chuck made his way slowly toward the start of the Cable Route beside Mark, maintaining his grip on Mark's elbow, until the two of them reached the others at the foot of the steel strands.

Ponch rubbed his hands together. "Almost time for the fun to begin," he exclaimed in an obvious attempt to recapture some of the night's lost energy.

"We're getting close," Dale joined in. He pulled a handheld video camera from his pack and handed it to Mark. "I'll use my phone for the close-in shots on top. Start filming from down here after we get up there, would you? I want to catch the first flames—plus the explosion."

23

Chuck took a quick breath. "Explosion?"

Dale punched him on the arm. "It's all under control."

Chuck stumbled a step sideways. If ever he was going to turn back, now was the time.

He swung his headlamp from face to face around the group. The others smiled back at him, their eyes bright with anticipation. Only Bernard's eyes displayed the uncertainty Chuck knew showed in his.

He cursed beneath his breath. It was pointless to ask questions; no one would confess to what they were up to. Still, none of those in the know appeared the least bit concerned.

"You jerks," he groused, triggering a round of laughter in response.

Dale said to Mark, "We can splice the footage together to eliminate the time lag in between. I made sure the battery is topped off, so that won't be a problem."

"Close up or wide angle?" Mark asked as his breathing calmed.

"Go in tight on the fires, then pull back and wait while the flames die out. I'll holler when it's getting close to time."

"Flames?" Chuck asked.

Rather than respond, Dale said to the group, "Let's head on up."

He took a cable in each hand and tugged himself up the pitched granite face, his headlamp painting a circle of light on the rock in front of him.

Alden dropped Mark's pack and scurried to the bottom of the Cable Route. Rather than trail after Dale between the cables, he pulled himself upward along the right side of the route, outside the confines of the steel strands. Caleb sprang to the opposite side of the route and hauled himself upward using the left-hand cable.

Quickly hand-over-handing up the right-side cable, Alden drew even with Dale. Caleb maintained a third-place position below and to the left of Dale and Alden as the three sped up the face, their headlamp beams flickering on the rock, their breaths harsh in the still night air.

Watching them, Ponch shook his head. "Boys will always be boys," he muttered.

Bernard chuckled. "You got that right, right, right."

Ponch set out, hauling himself upward between the cables at a more leisurely cadence behind the lead trio.

Bernard turned to Chuck. "Ready?"

Chuck said to Mark, "You good down here?"

"Golden."

Chuck followed Ponch and Bernard up the Cable Route, sliding his right hand, then his left, up the waist-high steel strands, his booted feet finding plenty of traction on the rough granite surface between the strands.

He reprimanded himself for his acquiescence to peer pressure even as he continued to ascend rather than head back to Camp 4.

As Ponch, Bernard, and Chuck neared the summit, Dale yelled down to them, "I won! I beat Alden!"

"By one measly step!" Alden hollered.

Chuck reached the top of the granite dome behind Ponch and Bernard, leaving the confines of the parallel cables for the compact, rounded summit. Quartz crystals trapped in the surface of the rock flashed like diamonds in the light of his headlamp.

The top of the dome rolled away on three sides, the rock steepening to near vertical as it plunged into darkness. On its fourth side, the cleaved granite dome ended in an abrupt stone cornice beneath which Half Dome's vertical north face, lined with climbing routes, plummeted two thousand feet straight down to the waters of Tenaya Creek. With the moon having set, the night sky sat close overhead, the stars distinct and shining.

In a few hours, hordes of daytime climbers would crowd the summit. For now, however, Chuck and the five others had the peak to themselves.

"He had both cables to pull himself up with," Alden complained of Dale. "I only used one."

"You got ahead of me for a while, I'll give you that," Dale said. "But I came back even though I've got twenty years on you." He clapped Alden's beefy shoulder. "You've got a few too many pounds on you, big boy."

"Not as many as the dude we left down below."

"A helluva lot more than Chuck's daughter, though. Amazing what she pulled off yesterday, all fifty pounds of her—without even resorting to the out move you snuck onto the route."

Alden shoved his chest into Dale. "What do you mean, 'snuck'?"

Dale grinned in the light of Alden's headlamp. "I don't mean anything," he said. "Nothing at all."

Alden stepped back. "I got no problem with being strong," he declared. He returned Dale's shoulder clap, with emphasis.

"Watch it!" Dale cried out, catching himself on the curved stone surface.

"Besides," Alden said, turning away, "the ladies like me just the way I am."

Chuck swung his headlamp between Dale and Alden. It appeared Dale, too, had spotted Alden speaking to Tara Rogan, the climber from Berkeley, at the start of the Slam.

Caleb broke in. "Let's do it."

"Do what?" Chuck asked.

"You're about to find out," Dale said. He turned to Alden. "Hand me your pack, would you, you big oaf?"

"I'll 'oaf' you, old man," Alden shot back. But he handed over his pack.

Dale opened the pack's top flap and pulled out a fifteen-pound bag of charcoal. He held it up in the light of his head-lamp.

"That's why I lost," Alden complained. "I had to carry that up here."

"I carried the bottle of lighter fluid," Dale countered, his tone lighthearted.

"Whoa," Alden scoffed. "That must've weighed a whole pound. Aren't you the strong man?"

Dale set the sack of charcoal on the ground and swept his headlamp around the summit. "Jimmy and I talked about where to set it up."

Caleb's headlamp beam dipped and rose as he nodded. "He and I talked, too. He told you about the shelf, right?"

"Yep." Dale aimed his headlamp to the west. "This way."

He hoisted the sack of charcoal and crossed the bare top of the dome. Beyond the pair of iron stanchions at the top of the Cable Route, the dome rounded gently to a shallow, concave rock shelf, two feet wide by ten feet long. On the far side of the shallow depression, the rock face fell steeply downward. Far beyond, the lights of Yosemite Village twinkled on the valley floor.

Dale set the bag of charcoal next to the shelf. "This must be it," he told the others as they gathered around him. "Looks perfect, just like Jimmy said." He pointed at the base of the Cable Route, in full view below and to the south. "Mark can see it from his position, and we'll be able to film it from up here, too."

"If anybody's looking from the valley, they'll get the full show," said Caleb. He held out a hand. "Charcoal first."

SCOTT GRAHAM

Dale slid the bag to Caleb, who ripped it open and poured half its contents into one end of the shallow depression in the rock and half into the other end.

"They need to be in two neat piles," Caleb said.

"Like volcanoes?" Dale asked with a mischievous grin. He knelt and set to work with his hands, forming the scattered briquettes at one end of the depression into a conical pile.

"Exactly like volcanoes," Caleb concurred, crouching at the other end of the rock shelf and assembling the second mound of charcoal pieces into a briquette cone like the one formed by Dale.

"Excellent," Dale declared, sitting back. He proffered a hand to Chuck. "Next."

"I don't know about this," Chuck said. "You're going to set a fire up here?"

"Two fires," Dale replied.

Chuck shook his head, his fingertips to the bridge of his nose.

"Everything will wash away with the next rainstorm," Dale assured him.

"What if the fires scorch the rock?"

"That'll wash away, too. It's no big deal, Chuck."

"Maybe it wouldn't have been that big a deal for us to do something like this—whatever 'this' is—back in the day. But we're adults now. We're supposed to be, anyway. This is a national park. You know, 'leave no trace' and all that."

"Leave no trace, leave no trace," Bernard echoed at Chuck's side.

"Chuck makes a good point," Ponch said, doubt entering his voice. "We got all the way up here to the summit together. Maybe that's all we—"

"Jesus!" Alden barked. "I had no idea you guys were such a bunch of weenies."

180

Caleb said to Chuck, "I had the same concerns you're raising. I talked to Jimmy about it. He was totally reassuring. We'll make sure we don't leave any sign of anything behind. It'll be all right, Chuck. Like we were never here."

"Says the guy who wanted to chuck a burning yule log off of here in the middle of the summer twenty years ago and set the whole valley on fire."

"Well, yeah, we did want to do that. But you talked us out of it, remember? And we listened to you. But this, tonight, is different. It's just a little charcoal, not a whole tree. And it's way up here on the summit, where there's only rock, no vegetation at all."

Chuck shone his headlamp around the circle, taking in the expectant faces of his friends. He exhaled sharply through his nose. "I got you guys to listen to me once. I guess it's too much to hope you'd ever listen to me again."

Dale held out his hand. "Gimme your load, weenie."

Chuck shrugged off his pack and dug out the two cans he'd carried to the summit. He held them out to Dale, the light of his headlamp revealing identical, unopened tin cans of sweet corn. "No trace. Promise me."

Dale took the cans. "I promise." He knelt next to his pile of charcoal. "Corn is perfect for this."

"Whatever *this* is," Chuck muttered.

"The high moisture content helps," Dale went on. "The sugariness, too. At least, I think it does."

"Sounds as if you're talking about one of your wines at Zanstar."

Dale put one of the cans to his nose and sniffed. "Strong bouquet of tannin. Aromatic depth. A buttery finish with hints of oak." He held up the can. "I'd say this is an exemplary varietal for our purposes."

He formed a bowl-shaped depression in the top of the

briquette pile and set the tin can in it.

"According to Jimmy, the can's gotta be upright," he explained.

When the can of corn didn't shift in its depression, he arranged more briquettes around it to within an inch of its top. He took the second tin can from Chuck and repeated the process in the other charcoal pyre.

"Okay, let's light 'em up," he said, a trill of excitement in his voice.

He took from his pack the plastic bottle of lighter fluid he'd hauled to the summit and squirted some of the bottle's contents on each of the conical briquette piles.

He walked to the top of the steel cables, gripped the topmost stanchions, and faced down the route. "Mark!" he called. "Be ready down there!"

Mark's faint cry came from the bottom of the cables. "All set!"

Dale took a lighter from his pocket and squatted beside the nearest charcoal volcano. He flicked the lighter and held the flame to the knee-high pyre. Fire erupted from the briquettes with a quiet *whoosh*, climbing above the can of corn.

Dale set the second pile aflame, traded the lighter for his phone, and filmed the twin pyres, panning between the two sets of flames licking skyward around the cans of corn.

After a few seconds, he checked the time. "It's 2:52," he announced. He pocketed his phone. "We've got between twenty and twenty-five minutes to wait—that'll be between 3:12 and 3:17."

"That specific?" Bernard asked.

"Jimmy says it's the same every time." Dale eyed the fires burning at the two ends of the depression a few feet away. "But we should move back, just in case one of them decides to go early."

Dale backed with Chuck and the others to the rounded summit, fifty feet from the burning cones of charcoal. The flames diminished as the lighter fluid wore off and the charcoal briquettes burned on their own. Waves of warmth from the glowing briquettes rolled past Chuck at the top of the Cable Route.

"I'll start filming again at the eighteen-minute mark," Dale said.

Chuck checked the time on his phone. Was it really almost three o'clock?

With cell service strong atop the dome, a text message from Janelle awaited him. *Where are you? When will you be back?*

On top of Half Dome, he thumbed back. *Not sure what I'm doing here.*

When he received no immediate response, he checked the timestamp on her message—2:32, not long ago. Though, he reasoned, the time might merely indicate when the message had reached his phone upon coming into service atop the dome.

He sent Janelle another text. *Back by dawn for the Slam. Promise!*

Stowing his phone, he sat down on the smooth stone surface of the summit and wrapped his arms around his knees. A slight breeze coursed over the peak, chilly but not cold. The others settled in, too, taking seats on the granite around him. Minutes ticked by. Chuck lay back and watched the stars, his head on his pack and his fingers clasped over his chest. After a minute or two, his eyes sagged shut.

He jerked awake when Dale announced, "Eighteen minutes. Rise and shine, everybody."

Chuck climbed stiffly to a standing position. The briquette pyres glowed red hot at opposite ends of the small depression. The briquettes crackled when a gust of wind swept across the summit, the pyres brightening to the orange-red color of a desert sunset. The bitter odor of burnt charcoal permeated the night air.

At Dale's urging, Chuck and the others formed a line atop the dome, facing the burning coals.

"Almost," Dale breathed. He held out his phone, filming the twin pyres. "I just wish Jimmy could be here to see this with us."

Chuck's pulse quickened. He took out his phone, punched it to video, and filmed the charcoal piles along with Dale.

"Headlamps off," Dale directed.

They switched off their lights. The night was inky black save for the pinpricks of the stars overhead and a faint glow on the western horizon where the moon had disappeared.

"Mark!" Dale cried down the steep rock face of the Cable Route.

"Yo!" Mark yelled from below, his voice bouncing up the rock.

"Are you ready?"

"All set!" came Mark's reply.

Dale counted off the minutes as he filmed the glowing stacks of charcoal. "Twenty-two." A minute later: "Twenty-three."

Chuck thought of the girls as he filmed the burning coals. If what was about to happen was what he expected, Carmelita and Rosie would get a kick out of watching his footage.

"Almost," Dale said between minutes twenty-three and twenty-four. "There's so little wind and they're burning so—"

The night exploded with a concussive blast. Blazing white light blinded Chuck. He staggered backward, throwing an arm across his face. Bits of flaming coal bounced off him and a wave of searing heat flattened his shirt to his chest.

Someone's elbow dug into his side as they all fought to remain upright atop the rounded summit. The light of the explosion winked out an instant later, replaced by enveloping darkness. The air was rank with the smell of smoke and ash. Chuck sucked a breath, tasting singed sweet corn on his tongue.

He shoved his phone in his pocket and blinked, his eyesight

returning. The others stumbled around the head of the Cable Route, dark forms on all sides of him. Dale clearly had misjudged the force of the blast—not that Chuck could blame him. Who could have imagined so much force could be generated by a single, exploding can of corn?

Chuck froze. There were two fires. Two cans.

The second blast, as powerful as the first, came before he could take so much as a single step in retreat. A second concussive wave pummeled him. The air around him lit brilliant white and another blast of heat washed past him. With the heat came a second round of red hot bits of charcoal, pelting him with the force of BB gun pellets. He put his hands to his face, his eyes closed.

The concussion from the second blast forced him backward. He took a gasping breath, coating his mouth with smoke and pulverized corn. He heard the distant tinkling of one of the cans, now empty, as it tumbled down the face of the dome.

Teetering on the sloped summit, he squinted between his fingers. The others milled around him as they, too, fought for balance.

Someone stumbled through the crowd, striking his shoulder a glancing blow. An instant later, a human form shot away from him, past the iron stanchions at the top of the Cable Route, and down, screaming, into the darkness.

PART THREE

*"Fingers of steel, zero body fat,
and lots of testosterone."*

—Famed female rock climber Lynn Hill,
describing the historically male-dominated
Yosemite Valley climbing scene

24

Chuck stared in horror, helpless, as the falling victim struck the rock face twenty feet below the summit of the dome, released a harsh "oomph," and again launched into the air.

The victim remained airborne, arms and legs flapping like those of a rag doll, until he faded into the dark void below. He screamed again, a terrorized sound, but his second scream ended abruptly, replaced by the crunching sound of his body striking the granite face once more, this time far below the summit of the peak.

Chuck leaned forward, retching. Whoever had just tumbled off Half Dome was, without doubt, dead.

He collapsed to his knees as cries of fear and confusion reached him from the smoky darkness.

Dale's voice: "What the . . . ?"

Caleb, agonized: "Jesus God!"

Alden bellowed, "What just happened? Can someone please tell me?"

Glowing charcoal embers littered the smooth granite. Headlamps clicked on and darted all directions, their beams lighting the dissipating smoke. From his kneeling position, Chuck turned on his own headlamp and swept it across the others, silhouetted in his light.

"Sound off when I say your name," he directed.

He began with those whose voices he'd already identified in the few shocked seconds since the accident. "Dale."

A headlamp bobbed a few feet away. "Here."

"Caleb."

"Yeah," Caleb answered from farther away, subdued.

"Alden."

"Still here, thank God."

"Bernard."

Silence.

"Bernard," Chuck repeated, louder.

"Yes," Bernard said shakily from behind one of the headlamps, followed by the sound of his hands striking his legs in quick, steady rhythm. "I can't . . . I couldn't . . ."

The tone of the screams must have triggered some sort of recognition in Chuck's mind, because he saved Ponch's name for last. "Ponch," he said, even as he knew he would receive no answer.

He waited. Nothing.

He wrapped his arms around himself, his eyes squeezed shut. "Ponch," he repeated. Tears stung his eyelids as guilt rose, boiling, in his chest.

Dale strode to the top of the Cable Route. "Mark!" he cried down the rock face.

"What happened?" Mark hollered back. "Is everyone all right?"

"No," Dale yelled. "Someone fell. Ponch. West of you. Go look. Go, go, go! I'm coming down."

Dale descended the steep granite wall, walking backward down the bare rock with alternating grasps on the parallel strands of steel.

Caleb went to the top of the route. "Oh, dear God," he said. He backed down the sloping stone face between the cables.

The others descended behind Dale and Caleb. Chuck came last, after a scan of the abandoned summit revealed nothing that hinted at what, beyond the force of the second explosion itself, might have led to Ponch's plunge from the top of the dome.

Maybe the second blast, close on the heels of the first, had startled Ponch so much he'd lost his footing and fallen off the peak. But that didn't seem likely, Chuck told himself, not when he considered his own surprise at the strength of the first blast and his shock at the second explosion so soon after. The blasts had startled him, but he hadn't lost his footing, much less come anywhere near falling from the summit, not even when he'd been jostled in the darkness by one of the others.

He stopped midway down the route, his hands locked to the cables, thinking back to the second explosion and the shoulder blow he'd received in the blast's immediate aftermath. The blow hadn't been enough to send him tumbling off Half Dome. But what if someone—perhaps even the same someone who'd bumped Chuck—had struck Ponch with enough force to send him cartwheeling off the top of the dome?

Chuck was certain whoever might have accidentally struck Ponch, if anyone, wouldn't admit to it. What point would there be in offering up such a confession?

He resumed his descent. An anguished cry echoed through the night air when he was three-quarters of the way down the coiled lengths of steel, the others nearing the bottom of the route below him.

"Ponch!" Mark screamed, his voice breaking. "Ponch!"

Chuck shuddered. Little more than twenty-four hours ago, Ponch had hiked up Sentinel Ridge and, together with Chuck and Janelle, located Thorpe's battered body. Now, Ponch had suffered a similar fate.

Chuck's throat constricted when he thought of Janelle and the girls back in Camp 4. Were they and Clarence safe?

He paused at the bottom of the Cable Route long enough to pull out his phone and check it for a message from Janelle. Nothing. Nor could he check in with her because there was no cell service here, lower on the peak.

Dale approached Chuck as he neared a tight circle of glowing headlamps a hundred feet west of the bottom of the Cable

Route, where the almost-vertical upper face of the dome moderated to a less severe pitch.

"Is he . . . ?" Chuck asked.

"Yes." Dale's voice shook. "He's dead."

Chuck's shoulders fell. "Ponch," he moaned.

He sagged, his knees nearly buckling. Why had he allowed the prank to go forward?

Finally, his voice weary, he said, "I'll climb back up until I can get a call to go through."

"Thank God," Chuck told Janelle four hours later, taking her in his arms upon his return to Camp 4. "You're okay."

"Me?"

"You. The girls."

She freed herself from his embrace. "You're the one who was up there." Her chin trembled. "It could have been you."

Chuck had called ahead, filling her in on Ponch's death. "I keep telling myself it must have been an accident."

Her chin stilled and her gaze grew sharp, a pair of dark lines furrowing her forehead between her brows. "You and I both know it wasn't. It couldn't have been, not after . . ." Her voice died away, but she could have finished the sentence any number of ways—not after Jimmy's accident, not after the close call with the tumbling boulder, not after Thorpe's death and the suspicious cut in his ankle.

Chuck detailed the night's events. "If you'd seen the explosions," he concluded. "They were way bigger than I expected."

"You never should have been up there in the first place."

Tears filled his eyes at the thought of Ponch's death. "That's what I keep telling myself. If only I'd put a stop to it."

He knuckled the corners of his eyes and looked around sun-drenched Camp 4, avoiding Janelle's gaze. Campers and climbers, unknowing, prepared breakfast and arranged gear in their sites. To the west, the YOSAR encampment was quiet, the team members high on the south flank of Half Dome, assisting the park rangers charged with securing the scene and performing the initial investigation into Ponch's death. In the reunion campsite next door, Jimmy leaned on his crutches, his face pale above his coiled beard, as he spoke with the others just returned from Half Dome with Chuck.

Janelle gripped Chuck's arm. "We both agree it wasn't an accident. It couldn't have been. Not in light of everything else."

"Meaning," he said, turning to her, "we have to get you and the girls out of here."

Clarence approached. "Is somebody going somewhere?"

Chuck provided more details to Clarence and Janelle about the explosions and Ponch's fall.

The YOSAR team and rangers had arrived on the scene two hours after Chuck's emergency call. The rangers had released Chuck and the others with the admonition they would be questioned later. As he'd crossed the valley floor toward Camp 4 with the others half an hour ago, Chuck had received a text from Owen Hutchins, Jr., with an assigned time of two p.m. for his interview at the campground office.

Finished describing the night's events, Chuck stared at the dusty ground of the campsite, barely capable of keeping his eyes open. The combination of the long overnight climb and lack of sleep was crushing, as was the brutal reality of Ponch's death on the heels of Thorpe's death, Jimmy's injury, and the toppled boulder.

He raised his head with tremendous effort and said to Janelle and Clarence, his words faltering, "I can't . . . I'm not sure . . ."

"You don't have any choice, *jefe*," Clarence said.

Beside him, Janelle nodded.

A rush of gratitude surged through Chuck. He wasn't alone. "What do we do?"

Carmelita poked her head from the tent.

"¡*Mamá!*" she cried, leaving the tent in pajamas and flip-flops. "Chuck! Uncle Clarence! This is it. This is the day. Round four. And I'm going to win!"

Janelle drew a breath. "I'm not sure we'll be able to stay, *m'hija.*"

Carmelita's eyes clouded. "What?"

"Something happened last night, another—" Janelle appeared to almost choke on the next word "—accident. To Ponch, one of Chuck's friends. I don't know that they'll even hold the last rounds of the competition."

Carmelita stamped her foot. "Yes, they will. They have to. I signed up. It's just the two of us now. Fifty-fifty, that's my chances. That's what Uncle Clarence said. That's really good. And we paid our money, right? Everybody did."

Chuck steadied himself where he stood, seeking mental footing as well. "Carm's right," he said to Janelle. "They've moved the Slam to this evening. The plan is to let the rangers secure the scene and conduct the initial investigation throughout the day and hold the competition later on. The park service is on board with the delay instead of calling it off. Two deaths in two days draws the kind of attention to the park nobody wants. Canceling the Slam would only draw more attention."

"See?" Carmelita said to her mother. "They're gonna have the Slam. And I want to be in it. I want to finish." She asked Chuck, "They're doing it tonight?"

"After sunset, at eight o'clock. Today's going to be tough for a lot of people. Holding the competition at dusk gives everyone something to look forward to." He said to Janelle, "Owen is going to interview me this afternoon. I can't leave until after that even if we want to."

Janelle took Carmelita's hand in hers. "We'll have to see how the day unfolds." When Carmelita's upturned face brightened, Janelle hurried on. "No guarantees, understand?" She pressed the tip of her daughter's nose with her finger. "We'll try. That's all."

Carmelita threw her arms around her mother's waist. "*Gracias, Mamá.*"

Chuck pivoted to watch with the others when the deep-throated *chuff-chuff-chuff* of a helicopter sounded from far down the valley. The beat of the chopper's rotors bounced off the walls of the valley as the craft flew past Camp 4, a blue flicker between the tree branches, aiming for the upper reaches of Half Dome, where Ponch's body lay. Throughout the campground, other campers stopped to watch, too.

When the rescue helicopter was far up the valley and the beat of its rotors grew faint, Janelle turned to Chuck. "I won't spend another night here. The minute the competition is over, we're gone."

Blood drained from Carmelita's cheeks at the harsh tone of her mother's voice.

Chuck rubbed Carmelita's upper arm and said to Janelle, "There's no proof of anything at this point. Besides, none of this affects you or the girls or Clarence. Or me, for that matter."

He hadn't mentioned being bumped atop the dome before Ponch's fall; he wasn't sure where that fit in the scheme of things, if at all.

"The boulder yesterday—that affected us," Janelle pointed out. She gazed around Camp 4, the look in her eyes that of a caged animal. "I have to get away from here. I swear to God, I'll go stark, raving mad if I have to stay here in the campground another minute."

25

Chuck, the girls, and Clarence walked together up the paved path from Camp 4 to Yosemite Village, headed for the Village Cafeteria. Janelle roamed a few steps ahead, her head swiveling and her eyes probing, the fact that she shared the path with scores of other visitors providing her no apparent reassurance.

Rosie pulled Chuck forward by the hand, struggling to keep up with her mother.

"Why are we in such a hurry?" she asked Chuck.

"Your mom is on a mission."

"Really? Cool. What kind of mission?"

"You'll have to ask her."

"*¿Mamá?*"

Janelle slowed until the others drew even with her, but her head continued to rotate. "I'm just keeping an eye on things," she told Rosie.

"I'm hungry," Rosie declared in response, still tugging Chuck forward.

"You're always hungry," Carmelita said.

Inside the cafeteria, they took trays and lined up at the head of the food line. The cavernous room smelled of ham and maple syrup and echoed with the clinking of silverware, the scraping of chairs, and the conversations of dozens of customers seated at long rows of tables.

The Latina woman who'd fried plantains for everyone after Carmelita's Columbia Boulder climb in Camp 4 stood behind the line of prepared breakfast items—eggs, ham, bacon, pancakes, and waffles in metal trays; dry cereal in portion-sized boxes; containers of yogurt stacked in glass-fronted coolers; and tall urns dispensing juice, milk, and coffee.

"*Hola*, Juanita," Janelle greeted the woman.

The two spoke in rapid-fire Spanish. Juanita matched Janelle's progress from the far side of the food line as Janelle sidled past the food, adding a muffin, sliced cantaloupe, and a hard-boiled egg to her tray. The faces of the two women darkened and their voices lowered as they talked. Chuck overheard Janelle say the word "Ponch." In response, Juanita referred to "*el Señor* Hutchins."

Clarence joined the women's conversation as he worked his way down the food line beside Janelle, loading his plate with bacon, ham, eggs, and a donut with chocolate icing. The three-way discussion grew animated. Chuck had picked up some Spanish in the years since he and Janelle had married, but the speed of the exchange between Clarence, Janelle, and Juanita was such that he caught only a handful of words, among them *desconfiado*, suspicious; and *peligroso*, dangerous.

At the end of the food line, Juanita wished Carmelita luck—"*suerte*"—and bid all of them farewell in accented English. The woman disappeared through a swinging door to the kitchen. Chuck settled their bill with the cashier and they headed for the unoccupied end of one of the communal tables in the cafeteria's eating area.

"She'd already heard about Ponch," Janelle reported to Chuck after they slid their trays onto the table and began to eat.

"No big surprise there," he replied. "News travels fast in the valley."

"She said she heard he was murdered."

Rosie looked up from sawing a syrup-soaked waffle with a plastic knife, her eyes round. "Somebody got murdered?"

"No, sweetie," Janelle said quickly. "It's just rumors people are making up about what happened on Half Dome last night."

"About Chuck's friend who fell, the one you told us about?"

"That's right."

"Okay," Rosie said simply. She went back to her waffle.

Janelle motioned Chuck and Clarence away from the table with a tilt of her head. They crossed the room and stood together near the front window.

Chuck spoke first. "With Thorpe, Jimmy, and now Ponch, it makes sense rumors are flying around the valley." He cocked an eyebrow. "Sometimes, in fact, it's those who start the rumors who most need looking into."

Janelle huffed. "Not if you're referring to Juanita."

"I heard her say Owen's name."

"He's the one you should be worried about."

Clarence said to Janelle, "You got that right, *hermana*." He turned to Chuck. "I been talking with *la gente* in their campsites. They got their own worries, and all of them revolve around the ranger dude. He's been all over them this summer, giving them a hard time."

"That's to be expected, I guess," Chuck said.

"They told me he got himself put in charge of Camp 4. They said he doesn't think the campground should be used by park workers, that it should be reserved for tourists."

"He's wrong about that. It's a public campground, open to all comers. Remember what the guy told us when we were eating plantains at their site? As crowded as the valley is these days, there's no place else for them to stay. Besides, what Owen thinks doesn't matter."

"He sees it different, I guess."

"What has he been doing to them?"

"Whatever he can come up with, sounds like. Telling them to take down their clothes lines, even though there's no rule against it. Busting them for doing laundry in the dishwashing sink in the bathroom—which, okay, technically they're not supposed to do. Writing them up for leaving food out on their tables in the middle of the day, when the bears aren't around, instead of in their bear boxes. Piss-ant things like that."

"Sounds like the same sort of stuff his dad used to pull on climbers in the campground back when I was here."

"They say he's getting worse. He keeps writing them tickets for big fines, which they refuse to pay, so he writes them up for even bigger fines. The way they tell it, he's crazy—as in, scary-crazy."

"That doesn't make him a murderer."

"Maybe, maybe not. But it makes him out to be someone who might not want you and me here, doing our work for the Indigenous Tribespeople Foundation."

"How so?"

"He seems like he's someone who doesn't like anything and anyone who rocks the boat, who's unusual in any way. The fact that we're looking into a couple of old murders in the valley? That's unusual."

"One look at him," Janelle added, "and you can tell he's someone who might go to extreme ends to make his point—like rolling a boulder down on us."

"We should focus on him," Clarence declared.

Janelle tipped her head in agreement.

"But he wasn't up on Half Dome last night," Chuck said.

"Maybe he's got an in with one of your reunion guys," said Janelle.

"Or Alden," Clarence added, "the rock-gym dude. You said he was up there with you."

"Why would anyone have wanted to kill Ponch up on Half Dome last night, though?" Chuck asked. *Or me*, he added to himself, thinking of the blow that had knocked him off balance after the second explosion.

Janelle glanced at the girls across the room. They giggled as they jousted with each other using their plastic utensils.

"I keep coming back to the boulder," Janelle said. "Everything else—Thorpe, Jimmy, Ponch—might or might not have been an accident. But the boulder was for real." She looked at Chuck and Clarence. "The thing I can't figure out is why somebody would do that—why someone would be against your doing the survey for the foundation. Any ideas?"

Clarence massaged the unshaven bristles on his chin and shook his head.

But Chuck snapped his fingers, his thoughts on the Yosemite Museum archives. "As a matter of fact, yes."

26

Outside the cafeteria, throngs of tourists made their way along the wide, paved walkway through the center of Yosemite Village. Families posed for pictures in front of the museum, with its river rock exterior and sloped, pine-needle-carpeted roof backed by the soaring north wall of the valley.

Chuck followed his family up the walkway toward the museum. His feet dragged. The morning already was warm, the heat adding to his exhaustion. His legs ached from his long trek up and down Half Dome, while his heart ached for Ponch.

Rosie skipped beside Clarence. "Museums are boring," she announced.

"I'm with you," Clarence said. He winked at her. "I think we deserve a payoff if we have to go in there."

"A payoff?"

"He means," Janelle told Rosie, "a bribe."

"If you consider an ice cream cone a bribe," Clarence said.

"Ice cream?" Rosie asked. "Like yesterday? Yea!"

Carmelita stopped in the middle of the path and planted her hands on her hips. The others stopped with her. "You just finished breakfast," she scolded Rosie. "I can't believe you."

"Ice cream, ice cream, ice cream!" Rosie cheered. She looked at her mother. "Deal?"

Janelle glowered at her brother. "I hope you get to be a parent someday." She sighed and said to Rosie, "Deal."

They set off once more. As they climbed the steps to the museum, the building's front doors swung open, and Dale and Owen exited together. Deep in conversation and taking no notice of Chuck and the others, the two men descended the wide, flagstone stairway and walked away from the building.

"Go on in," Chuck said, waving Janelle, Clarence, and the girls on up the steps. "I'll be right behind you."

"Our plan is to stick together today," Janelle said. "Remember?"

"I'll be right back. I just want to see what they're up to."

Chuck hurried down the steps to the walkway without giving Janelle the chance to protest further. Ahead, Dale and Owen crossed the central village plaza, their heads bent toward each other. They passed the sprawling Visitor Center complex while continuing their conversation.

Chuck remained fifty feet back as they turned off the main pathway next to the village post office, made their way beneath the widespread branches of a black oak beside the building, and passed from sight.

Chuck slowed, not wanting to come upon the two men unexpectedly. He reached the near corner of the post office and peered around it. No sign of them. He walked beneath the oak to the building's far corner and leaned around it.

A parking lot stretched behind the post office. Cars filled the lot, glimmering in the late morning sunshine. Dale and Owen stood next to a light green ranger sedan parked in the middle of the lot, a bar of emergency lights bolted to its roof. Owen gathered himself and slammed Dale in the chest, shoving him hard against the passenger door of the car. The ranger pressed Dale to the sedan, his elbow to Dale's throat, his face red.

"Enough?" Owen demanded of Dale, his raised voice carrying across the parking lot to Chuck. "Or do you need more convincing?"

Dale lifted his hands in surrender. He did not struggle. Owen released him. Stepping back, the ranger tucked his gray uniform shirt into his green slacks, then smoothed the front of his shirt with both hands. He pulled out a key fob and pressed it.

The headlights of the ranger vehicle blinked as the car unlocked.

Dale stood still, his eyes on Owen. The ranger glared at him, waiting. Dale's shoulders fell and he opened the passenger door and lowered himself into the ranger car without speaking.

Owen slid behind the wheel and they drove off, disappearing among low administrative buildings arrayed in haphazard fashion behind the post office.

Chuck backtracked to the central village walkway. Pausing in front of the Visitor Center, he squeezed his temples with his thumb and forefinger. It made no sense that Dale and Owen were together. It made even less sense that Owen had assaulted Dale, and that Dale had not retaliated.

No possible explanation came to him. He set out for the museum, his thoughts turning to his scheduled interview with Owen. When the time came for his questioning on the subject of Ponch's fatal plunge, Chuck would have to be strategic with his own questions, aimed at the ranger, as well.

Upon his return to the museum, Chuck found his family standing with Caleb, Mark, Bernard, and Jimmy at the back of the entry lobby, near the stairway to the museum's basement archives. The group was gathered in front of a display depicting naturalist John Muir's initial years in Yosemite Valley, when Muir had worked in a valley sawmill, producing lumber from wind-felled trees, and had roamed the nearby canyons and mountains on his days off.

For two decades after first coming to the valley in 1868, Muir had championed the creation of Yosemite National Park, leading to its approval by Congress in 1890. Muir cofounded the Sierra Club two years later, in 1892, in large part to protect Yosemite from those who sought to profit by overdeveloping the newly declared park.

"We caught the shuttle bus here," Jimmy explained to Chuck as he walked up to the group.

Caleb pressed the flat of his hand to his forehead. "None of us could sleep."

Jimmy pivoted on his crutches to face Janelle, Clarence, and the girls. "I want you to know how sorry I am about your visit here," he told them. "I know you came to Yosemite with Chuck to see what the rest of us love so much about this place, not. . ." His beard quivered and he fell silent.

"Where's Dale?" Chuck asked him.

Jimmy pressed his mouth shut, his mustache meeting his beard over his tight lips.

When Jimmy didn't speak, Mark said to Chuck, his tone bitter, "He sold out. He's with Owen."

"Sold out?"

"He was the first to be questioned, in the campground office," Mark explained. "I was supposed to go second, but they came outside and drove off in Owen's car. They didn't say a word to me. I waited for a while, but they didn't come back." He glanced at Jimmy, Bernard, and Caleb. "We decided there was no point in hanging around. Owen has our phone numbers and there's good signal strength in the village. He'll get hold of us when he's ready."

Chuck tucked his fingers in his pants pockets. Mark and the others clearly hadn't seen Dale leaving the museum with Owen. "What brings you guys here?" Chuck asked, thinking of his own reason for visiting the museum.

Bernard's hands fluttered like butterfly wings at his sides. "We went through the Visitor Center yesterday."

"This is the first time I've ever been in this place," Caleb admitted. He cracked a wan smile. "I wouldn't have been caught dead in museums back in the day."

Rosie tugged Clarence's arm. "I'm bored. Can we go get ice

cream now?"

"It's fine by me, but you need to ask your mom."

The corner of Janelle's mouth twisted downward. She said to Rosie, "You lasted ten minutes in here, *m'hija*. That's a record for you." She took her hand. "Okay. *Vámanos.*"

Jimmy lifted a crutch from the scuffed flagstone floor of the museum and aimed it at Carmelita. "Are you all set for tonight, little lady?"

She nodded.

"You're quite a climber, you know that?"

Carmelita's eyes lit up.

"There'll be a huge crowd tonight. You and Tara will start things off." Jimmy lowered his crutch. "Just between you and me, I think Tara's a little scared of you."

Carmelita's face reddened.

Chuck asked Jimmy, "Did you say Carm and Tara are going first?"

"Yes. It was Alden's idea. Climbing comps are doing it more and more—placing different routes for male and female competitors. Everyone knows men and women climb differently. Men are stronger. That's just a basic fact of human physiology. Women have plenty of strength, of course, but they tend to have way more finesse than men, too. That's what makes them so much fun to watch when they climb—the way they move, so balanced and graceful, like they're doing ballet up there on the wall."

"Especially, I take it, on routes that play to their abilities."

"You got it. We'll start the competition with a route set specifically for Tara and your little girl here; that is, with the holds placed to reward finesse as well as strength—what's known as a combo route-set." Jimmy pivoted on his crutches to face Carmelita. "Tara already knows the two of you are going first. You deserve to know, too, so you'll be ready right at the start." He

SCOTT GRAHAM

rocked forward on his crutches. "I can't wait to see you in action tonight."

Mark's phone buzzed. He pulled it out and studied its face. "Owen wants to meet me back at the campground in thirty minutes," he reported to the others. He typed on his phone with his thumbs and returned it to his pocket. "I'd better get going."

"I'll be next," Caleb said. "I'll go with you."

Jimmy turned to Bernard. "You're scheduled after them. Are you ready to head back?"

Bernard nodded hard several times, the staccato jerks of his head timed with hand taps to his thighs.

Jimmy turned to Chuck. "What about you?"

"He's got me set for two o'clock."

"Sounds like he's saving you for last. I wonder why?"

"So do I."

27

Chuck watched Jimmy and the others cross the front lobby and leave the building. He turned to Clarence, Janelle, and the girls.

Clarence tilted his head at the stairwell. A length of his long, black hair escaped from behind his ear to dangle beside his face. "That way?"

"Yep."

Clarence tucked the hair back behind his ear. "It's a Sunday morning, you know."

"The archives are overseen by the Yosemite Historical Society. Volunteers keep them open seven days a week from Memorial Day through Labor Day."

"I'll take the girls," Janelle offered to Chuck, "provided you make it quick."

"It shouldn't take long," he told her.

"I've heard that before."

"I promise."

"I've heard that before, too."

"At least you'll know where to find us this time."

She exhaled through her nose. "True." She turned to Rosie. "¿Helado?"

"¡Buenisimo!" Rosie cheered.

Janelle led the girls out of the museum. Chuck descended the stone steps with Clarence to the museum's lower level. At the foot of the stairs, an elderly woman sat reading a book at a desk in a small foyer. Behind her, a floor-to-ceiling glass wall, broken by a metal door, separated the foyer from a narrow room lit by fluorescent lights and lined with head-high metal shelves. Aged, leather-bound books and cardboard document boxes of various sizes filled the shelves.

The woman closed her book and placed it face down on the desk. Her gray hair was combed close on the sides of her head. A tag on her breast identified her as Irene.

She clasped her sun-spotted hands on top of her book and asked, "May I be of service to you?"

Chuck looked past her through the windowed wall. "Are those the Yosemite Museum archives?"

"Indeed, they are." The historical society volunteer smiled, causing wrinkles to gather like waves at the sides of her mouth. "Most people come down here by mistake, looking for more museum displays."

"The archives don't attract a lot of visitors?"

"More than a few, I'd say, but not many," the volunteer, Irene, said. "We've digitized and placed so much of the collection online over the years that it's almost put me out of a job—not that the pay is very good."

Introducing himself and Clarence, Chuck explained their purpose in the valley on behalf of the Indigenous Tribespeople Foundation. "I've spent a lot of time accessing the archives online the last few months myself," he concluded.

"The ITF is a great organization," Irene said. Her manner of speech was crisp and precise. "They do fine work correcting the historical record."

"Attempting to correct it, at any rate."

"I and others have spent a good deal of time with their researchers on the phone over the last couple of years. So far, I'm happy to say, we've been able to provide them everything they've asked for in digitized fashion."

"I found pretty much everything I needed through your website, too," Chuck said.

"*Pretty much* everything?"

"I need to gather one last detail for the foundation. They're meticulous in their research, as you already know. They even go so far as to track, as best they can, who else is looking into the same stories they're studying."

A twinkle appeared in Irene's eyes. "They do have their enemies, don't they?"

Chuck lifted his eyebrows.

"No need to look surprised," she said. "I may be down here in a museum basement on a Sunday morning reading a romance novel, but I know how the world works. Someone at the foundation understands that while it's good to know who your friends are, it's far better to know who might be working against you." She looked up at Chuck and Clarence from her seat. "We don't track visitors to our website. But that's not why you're here, is it?"

Her eyes fell to a registration book resting on the front corner of the desk. A place-holding ribbon extended from the middle of the closed book's pages. She spun the book to her and opened it to the pages marked by the ribbon. The two pages were lined with neat columns of signatures and dates left by those who had signed in to study the physical archives in the glass-enclosed room behind the desk.

"Here we are," she said. Turning the registration book, she flopped it open in front of Chuck and Clarence. "Help yourselves."

Chuck scanned the columns. The two pages accounted for visitors to the archives dating back nearly a year, their names and the dates of their visits handprinted alongside their accompanying signatures.

He checked the most recent visitor. His intuition had been right. Owen Hutchins, Jr., had signed in thirty minutes ago, along with Dale. The two had signed out ten minutes later.

Chuck worked his way backward by date, scanning the list

SCOTT GRAHAM

of visitors. Two weeks ago, Owen also had signed in as a visitor to the archives. Chuck continued to study the list. The ranger's name and signature appeared another time a week earlier, and yet again two weeks prior to that.

Based on his cursory glance at the two pages, Chuck counted five times Owen had visited the archives in the previous few months. He flipped the page, moving farther backward in time. On the preceding two pages, he spotted three additional visits by Owen to the archives in the past year.

Returning to the most recent two pages of listed visitors, Chuck double-checked the dates of Owen's visits. One had been the day after the public announcement by the Indigenous Tribespeople Foundation that Bender Archaeological, Inc., had been awarded the survey contract aimed at assessing the veracity of Stephen Grover's account of the killings of the two prospectors in the valley.

Chuck cut a sidelong look at Clarence.

Irene chuckled. "Methinks you found what you were looking for," she said.

Chuck and Clarence caught up with Janelle and the girls. From the ice cream parlor, they visited the village's gift shops and the Ansel Adams Gallery, dedicated to preserving the legacy of Adams' stunning black and white photographs, captured over the course of decades, of the valley in winter, spring, summer, and fall.

They grabbed sandwiches from Degnan's Deli at the edge of the village and jumped a shuttle to Majestic Yosemite Hotel, the park's premiere example of the architectural style known as National Park Service rustic—lodges constructed in national parks throughout the twentieth century of natural stone and massive beams to complement the parks' natural landscapes.

They wandered through the hotel's cavernous lobby, the room's high ceiling hand-painted with tribal and Hispanic motifs harkening to California's early years. From the back patio, they looked nearly straight up at Glacier Point, half a vertical mile above. Chuck craned his head, staring at the distant granite prow. Two days ago, Thorpe had leapt from the point only to die in Sentinel Gap.

Guests chatted over cocktails and iced tea on the hotel veranda around Chuck. But Thorpe was dead. Ponch, too. Jimmy was lucky to be alive, as were Chuck and his family after the close call with the tumbling boulder.

He gathered Carmelita and Rosie to him and shivered despite the midday heat. Janelle was right. The sooner they left Yosemite, the better.

Chuck arrived for his interview with Owen just after two o'clock, entering the small A-frame office at the entrance to Camp 4. Owen looked up from forms stacked on the desk in front of him with hooded eyes, his face drawn. He was aging before Chuck's eyes, turning into a sallow-cheeked, baggy-eyed version of his father over the course of a single weekend.

He waved Chuck to the wooden bench against the front wall, leaned back in his office chair, and put his hands to his face, covering his eyes.

Chuck lowered himself cautiously to the bench. "You seem tired," he ventured.

The ranger lowered his hands. "I could say the same about you."

Chuck ran the back of his wrist across his mouth. No doubt Owen was right.

The ranger sat forward. When he spoke, weariness deadened his voice. "All of you guys are so screwed up."

Chuck frowned. "I'm not sure I—"

Owen continued, cutting Chuck off. "I've never understood you climbers. You're all so competitive, so fixated on cheating death and pretending you're so brave."

"The other rangers get along with the climbers in the valley these days," Chuck said. "They even climb together now and then."

Owen eyed the scarred desktop. "I know."

"You don't understand the other rangers either, is that it?"

Owen raised his head. "Before my dad died, he told me I had to keep up the 'good work.' That's what he called it. Can you imagine?"

"From what I've seen since I've been here, everyone seems to be on the same side now. You can be, too. I can't imagine it would be that hard. In fact, you're already trying, aren't you? I heard you spent a good chunk of time with Dale this morning."

Owen straightened in his seat. "I questioned him, like everyone else, that's all."

"You left the office with him. Mark saw you."

"Sure."

"Because?"

"He was my first interview. I needed some answers."

"Where'd you go to get your answers?"

"Am I conducting this interview or are you?"

"I'm just wondering if you're going to want me to go somewhere with you, too."

Owen settled back, his hands on the arms of his chair. "We drove to the head of the valley for a closer look at Half Dome. He told me about the charcoal volcanos, your group's little stunt. He pointed out to me where everything was set up, how it all happened. He said he'd planned to pick up the cans, and that the next rainstorm would wash away the ashes."

"You drove back to the campground with him after that?"

"I saw what I needed to see. We came back here and finished up."

"Without going anywhere else?"

Owen hesitated. "Right."

Chuck kept his eyes on the ranger. "You forgot to mention that you signed in and visited the archives with him, in the basement of the museum."

Owen's fingers tightened around the arms of his chair. "Again, who's conducting this interview?"

"I'm just wondering why you didn't see that as worth mentioning."

Owen shrugged. "Okay. Fine." He released his grip on the chair. "Yes, Dale and I visited the archives. I admit to being an archive groupie. There are amazing things down there—maps, old photos, journals, diaries. I like going through them in my spare time."

"You didn't take Dale there in your spare time."

"There's a photo I wanted him to see before we drove up the valley. It wasn't absolutely necessary. It's an Ansel Adams print of Half Dome in winter. The lower half of the lens was fogged when Adams took the picture, so the bottom is fuzzy. That's why it's never been used in any of his books or posters. But the top half of the photo, of the dome itself, is crystal clear, extremely detailed. I wanted to see if your friend could pick out the depression he told me about, the one you guys used for your fires."

Chuck studied the ranger. "You and Dale argued," he said, "in the parking lot behind the post office."

Owen didn't blink. "No, we didn't."

"You assaulted him. I saw you."

The ranger didn't move. "I have no idea what you're talking about."

Chuck sat up straight on the hard bench. Owen was lying. That much was obvious. But when had the ranger's lies begun?

Owen's office chair squeaked as he shifted in his seat. "We've spent enough time on your questions. It's my turn now."

Chuck hesitated. There was no reason to keep pressing the ranger. No amount of additional interrogation would elicit any more information. "What more can I tell you that the others haven't?"

"The SAIT—the Serious Accident Investigation Team—is already being formed for Thorpe's accident. Sounds like they'll investigate what happened last night on Half Dome, too. In that regard, there's one primary question they want me to ask of everyone while you're all still here in the park, to help determine the nature of their investigation. You probably know what it is. I've been asking it of everybody."

"I haven't talked with anyone else."

Owen folded his hands over the papers in front of him. "Do you believe Henry Stilwell's death this morning was an accident?"

"You mean Ponch?" Chuck leaned back against the A-frame's plywood wall. "What kind of a question is that?"

Owen didn't move, his fingers locked, his eyes on Chuck. "My assignment here today is to perform a preliminary examination of what we in the park service refer to as a bad outcome. Most bad outcomes in Yosemite are the result of accidents. But not all of them."

"What are you suggesting?"

"I'm not suggesting anything. Every time I conduct an accident investigation, preliminary or otherwise, I do so with the aim of uncovering any wrongdoing that may have led to each bad outcome, and to learn whether any discovered wrongdoing was incidental—or purposeful."

Chuck held Owen's gaze.

The ranger continued. "I initiate each of my examinations as if I'm looking into something more than a simple, straightforward accident. I've found it's easier to start that way."

"You're saying you begin with a presumption of guilt."

Owen rolled back from the desk and rested his elbows on the arms of his chair. "You have to understand, we're looking out for the interests of someone who, generally, is either dead or badly injured—the victim of a fall from a cliff, a car wreck, a drowning. Because they're unable to speak for themselves, it's our responsibility to ask questions for them."

"You require people you interview to prove their innocence, the exact opposite of how the legal system is supposed to work."

"I never make any assumptions at the outset."

"You just did with the question you asked me. You made a full-on assumption about what happened to Ponch—which, I can only assume, is something you learned from your dad."

Owen sat up, his back stiff. "He only ever did what he thought was right."

Chuck straightened, too. "Doing what's right means giving people the benefit of the doubt, not treating them as suspects."

Even as Chuck said the words, his own suspicions remained, vibrating inside him like a tuning fork. Owen's explanation of his numerous visits to the Yosemite Museum archives had the feel of the truth about it, as did his explanation for his visit to the archives this morning: to view the Ansel Adams photo along with Dale, his first interview subject. But if the ranger had told the truth about all that, why had he not admitted to his altercation with Dale?

What was Owen hiding?

28

Chuck held his position until Owen slumped in his seat.
"Just answer my question," he said. "Please."

Chuck sat still. There was nothing to be gained by sharing his suspicions regarding Ponch's fatal plunge with Owen, not after the ranger's own lack of truthfulness. "Do I think Ponch's death was more than just an accident? No, I don't."

"You believe the explosions startled him and caused him to fall?"

"Yes."

"Okay." Owen rolled in his chair back to the desk and made a notation on the form in front of him. "That will be all."

"That's it?"

"If you have nothing more to add." The ranger picked up the handwritten sheet on the top of the stack, looked at it, set it back down. "Since you got here, you've been on hand everywhere there's been trouble. That's why I wanted to interview you last today." He paused. When Chuck said nothing, he continued. "At this point, I have several descriptions of what happened last night on Half Dome from everyone else. If, as you say, you're convinced it was an accident . . ." He let the end of the sentence dangle.

Chuck licked his lips. Clearly, Owen didn't trust him and therefore saw value in questioning him further. Or was this some sort of trap? "It was dark. We were all crowded on top. The second can exploded, and Ponch fell."

"Nothing else?" the ranger asked.

"Nothing else."

* * *

Chuck returned to camp from the A-frame. He considered confronting Dale about his altercation with Owen. But, like Owen, Dale was sure to deny the argument had taken place, which meant questioning him would serve only to make him aware of Chuck's suspicion. Instead, Chuck kept his distance from Dale as well as from Mark, Caleb, and Bernard throughout the afternoon, noting that the men did the same among themselves, resting in their tents or reclining in their camp chairs with their noses in books or their eyes on their phones.

As the afternoon gave way to evening, Chuck spotted Jimmy through the trees, talking with Alden at the front of the campground. The two disappeared beneath the sheet covering the tower, presumably to set the finesse-oriented route for Carmelita and Tara, the Berkeley climber, who was nowhere to be seen.

Chuck teamed with Janelle in preparing an early dinner of pasta and salad. With the start time for the competition approaching, Carmelita swirled noodles on a plate with her fork but didn't lift any to her mouth.

"Climbing on an empty stomach won't be a bad thing," Chuck assured her. "You'll regain your appetite when it's over. You can eat something then."

Rosie swung her feet below the bench seat of the picnic table and asked with her mouth full, "Are you nervous, Carm?"

Carmelita nodded.

Leaning across the table, Janelle rested her hand on her older daughter's slender forearm. "It's okay, baby. Nobody expected you to get this far. Just do your best."

Carmelita nodded again, her eyes downcast.

"You're gonna kill that lady climber, *hermana*," Rosie declared. She made tearing motions with her hands. "You're gonna rip her to shreds. Rip, rip, rip!"

"Rosie, please," Janelle admonished.

But when Carmelita raised her head to glance at her sister,

Chuck spotted a smile playing at the corners of her mouth.

Jimmy made no mention of Ponch's death when he introduced himself and welcomed the gathered onlookers to the start of round four of the Slam a few minutes after eight, as evening shadows settled in the valley. Ponch's fall was too fresh, too raw, Chuck decided, and Jimmy's role in having proposed the prank that led to it too personal.

Chuck's own shame burned like acid inside him. Why had he not pushed harder to stop last night's escapade? If he'd kept at it until he convinced the others to abandon the prank, Ponch would still be alive.

The crowd of spectators, some standing, others seated in camp chairs, was triple the size of the gathering for yesterday's opening rounds of the Slam. Juanita and other park concession workers were among the onlookers. YOSAR team members speckled the crowd, too, while Owen stood to one side, as he had the day before, the badge on his chest polished to a high sheen.

Spotlights on extended poles lit Jimmy and the climbing tower behind him, warding off the approaching darkness and providing a stage-like atmosphere for the conclusion of the competition.

Standing in front of the crowd at the foot of the tower's billowy shroud, Jimmy spoke into a cordless microphone, another addition, along with the lights, to the closing rounds of the competition. He offered only a few subdued words of welcome, his voice issuing from speakers at the foot of the spotlight poles, and held out the microphone to Alden.

The tower attendant bounded to the base of the climbing wall, accepted the cordless mic from Jimmy, and turned to face the audience with a wide grin while Jimmy crutched away from the tower to stand in the crowd with Dale, Mark, Caleb, and Bernard. In true master-of-ceremonies fashion, Alden wore black slacks and a purple dress shirt beneath a black suit coat, the coat's sleeves and those of the dress shirt rolled up his thick forearms. When he lifted his hand to wave at the spectators, the fitted coat rose and drew in at his sides, accentuating his broad shoulders and revealing his climbing harness, strapped over his slacks at his waist.

"Welcome!" he roared, his enthusiasm a stark contrast to Jimmy's muted greeting. "I can't believe how many of you have turned out for our competition tonight. Way more than we've ever had before. And I'll tell you what, you're in for a real treat this evening, starting with an intriguing one-on-one matchup on the women's side of the bracket, on a route designed just for them."

He put his hand to his eyes, shading the spotlights, and peered into the audience. "Ladies, come on up here, would you, please?"

Tara left the crowd and approached Alden. The two exchanged no words before she spun to face the spectators. After a nudge from Janelle, Carmelita snaked her way out of the crowd to Tara's side and turned to the crowd as well.

Carmelita was dressed in the same T-shirt and loose leggings as yesterday. Tara again wore black, body-hugging tights low on her hips. She wore a different top, however, this one a skimpy sports bra with thin straps, cream-colored to match her tanned skin so that, from a distance, she appeared topless in the glare of the spotlights save for the ring glittering in her exposed belly button.

Tara shook out her long, golden hair and tossed it over her shoulder. Carmelita, a full head shorter, looked at her feet, her hands locked behind her back.

Chuck had spotted Tara when she'd pulled into Camp 4 an hour ago in an aging Ford Econoline van repurposed as a camper. While the sun descended behind El Capitan, she chatted with other climbers at the front of the campground, bending forward in deep stretches every once in a while. Chuck kept watch to see if she spoke with Alden—not that there was anything he could do about it. As best he could tell, though, the two did not converse during the lead-up to the competition, nor did he catch Tara sneaking a peak beneath the tower's nylon sheet at the climbing route awaiting her and Carmelita.

Dwarfing the two female competitors beside him, Alden put the microphone to his mouth. "As many of you know," he said, "today's women rock climbers are among the best climbers, regardless of gender, on the planet. In the past, strength moves by big guys—" he bent one arm, stretching the fabric of his jacket as he showed off his bulging bicep "—were the primary way climbers sent the toughest routes. But today's most difficult unconquered faces, with their fewer and tinier holds, require finesse moves rather than brute strength. That has led to skinny male climbers—unlike me—occupying the highest echelons of the climbing world, along with more and more female climbers."

Alden cast a glance of obvious admiration at Tara and Carmelita.

"Which brings us to tonight," he continued, "with world-renowned Tara Rogan from Berkeley, California, and the new kid on the block—and I do mean *kid*—twelve-year-old Carmelita Ortega from Durango, Colorado. Please join me in welcoming Tara and Carmelita back with us tonight."

The crowd applauded as Alden directed a thumb over his shoulder at the covered tower.

"When I drop the sheet, I want all of you to notice how incredibly difficult this route will be for our contestants," he said. "Jimmy and I believe the route we've set is one of the toughest ever placed in a climbing competition. Tara and Carmelita have fully recovered from yesterday's rounds and are prepared to give the route their ultimate effort this evening, right out of the blocks."

Alden dug a coin from his pocket. "We'll flip to see who goes first," he said. He proffered the coin in his palm to Tara and Carmelita for their inspection. "Tara, why don't you call it?"

Alden held the microphone to her mouth.

"Tails," Tara said.

"Tails it is," Alden repeated into the mic.

He flipped the coin into the air and allowed it to fall to the ground. The three bent over it. Disappointment showed on Tara's face when she straightened.

Alden announced, "It's heads!" He turned to Carmelita. "What do you think? Do you want to go first?"

He reached past Tara to hold the microphone in front of Carmelita's clamped lips. She stared at the coin, still lying on the ground.

Alden brought the mic back to his mouth and singsonged with a half-smile, "We're wait-ing."

In the crowd, Chuck whispered to Janelle, "Second. She should go second. Just like in football. It's always best to be the last one holding the ball."

Alden held the microphone to Carmelita's mouth. She gulped. The noise, audible through the speakers, prompted laughter from the spectators.

"Um," Carmelita said.

Tara bent and said something in Carmelita's ear.

Carmelita raised her head to look at Tara, her hazel eyes wide open. "I'll go last," she said into the outthrust microphone.

Tara's lips formed a rigid, white line. She scowled at Carmelita.

Alden brought the microphone back to his mouth and crowed to the audience, "All righty then! Tara will go first, and little Carmelita will follow." He turned to the two of them. "I'll give you a couple of minutes to make sure you're all set before I ask you to make your way to the back of the tower together."

Tara returned to the spectators. When Carmelita didn't move, Alden gave her a gentle shove while he smiled at the onlookers. She took a stumbling step forward, then darted into the crowd, straight to Janelle's side.

From the foot of the tower, Alden cried out, "Let's hear it for day two, round four of this year's Yosemite Sa-lammm!"

The spectators cheered. Chuck knelt and tightened the laces on Carmelita's climbing shoes a final time. Rising, he helped her strap on her helmet and offered her a bottle of water. While she sipped, he put his mouth to her ear and asked, "What did Tara say to you?"

She replied so only he could hear. "She said I should go first to get it over with."

Chuck grinned. "You're one smart girl, you know that?" He lifted his fist and she bumped it with her own.

On the opposite side of the crowd, Tara drank out of a bottle, wiped her mouth with the back of her hand, and wormed her way from among the gathered onlookers, heading for Alden and the sheet-covered wall.

Alden edged sideways, placing himself squarely in Tara's path to the back of the tower. He raised a hand and smiled, prepared, it seemed, to exchange pleasantries with her as she passed him on her way around the climbing wall. But the dark gleam in his eyes indicated he had more to offer her than mere good wishes.

Chuck wormed his way forward, elbowing people aside, as Tara neared Alden. The tower attendant lowered his chin when she came within a step of him, his face shaded from the spotlights. He opened his mouth to speak at the same instant Chuck broke from the front of the crowd, thirty feet away.

"Yo," Chuck called out.

Alden jerked visibly and raised his head to stare at Chuck.

Chuck hustled forward. "I've got something I want to ask."

At Alden's side, Tara observed Chuck's approach, her eyes glistening with unconcealed animosity beneath the brim of her helmet.

"What is it?" Alden asked, his face hard.

"What about—" Chuck hesitated as he worked to come up with a question. "What about Carmelita's belay? Are you still okay with me doing it?"

Alden clenched his jaw, the muscles at the sides of his face rippling. "Tell you what," he said as Chuck stopped before him. "Just to make sure everything's above board, I think I'll belay both climbers." Alden turned to Tara. "How's that sound to you?"

"Whatever you think," she said with a shrug.

Chuck shrugged, too, feigning nonchalance. "Sure," he said, having no choice but to agree.

The three faced each other in silence.

When Chuck made no move to return to the crowd, Tara rolled her helmeted head around her shoulders, her silky hair shining behind her. "I guess I'll go on back so you can do your unveiling," she said to Alden.

She rounded the tower to the vehicle-filled parking lot. Chuck motioned to Carmelita. Leaving her mother's side, she edged through the crowd.

"All set?" Chuck asked her when she reached him and Alden at the foot of the tower.

She nodded once, a slight tip of her chin.

"Go get 'em," he urged her.

She ducked her head and disappeared behind the tower.

Chuck faced Alden. "I'm looking forward to seeing what you've got in store for them."

"You and everybody else," Alden said, his voice cold. "Now, if you'll excuse me."

Chuck returned to Janelle's side in the audience. Alden untied the rope holding the nylon shroud in place.

"Three! Two! One!" he counted down into the microphone for the benefit of the onlookers, his voice once again animated.

He released the line, allowing the sheet to fall to the ground. The spectators murmured breathlessly to one another as they studied the route.

At first glance, and second and third, the new route looked impossible to Chuck. Alden and Jimmy had gone with extreme minimalism, placing only a handful of holds on the wall. Sizable blank spaces pocked the tower from bottom to top, the first only a few feet off the ground. The few holds bolted into place were small and sloped outward, providing little purchase for fingers or toes.

"*Dios mío*," Janelle muttered at Chuck's side.

"Pretty outrageous," he agreed, his voice low. "But it might favor Carmelita. She's lighter than Tara. Instead of a multi-hold route that requires experience to recognize the best solutions along the way, this is all about what's not there. It's like the routes with the blank spaces from yesterday, only more so." He aimed a finger at the largest blank spot on the tower. "Like that space there, two-thirds of the way up."

Even as he pointed out the large blank space to Janelle, something about it caught his eye. He squinted at it, then exhaled sharply.

29

A tiny, dark circle showed near the bottom of the blank space. The circle, little more than a speck against the fiberglass wall, was far too small to be a climbing hold. It sat in line with other specks, slightly lighter in color, that together formed a horizontal border across the convex face of the wall. Chuck recognized the specks as the heads of screws securing one of the rounded fiberglass wall panels in place on the tower. The darker speck was a single loosened screw head in the middle of the line of screws.

It appeared Alden had rotated the head of the screw out of the wall just enough to provide purchase to the toe of a climbing shoe worn by anyone aware of the screw's slight extension. The loosened screw cast a slightly greater shadow on the wall than the heads of the other screws, enough to catch Chuck's suspicious eye, but almost certainly not enough to catch the attention of anyone else, Tara and Carmelita included. Chuck could only hope his hurried approach to the tower a few minutes ago had precluded Alden's attempt to tell Tara about the extended screw head.

"We're ready for you, Tara," Alden called around the tower, the microphone to his mouth. His amplified voice echoed across the campground from the speakers.

Tara emerged from the back of the forty-foot-high structure. She gazed at the wall, her eyes tracking from bottom to top, as she dug her hands into the chalk bag slung from the harness at her waist. Alden set the microphone on the ground, attached the climbing rope to Tara's harness, and backed away from the wall. He gripped the opposite end of the rope, which ran through the belay device attached to his own harness.

Tara shot a joking look of consternation at Alden, then directed the same look at Jimmy, perched on his crutches at the front of the crowd. He released the crutches' grips and turned his hands palms up. The spectators chuckled.

Tara turned her back on him, her hair below her helmet shimmering in the spotlights. She stood unmoving, inches from the wall. The crowd quieted as she raised herself on her toes and lifted her arms from her sides like a high diver, her hands outstretched.

Grasping the lowest holds on the tower, Tara hoisted herself off the ground. She moved upward slowly, working her way from one widely spaced hold to the next, her muscles tensed. Within a minute, her breaths came in harsh gasps.

Chuck bit down on the inside of his cheek as Tara extended her hand blindly above her head to find a particularly tiny hold with her outstretched fingers. She tugged herself upward, overcoming a sizable blank space at the halfway point on the wall, and continued her painstaking climb until she reached the largest of the blank spaces—the one offering purchase on the loosened screw head to anyone in the know.

Chuck glanced back and forth between Tara and Alden as Tara hesitated at the bottom of the blank space, her fingers kinked where she clung to sloped holds. She leaned back, studying the gap and the small hold placed at its top.

Alden stared at her from the foot of the tower, his brake hand gripping the rope at his waist.

Tara shot her right hand upward and pushed off from her toeholds. She stretched her trim body full out, reaching for the hold bolted above the blank spot, her face to the wall. At the same instant, unnoticed by the audience, Alden gave the climbing rope a brisk yank through his belay device with his brake hand. The sudden tug took up all the slack in the rope at once, providing Tara an extra bit of upward momentum as she leapt up the tower. Her fingers caught the hold at the top of the large gap and she pulled herself upward with an audible grunt. Again, Alden tugged downward on his end of the rope, continuing to aid Tara's ascent while the spectators' eyes were on Tara, high above.

Clinging with her right hand to the hold above the blank spot, Tara shot her left hand to a second hold at the top of the space. Alden took up the new bit of slack in the rope with another tug, helping Tara as she fought to hold her place on the wall.

The champion woman climber lifted herself higher on the two tiny holds. Her feet scrabbled for traction on the blank stretch of wall. Here, Chuck knew, was where knowledge of the extended screw head would come in handy. But, he noted with satisfaction, neither of Tara's toes, sliding on the fiberglass surface, came anywhere near the loosened screw. Instead, her feet continued to fight for purchase until she let out a sharp breath and her fingers slipped from the holds above the blank space, causing her to fall away from the wall.

The rope, taut from Alden's braking device to Tara's harness, caught her after she dropped only a few inches. She swung from the stanchion extending from the top of the tower, her head down, cursing under her breath. Finally, she placed her feet on the wall and walked backward down the tower as Alden lowered her to the ground.

Cheers from the crowd rose to a crescendo as the onlookers recognized how high Tara had climbed on the seemingly insurmountable route set by Alden and Jimmy. She turned to the spectators at the foot of the tower and acknowledged their acclaim with a small wave, her face downcast, as Alden unclipped the rope from her waist.

Audience members embraced Tara when she reentered the crowd. Alden retrieved the microphone and addressed the audience: "As most of you know, the rules state that a climber must top out on the tower to complete the route and, in this case, win the competition. If Carmelita fails anywhere on the wall, we'll reset the route for both competitors and move on to their next one-on-one round."

A spectator to Chuck's right muttered to a companion, "Looks like we're gonna be here awhile."

When Alden called Carmelita's name, she appeared from behind the tower to a boisterous ovation. Rosie and Clarence offered particularly spirited cries of support, their hands cupped around their mouths. Alden placed the mic on the ground, attached the rope to Carmelita's harness, and stepped back, his brake hand on his end of the rope.

Carmelita coated her hands with powder from her chalk bag and set off up the wall, climbing fast.

Chuck gnawed his cheek as she sped upward. Even as he fought the urge to call out to her to slow down, he knew her instincts were correct. Completing the grueling route to the top of the tower would depend on wise retention and use of energy, by moving fast, along with loads of skill.

Carmelita overcame the lowest blank spot on the wall without hesitation. She paused at the base of the second blank space, studying the holds above it. Chuck glanced at Alden, who used his free hand to give the rope above his belay device a slight twitch. The subtle vibration traveled up the rope, through the pulley, and back down to the rope's attachment point at Carmelita's waist.

Carmelita wobbled when the nearly imperceptible pulse struck her climbing harness and traveled into her body. Her toes slipped from the holds on which they'd been balanced. The onlookers gasped as Carmelita fell several inches down the face of the wall until her fingers, grasping tiny holds above her head, caught her and halted her plunge.

She huffed with obvious exertion and lifted herself back into place on the wall, regaining her toeholds but burning valuable energy in the process.

Moving even more quickly now, she shot first her right hand, then her left, to holds above the blank space and scrambled higher on the wall, her arms and legs spread wide like a spider.

Rather than haul in the excess slack in the rope running from his brake device to Carmelita, Alden allowed the rope to trail downward away from his waist as Carmelita ascended, requiring her to deal with the added weight of the dangling rope with each move. Only when the rope drooped all the way to the ground did Alden take up some of the slack running from his waist to the top of the tower and back down to Carmelita.

Enraged, Chuck left Janelle's side and pushed his way through the spectators as Carmelita approached the largest blank space on the wall, three quarters of the way up the tower, where Tara had fallen. After working his way around to the side of the tower, Chuck stepped out of the crowd and glared at Alden's back.

Carmelita reached the bottom of the large blank space on the wall. Below her, at the foot of the tower, Alden took hold of the rope with his non-brake hand, ready to give the line another twitch.

"Don't," Chuck said menacingly, just loud enough for Alden to hear.

Alden froze. He glanced over his shoulder at Chuck and lowered his free hand to his side.

High on the tower, Carmelita leaned back and surveyed the tiny hold atop the expansive blank space. She sank low on her toeholds and sprang cat-like up the face of the wall.

The onlookers fell silent. Carmelita hung suspended in midair at the top of her upward leap. She stretched her hand high above her head, grabbed the tiny hold with her fingers, and hung from it atop the blank space, her body swinging free below.

Chuck bit the inside of his cheek so hard he tasted blood. Here was where Tara had fallen despite the aid of Alden's upward tug on the rope.

Carmelita wedged her toes against the blank patch of wall beneath her, neither foot coming anywhere near the extended screw head. She maintained her tenuous grip on the upper hold and climbed her feet up the wall. With her lower body contorted, she shot her left hand to a higher hold and immediately followed with her right hand to another hold still higher on the wall. She scrambled upward until she gained tenuous purchase with her fingers as well as her toes on minuscule holds above the large blank space.

Thunderous cries erupted from the crowd as she continued to climb, still moving fast, and still overcoming the swinging, off-putting excess slack left in the rope by Alden.

Chuck kept an eye on Alden as Carmelita neared the top of the tower. Alden's free hand trembled but remained at his side.

A triumphant roar rose from the spectators as Carmelita completed the climb by tapping the tower's fiberglass top. Standing together in the crowd, Dale, Caleb, Mark, and Bernard pounded one another's backs. Jimmy grinned. Even Owen, on the opposite side of the semi-circle of onlookers from Chuck, clapped politely, his ever-present clipboard tucked beneath his arm.

Carmelita released her holds and leaned back from the tower, ready to descend. But the rope did not take her weight. Instead, she plummeted straight down the face of the tower, free-falling toward the ground just as Jimmy had two days ago.

30

R osie screeched as Carmelita fell, but Chuck did not move. Carmelita spread-eagled her arms and legs, facing the wall, and held her position until the slack left in the rope by Alden played through the pulley at the top of the tower and the rope tightened, bringing her to an abrupt halt five feet down the wall. She bounced lightly off the tower's face, using her outspread arms and legs as springs, then leaned away from the wall and walked backward as Alden lowered her, the rope running steadily through his brake hand.

Regaining their voices, the spectators hooted and hollered for Carmelita when she reached the ground and Alden freed the rope from her waist. She turned to the crowd with her head bowed, shaking out her hands at her sides.

Alden picked up the microphone and addressed the onlookers, who surrounded the front of the tower at the edge of the spotlights, their backs to what was now full darkness.

"There we have it," he announced, his voice lacking its earlier enthusiasm. "This year's women's open Yosemite Slam champion, Carmelita Ortega."

Carmelita raised her head as the crowd cheered. She stood in place while the acclaim washed over her, the pride in her eyes glowingly evident. As soon as the applause ended, she beelined for Janelle.

"We'll take a few minutes' break to reset the route for the men's competition," Alden announced. He detached himself from the rope and headed for Tara.

Trailing Alden, Chuck crossed the open area at the foot of the tower with his hands twisted into fists. In the crowd ahead,

Tara's face turned crimson when she caught sight of Alden approaching her. She turned from him and walked away through the onlookers, her back stiff. Alden came to an abrupt halt in the lit area between the tower and spectators, watching Tara's departure.

"What the hell?" Chuck demanded, coming up on Alden from behind.

Alden turned to Chuck. "I . . . I . . ."

Chuck stopped inches from him. "You did everything you could to throw the competition."

Alden gulped. Guilt flooded his eyes. He aimed a finger at Tara as she strode off. The spotlights winked off the smooth skin of her bare shoulders, her wavy hair rippling down her back, her legs smooth and muscled in her skintight climbing pants. "How am I supposed to say no to that?" he asked plaintively.

Chuck drew back his fist.

Then he hesitated.

Before Janelle and the girls had entered his life, he'd have torn into Alden, heedless of the consequences. But he was a husband now, a stepfather.

He lowered his fist. "If . . . you . . . *ever*," he threatened.

Alden's chin rose and fell above his thick neck. "Never," he said, his voice shaking. "Never again."

Chuck spun away, his shoulders bunched. He spied Carmelita through the crowd, clutched in her mother's embrace. He opened and closed his hands, releasing his anger, anxious to commend his daughter for her incredible climb.

Cheers of encouragement for the first male competitor of round four resounded through the deserted campground when the Slam resumed thirty minutes later. In the darkness on the far side of Camp 4, Chuck folded the final camp chair from the emptied Bender Archaeological campsite and stuffed it with the others into an oversized duffle bag.

Janelle walked the perimeter of the site, her phone light directed at the ground, checking for any items missed while packing. Chuck straightened from the duffle bag and scanned the site from where he stood as he waited for Janelle to circle back to him. He crossed his arms over his chest. They'd broken camp quickly. The picnic table was bare, the family tent and Clarence's solo tent collapsed and carted off by Clarence and the girls to the truck in the parking lot.

Like the rest of the campground, the reunion campsite next door was quiet; Jimmy, Dale, Caleb, Bernard, and Mark were among those watching the resumption of the men's competition at the tower. A yellow dome tent among the other pup tents ringing the reunion site caught Chuck's eye.

Chuck pointed at the tent as Janelle came up to him. "That's Ponch's. My heart hurts just looking at it."

"Mine, too," Janelle said. She sighed. "He's why we're getting out of here." She turned off her light. "We're making our escape, just like those gold prospectors of yours."

"I'd almost forgotten about them. Aside from Carmelita's winning the Slam, the only good thing from this weekend is your finding the ring, which points straight at Rose as having gotten away with murder."

"But the questions about Ponch and Thorpe? And Jimmy's fall?" Janelle shook herself, the wiggling movement of her body visible to Chuck in the filtered light reaching the campsite from the bathroom in the center of the campground. An additional flutter of movement showed in the shadows beyond Janelle's shoulder to the north, in the direction of the side-by-side park worker campsites near Columbia Boulder, as she continued, "Those questions can stay unanswered forever as far as I'm concerned. I just want to find a motel room as far away from the valley as possible tonight, and head back to Durango first thing in the morning."

Chuck looked past her. No more movement showed itself in the darkness. But he'd seen something. He was sure of it.

He picked up the chair-filled duffle and offered it to Janelle. "Think you can handle this?"

"Sure." She slung the bag over her shoulder by its strap.

"I'll be right behind you. I want to take a look around the reunion site, make sure I didn't leave anything over there."

He handed her the truck key. She headed for the front of the campground, the duffle riding low on her back. Jimmy's voice rang out from the climbing tower as he announced the name of the next climber in the competition, taking a turn at the master-of-ceremony duties.

Peering north, Chuck made out the two park worker campsites in front of the dark bulk of Columbia Boulder. The sites, bubbled with tents and backed by hanging laundry, were deserted.

He stood motionless, staring. Nothing.

He counted to five, watching the campsites. Still nothing.

He released his breath. Clarence and the girls would have the bed of the truck loaded by now. It was time to go.

Turning away, he crossed the campsite. When he reached the gravel path leading through the center of Camp 4, a muffled groan sounded behind him.

31

Chuck spun, listening. The groan had come from the area around the worker campsites, where he'd spotted the movement in the darkness. The groan had been deep and raspy, that of a male.

Jimmy's amplified voice carried through the trees. Cheers from the spectators reached Chuck, too, as did the rustle of the evening breeze sifting through the branches above his head.

He waited, tense.

Hearing nothing more, he crept toward the campsites, placing one careful foot in front of the other.

Hunched low, he slipped into the nearer of the two sites, only to find it empty. He continued into the farther site, but spotted nothing out of the ordinary there, either, just the workers' hoop tents and strung clothes.

He straightened in the center of the second site. Noisy hurrahs rose from the crowd gathered at the climbing tower. When the cheers died away, another groan sounded, directly ahead of him near Columbia Boulder.

He hurried through the second campsite, past the line of softball-sized rocks marking the north Camp 4 boundary. Two-story-high Columbia Boulder reared above him in the dim glow of the bathroom lights from the center of the campground. A bulky shadow the size and shape of a human body lay on the ground at the base of the massive boulder.

Chuck yanked his phone from his pocket and rushed to the shadowed shape. Metal gleamed on the human-sized form—a ranger badge.

Owen Hutchins, Jr., lay on his back at Chuck's feet.

SCOTT GRAHAM

The ranger groaned a third time.

Chuck tapped frantically at the face of his phone. Before he could activate its light, a voice said from behind him, "Don't do that."

Ice chilled Chuck's veins. He turned and came face to face with Alden.

The tower attendant stood in the shadows ten feet away, barely visible in his black slacks and suit coat—though there was enough light to reveal that he held a pistol in his right hand, aimed at Chuck's midsection.

"You wouldn't dare use that thing," Chuck challenged. "Everyone would come running."

"I'd just tell them Owen did it," Alden said. "This is his gun. Everybody knows he has it in for you."

Chuck's heart pounded. "What is it you want?"

Alden held out his left hand, his palm cupped. "The ring. Jimmy said it's worth a fortune. I can't let you leave here with it. I won't."

Chuck stared, dumbfounded, at him.

"I saw you were leaving," he said. "I gave Jimmy the mic and got Owen to come over here with me and I popped him on the head." He waggled the ranger's pistol. "I was coming to find you, but you came to me instead."

"The ring is in my gear duffle, at the truck."

"We'll head over there. Don't try to run." A sinister note entered Alden's voice. "You thought you could threaten me about Tara and the Slam. Now it's my turn. We know where your girls are."

Chuck shuddered. Was Alden's threat, aimed at the girls, for real?

More cheers rose from the spectators at the tower.

Alden kept the gun trained on Chuck. "We've got plenty of time. The competition will go for at least another hour."

236

"I'll get you the ring." Chuck glanced at Owen's prostrate form on the ground. "There's no need to hurt anyone else."

"Oh, but I already have."

Chuck's brain churned. "Ponch?"

"Collateral damage, I'm afraid."

"It was you who bumped into me on Half Dome, wasn't it?"

"I had you all lined up. But the explosion was bigger than I expected. Brighter. I bounced off of you and hit him instead."

"Why?" Chuck demanded.

"Duh," said Alden. "The ring."

"Knocking me off Half Dome wouldn't have gotten it for you."

"It would have made it easy for me to get it from your wife. After your little tumble, she'd have given it up in a flash."

A human form emerged from the shadows thirty feet beyond Alden's shoulder. A second later, an additional form materialized alongside the first. Both forms crept toward Alden from behind.

Intent on keeping his conversation with Alden going, Chuck beckoned him forward and squatted beside Owen. "He's not groaning anymore. He might be dead."

Alden stepped closer. "Good riddance."

"You won't get away with this, you know."

"Wrong. The ring is my lottery ticket. I'll find a buyer for it on the internet. That part will be easy. I'll get myself a new identity and bounce from crag to crag—Thailand, Greece, Spain, you name it. I'll climb my way around the world and have me all the ladies I want. No more sorry-ass Sacramento Rock Gym, and no more Jimmy, either, with his worthless promises."

Chuck pressed his fingers to Owen's wrist. "Lucky for you he's got a good pulse. He just needs—"

"Oof!" Alden exclaimed, his breath escaping. The gun shuddered in his hand and fired, the blast concussing the night air.

32

The bullet tore into Chuck, the force of the shot throwing him across Owen's body. Alden dropped the gun and collapsed in a heap beside the downed ranger.

Chuck sat up between the sprawled bodies of Owen and Alden. He probed the bullet wound with his fingers. Pain stabbed his brain. His searching fingers discovered that the bullet had missed his torso, passing instead through the flesh of his inner, upper arm. He clutched his injured arm and staggered to his feet. Blood from the wound ran past his elbow. The pain was sharp but bearable, blunted by adrenaline coursing through him.

Janelle and Clarence stood over Alden in the shadowy darkness. Clarence dropped a brick-sized rock from his hand and scooped Owen's gun from the ground.

Cries of alarm sounded from the front of the campground. Chuck looked through the trees toward the climbing tower. Spectators milled in the spotlights at the base of the tower, pointing into the campground. Several pressed phones to their ears.

Alden lay face down in the dirt. He moaned. His legs twitched and he reached a hand for the back of his head.

"You didn't kill him," Chuck said to Clarence.

"He didn't get what he deserved, then."

"I need you to tie him up."

"*Por supuesto.*"

"The girls," Chuck said, turning to Janelle, his tone urgent. "Where are they?"

Her face was pale in the shadowy light. "With Juanita."

"The Latina woman?"

"They're in the crowd, safe, with everyone else."

"You barely know her."

Janelle held herself erect. "I know her well enough. You didn't follow me to the truck. Clarence and I had to come looking for you."

"I have to get over there," Chuck said, thinking of Alden's threat—and his use of the term *we*. "The girls."

Janelle's voice trembled. "What do you mean, 'the girls'?"

By now, a handful of spectators, silhouetted by the spotlights directed at the tower behind them, made their way through the campground toward Columbia Boulder.

"There isn't time to explain."

"I'm coming with you," Janelle said.

A wave of nausea rolled upward from Chuck's stomach, causing him to stagger.

Janelle lifted his wounded arm away from his body. Blood dripped from the wound to the ground.

"It's okay," Chuck said, tugging his arm from her grasp.

"I'll be the judge of that," Janelle said, but her eyes roved toward the tower and the girls.

"I'll be all right," he insisted.

"Press your arm against your side," she directed. "Hard. Don't let up. You have to maintain pressure. Got it?"

"Got it."

"Let's go."

Chuck pressed his injured arm to his ribs as instructed. The flow of blood from the wound slowed to a trickle, but the pain intensified. Wincing, he said to Clarence, "You're in charge here. Don't let anybody touch the gun until the rangers get here, and be ready with it yourself. I don't trust anyone right now."

"You got it, *jefe*," Clarence said.

The screech of a siren reverberated down the valley, coming from Yosemite Village, as Chuck led Janelle past the boulder and into the thick stand of trees north of the campground. They wound through the forest until they drew even with the bathroom.

Half a dozen members of the YOSAR team, ball caps low over their eyes, entered the circle of light around the building. They melted into the shadows beyond the bathroom. Behind them, two Latino men entered the lit area surrounding the bathroom. Dale came into the light next, following the two men.

Cries of surprise rose from the foot of Columbia Boulder, where the YOSAR team members aimed phone lights at Owen and Alden on the ground, with Clarence standing over them. From up the valley, the sound of the siren grew to a piercing wail as the emergency vehicle neared the campground.

"Dale!" Chuck hissed from the trees.

Dale halted. So did the two Latino men, their heads turning toward the sound of Chuck's voice. The two men continued toward Columbia Boulder after a pause, while Dale walked toward Chuck and Janelle.

"Chuck?" Dale ventured as he approached the north edge of the campground.

Chuck stepped from the shadows of the trees with Janelle.

"It *is* you," Dale exclaimed. "What the hell's going on?"

"That's what I want to ask you," Chuck said. A second wave of nausea rocked him back on his heels as the pain from his wound increased. "That's close enough," he warned when Dale was five feet away.

Dale stopped.

Chuck dug his phone from his pocket with his right hand, his throbbing left arm pressed to his side. Blood ran down his ribcage, gathering at the waistband of his jeans. Working his phone with his thumb, Chuck turned on the light and shone it in Dale's eyes.

Dale shielded his face with his hand. "What is this, some sort of interrogation?"

"That's exactly what it is."

Lowering his hand, Dale looked straight at Chuck. "If this has anything to do with Ponch's death, I'll tell you everything I know, everything I'm thinking."

Chuck kept the light steady on Dale's face.

"The explosion would not have sent Ponch over the edge," Dale said. "I'm convinced of it. Someone had to have pushed him."

Chuck asked, his voice tight, "The same way Owen pushed you today behind the post office?"

In the light of Chuck's phone, Dale blanched. "I didn't . . . I wasn't . . ." He took a deep breath. "That was a mistake. I fully admit it. Owen seemed so sad, so alone, like he needed comfort. I just . . . I couldn't help myself."

"What did you do to him, Dale?" Chuck demanded.

"I tried to hug him, that's all."

Chuck's jaw dropped. "You made a pass at him?"

"My gaydar was off. It happens. He didn't take it too well."

"You're . . . you're . . . unbelievable," Chuck muttered. He killed the light and pocketed his phone.

The ranger vehicle skidded into the gravel parking lot and sped around the perimeter of the lot to the front of the campground, its siren blaring and roof lights flashing.

"The girls," Janelle urged. She tugged Chuck's uninjured arm as the vehicle slid to a stop beside the climbing tower and the wail of its siren died away.

Chuck began, "I need to ask—"

But Janelle cut him off. "Carm and Rosie first. You said so yourself."

She dragged him toward the climbing tower. Chuck glanced back to see Dale continue on in the direction of Columbia Boulder.

Janelle maintained her grip on Chuck's right arm, jogging

with him toward the tower. Chuck's injured left arm jostled against his side. Lightning bolts of pain shot through him. Blood flowed from the wound, less than at first as the injury began to clot, but enough to make his side wet and sticky.

Ahead, the front doors to the park ranger vehicle swung open. Two uniformed rangers, a man and a woman, stepped out, their hands on the guns at their hips. Onlookers pointed the two toward Columbia Boulder. The rangers drew flashlights from their belts and entered the campground at a fast walk, the beams of their lights bouncing off tents and picnic tables.

Chuck and Janelle angled away from the approaching rangers. After the officers passed, he hurried with her toward a knot of people standing at the foot of the tower, Juanita among them.

Rosie and Carmelita broke from the group when Chuck and Janelle drew near. The girls buried themselves against their mother, their arms wrapped around her waist.

Chuck scanned the brightly lit area in front of the tower. Spectators and climbers stood in clusters, talking and gesturing toward the campground. Caleb, Mark, and Bernard stood with their heads close, engaged in what appeared to be an intense discussion.

They turned when Chuck hurried over to them.

Chuck searched the darkness beyond the three men. "Where's Jimmy?"

33

"Jimmy?" Caleb asked, frowning. He pointed into Camp 4. "He probably headed that way."

Chuck turned a quick circle. He was certain Jimmy hadn't passed through the campground to Columbia Boulder, nor was there any sign of him at the tower. But he couldn't have gone far on his crutches.

The wails of more sirens rose from the east as additional emergency vehicles left the village and sped down the valley toward the campground.

Chuck wiped his sweating face with his right hand.

He didn't have much time. He needed to think, to focus.

Alden had wanted the ring.

Chuck dropped his hand to his side.

Greed. A century and a half ago, Rose. Now, Alden.

But it was Jimmy who had told Alden how much the ring was worth.

Pressing his wounded left arm to his ribcage, Chuck rounded the climbing tower, leaving Caleb, Mark, and Bernard behind.

The spotlights struck the tower, throwing a long shadow across the parking lot. The big, boxy Bender Archaeological pickup truck was parked in the second row, deep in the tower's shadow.

Chuck stole to the first row of vehicles and supported himself on a parked car, his thoughts growing foggy and disjointed. He collapsed to his elbow on the trunk of the car and stared into the shadow cast by the tower. He blinked to clear his vision. The pickup truck sat between a pair of mini-SUVs on the far side of the second row of cars, and well above a small sedan parked nose to nose with it on the near side of the second row. The quiet *snick* of metal on metal came from the rear of the truck.

Chuck stifled his breathing. He entered the shadow of the tower, crossed the gravel driving lane to the second row of cars, and ducked behind the sedan that faced the truck. Peering woozily around the low-slung car, he caught sight of Jimmy standing at the opened tailgate at the back of the pickup. Jimmy's crutches, tucked beneath his arms, tapped the edge of the tailgate as he unzipped and pawed through the pockets of Chuck's gear duffle.

Chuck crept through the shadow along the side of the sedan, the screech of sirens from the approaching emergency vehicles providing him cover. He wavered at the front of the car. By now, blood from his wound soaked his pants from his waist to his knee. White stars flashed before his eyes. He toppled sideways between the sedan and truck, striking the grill of the pickup with a resounding *thump*. He bounced off the truck and collapsed across the sedan's hood.

A second ranger vehicle turned into the parking lot, its siren blaring. The car's headlights swept across the lot, lighting Jimmy as he crutched alongside the truck toward Chuck.

"Where is it?" Jimmy demanded, rounding the front of the pickup. "Where is it, goddammit?"

Chuck lay sprawled on the hood of the sedan, unable to move.

"Ah," Jimmy observed. "Not doing so well, are you?"

"Alden shot me," Chuck said, his voice weak.

Another set of headlights swept through the parking lot as a third ranger sedan swung into the campground. The flash of the vehicle's headlights across Jimmy's face revealed a predatory look in his eyes.

The headlights swept on, returning Jimmy to shadow. Chuck could only watch, dazed, as Jimmy lifted one of his crutches and brought it down hard on Chuck's wounded upper arm. Chuck cried out and tumbled to the ground between the truck and facing sedan. Pain from his arm sizzled through his back and neck.

Jimmy crutched forward, swinging his left leg in its soft ankle cast, until he loomed over Chuck.

Chuck summoned the last of his strength and lashed out with his foot, striking the cast a solid blow at the spot where, two days ago, Jimmy's left foot had protruded sideways at his ankle.

Jimmy howled, his screech drowned by the dying sirens of the arriving emergency vehicles. He dropped his crutches and fell to the gravel beside Chuck, between the truck and sedan.

"Jesus!" Jimmy cried out between agonized moans, gripping his lower leg.

"You're finished, Jimmy," Chuck muttered, his words slurred.

Jimmy released his leg and collapsed to his back at Chuck's side, choking back a groan. "The hell I am."

The flow of blood returning to Chuck's brain as he lay on the ground enabled him to think clearly. "Alden knocked Ponch off Half Dome. He said he was aiming for me."

Jimmy took a shaky breath. "It was his idea to go after you up there, not mine."

Chuck twisted his head to look at Jimmy. "He wanted the ring."

"I want it, too. I need it."

"He said the same thing. He said you made promises to him you didn't keep."

"*Couldn't* keep." In the dim light, Jimmy's face turned to stone. "Thorpe," he snarled.

"You met up with him, didn't you?"

"Thursday night," Jimmy confirmed.

"You cut his wingsuit."

"One little snip. Just enough to mess it up a little, to make sure he turned away from the gap and pulled his chute early. He didn't deserve the big, fancy arrival he was planning for the reunion."

"The seam separated all the way up into the airfoil. One of the stays came loose. It slashed his ankle. I'm sure that's what made him wreck."

Jimmy didn't respond.

"You knew," Chuck said, his voice harsh, demanding. "That morning, as soon as he went missing."

"Yes."

"You released the auto-belay. You fell on purpose."

"I had no other choice. I couldn't have people looking my way."

Chuck cocked his head. Jimmy hadn't wanted anyone looking his way after Thorpe's death—because of something the two of them had been involved in, together.

"MoJuice," Chuck said.

"MoJuice," Jimmy repeated in agreement.

"The energy drink. The one you have a stake in."

"If they'd ever fucking IPO it." Jimmy shifted on the ground, grimaced, and again clutched his leg.

Chuck stared at Jimmy's profile, the scorpion-tail beard curling skyward. A century and a half ago, the prospector, Rose, likely had murdered his fellow mine owners for money. Two days ago, Jimmy had done essentially the same thing to Thorpe, for the same reason.

Chuck said, "The MoJuice people have been claiming for years they're about to go public—this year, too, right?"

"Thorpe's girlfriend," Jimmy growled in response, "in Fresno. He told her the IPO was sure to happen. She started spending money like she'd turned on a spigot, and she got him going, too."

"His new camper van."

"And lots more. She bought a house, electronic crap for her kids, a car for her parents. She convinced Thorpe my working for Camp 4 meant I'd gone over to the dark side, that I wasn't a renegade anymore and wasn't worthy of MoJuice. She got him to file suit to remove me from the agreement on some technicality. He offered to buy me out for, like, pennies on the dollar. I told him to go to hell. I wouldn't take it. I couldn't." Jimmy turned his head to Chuck. "He wasn't supposed to die. I only wanted him to drop the suit. I was just trying to put some fear into him."

"The same as with me and my family," Chuck said. "You tried to scare us, too."

"It didn't work," Jimmy confirmed, "which shouldn't have surprised me, knowing you. But I had to try. I talked to Alden from the hospital. He told me Owen had mentioned your wife was making a big thing about the airfoil. I knew you'd put two and two together if you stuck around. I sent Alden after you when you crossed the valley. All things considered, though, I'm glad you didn't scare so easy."

"Because of the ring."

"People think Thorpe and I got rich off our sponsorships." Jimmy let out a harsh guffaw. "What a crock. I've been broke every day for the last twenty years. If MoJuice would just IPO, I'd be a millionaire. I could pay Alden fair and square for all the time he's put in for me, like I've promised him. But those 'Juice assholes just keep on keeping themselves private."

Chuck turned his face to the star-studded slice of sky showing between the two vehicles. The air beneath the parked cars smelled of exhaust and motor oil. His eyelids fluttered, his clarity of mind giving way once more to anemic fog and bleariness. "You're a murderer, Jimmy," he said, his words coming with great exertion. "You murdered Thorpe."

"I scared him," Jimmy countered, his voice sharp. "That's all

I wanted to do."

"You cut his airfoil. That's murderous intent. They'll put you away forever."

"No, they won't," Jimmy hissed. He sat up and glowered down at Chuck, his eyes burning. "No one else knows. And no one else is going to know."

Chuck stared dully up from the ground as Jimmy untied his bandanna from around his neck. He put the red cloth to Chuck's nose and mouth and pressed down, crushing the back of Chuck's head into the gravel and cutting off his air supply.

Chuck clawed at Jimmy's wrists, unable to breathe through the bandanna and Jimmy's pressing hands.

Jimmy threw his good leg over Chuck. "They'll think you bled out," he said through bared teeth. Rising between the facing vehicles and locking his arms, he bore down on the bandanna covering the lower half of Chuck's face.

Chuck convulsed. He thrashed the air with his hands and pounded the gravel with his heels.

Jimmy lifted his shoulders, grunting with effort, his fingers clasped over Chuck's nose and mouth.

Chuck lost focus, his eyes closing. Then, in an instantaneous clamor of noise and motion, the truck roared to life and sprang forward, smashing Jimmy between the front of the pickup and the facing sedan.

The truck engine growled and its rear wheels spun, pinning Jimmy in place between the vehicles, his body limp and lifeless.

Chuck slapped the bandanna from his face and drew a deep, shuddering breath.

The truck's wheels stopped spinning and its engine died. A pair of feet in familiar white sneakers appeared below the pickup's underbody as Janelle stepped from the cab.

She dragged Chuck from beneath the vehicles and collapsed to a sitting position beside him. She cradled his head in her lap and stroked his forehead, her falling tears dotting his face.

He lifted a shaky finger to wipe a streak of wetness from her cheek. "It's okay," he told her, his voice weak. "I'm all right."

"I couldn't think what else to do," she said, her words catching in her throat.

"You did great." His hand fell to his chest. "You weaponized yourself."

She raised her chin. "You're right," she said. "I did." Through her tears, her eyes glinted, unwavering. "Don't nobody mess with an Ortega."

ACKNOWLEDGMENTS

With each installment in the National Park Mystery Series, my appreciation grows for the time, effort, and intelligence provided by my early-draft readers. This time around, those readers include Anne Markward, Chuck Greaves, Margaret Mizushima, John Peel, Kevin Graham, and always my first reader, my wife Sue. My thanks go as well to Kirsten Johanna Allen and Anne Terashima of Torrey House Press for their keen editorial skills, and for their work on many levels to protect and preserve our national parks and public lands across the West.

The assistance of Yosemite National Park research librarian Virginia Sanchez and archivist Paul Rogers proved particularly helpful in verifying the historical plot points of *Yosemite Fall*. In addition, I gratefully acknowledge the public-domain use of the nineteenth-century writings of Stephen F. Grover and Lafayette H. Bunnell, whose fascinating journal entries augment the story told here.

I offer my sincere gratitude to independent bookstores and booksellers across the West for their unflagging support, which has been critical to the growing success of the National Park Mystery Series.

Finally, I extend my appreciation to the people of California's present-day Southern Sierra Miwok tribe and all descendants of the Yosemite people, whose ancestral lands today form the beautiful heart of Yosemite National Park.

ABOUT SCOTT GRAHAM

Scott Graham is the author of eight books, including the National Park Mystery Series from Torrey House Press, and *Extreme Kids,* winner of the National Outdoor Book Award. Graham is an avid outdoorsman who enjoys mountaineering, skiing, hunting, rock climbing, and whitewater rafting with his wife, who is an emergency physician, and their two sons. He lives in Durango, Colorado.

ARCHES ENEMY

A National Park Mystery
by Scott Graham

Forthcoming June 2019 from Torrey House Press

TORREY HOUSE PRESS, LLC

SALT LAKE CITY • TORREY

PROLOGUE

Her death was her own damn fault.

He'd done everything right—research, surveillance, charge level, timing. His planning and execution had been perfect, his actions beyond reproach.

Which was why not a single question came his way. Instead, her friends directed their anger at NatResources while they mourned her "passing," to use their spineless phrase. They didn't even cancel that weekend's Moab Counts 10K, the annual citizens' run she'd directed each November for more than a decade. Instead, they declared that year's race a "celebration of her life"—again, their pathetic term. She was *dead*, for Christ's sake. But they couldn't even bring themselves to say the word.

He jogged with everyone else that cold, sunny Saturday morning along the bike path beside the Colorado River away from town and back again. While he ran, he maintained a teary-eyed look on his face, proving himself just another wimp-ass, heartbroken local.

When, in fact, he was anything but.

The notion had popped into his head a year earlier.

He'd been out for an autumn run on Behind the Rocks Trail, following its serpentine path through the maze of red sandstone fins that jutted skyward south of town. The tall, thin slabs of rock sliced the landscape into linear strips of wind-swept dunes separated by shadowed slot canyons.

Tremors surged through the ground every few seconds during his run. The seismic vibrations pulsed upward through his legs and reverberated in his torso. With each mini-earthquake came the same question, over and over again. What if he could send his own seismic wakeup call to every citizen of Utah? *Thump.* What if? *Thump.* What if?

For decades, Utah's politicians had fed voters the same tired line: Utahns could sell their souls to the petrochemical devil while continuing to attract millions of big-spending tourists to the state's incomparable canyon country. In recent years, fierce young environmentalists from the Wasatch Front had disputed the politicians' long-unquestioned claim. Hoisting the torch of Edward Abbey high above their heads, the conservation warriors declared nothing would be left of Utah's stunning red rock country but savaged earth if the petrochemical giants kept on mauling the land with their bulldozers, excavators, backhoes, and graders.

So far, the environmentalists' protest marches and online petitions had resulted in zero change. It was up to someone else to shock the citizens of Utah out of their willful ignorance before it was too late, and with each vibration that pulsed up from the ground through his body on his morning runs south of town, he realized with greater clarity who that someone was.

He began by purchasing a laptop off Craigslist and wiping its hard drive clean. He linked the computer to the internet and conducted his research only through his new, secret online portal. He made further purchases in cash at far-flung ranch supply stores throughout the winter, until he collected everything his research told him he needed.

All through those long months, the seismic truck continued its work south of Moab among the sandstone fins, its proposed move north of town bogged down in the courts.

Spring passed. Summer. By October, a year since he'd first felt the vibrations on Back of Beyond Trail, the truck's pulses were a living thing inside him, a thrumming reminder of what he was prepared to do, and why.

The cottonwoods glowed with autumn gold, the brilliant yellow trees resplendent in the slanted fall sunlight. The leaves snapped free of their branches by the thousands each crisp, cold morning, fluttering to earth in shimmering cascades.

Finally freed by the courts, the massive thumper truck trundled through town early one morning the first week of November, its passage noted by only a handful of sign-waving protesters. It turned off the highway twenty miles north of town and crawled across public land on a winding two track to Yellow Cat Flat, just outside the northern border of Arches National Park.

The limbs of the cottonwoods in town were bare and skeletal a few days later, when the year's first winter storm drew a bead on Moab. He checked the truck's timetable on the Geo-Resources website as the storm bore down, set to bring decreasing temperatures, whipping winds, and icy sleet to southern Utah. He shuddered and took a deep, calming breath. When the storm arrived in two days, the truck still would be thumping its way across Yellow Cat Flat, immediately north of the park.

He double-checked the detonator and retested the timer and battery. He remeasured the premixed amounts of mercury fulminate, ammonium chlorate, and nitroglycerine, making sure they were exact.

The storm crossed into Utah late in the afternoon on November 14. As darkness fell, gray clouds gathered over the state, bringing heavy snow to the northern mountains and sleet to the red rock country in the south.

That night, he deleted his online account and powered down the laptop. He drove north out of Moab over the Colorado

River bridge, slowing to toss the computer over the guardrail into the dark waters below.

He remained on the highway, bypassing the entrance to the national park to avoid the park welcome station and the twenty-four-hour webcam on the building's roof that recorded the license plates of all entering vehicles. He swung off the highway into the Klondike Bluffs Trailhead parking lot fifteen miles north of town.

Cold gusts of wind and icy blasts of sleet bit into him when he climbed out of his car. Low, scudding clouds hid the stars. Though it was after midnight, sedans, SUVs, and tractor-trailer rigs coursed along the wet highway, their wipers flapping in the storm.

He shouldered his pack, clicked on his headlamp, and hiked away from the parking lot. The distinctive rise of Entrada sandstone at the heart of the national park loomed to the east. Two miles from the highway, he left the trail and crossed the unmarked boundary into the park, wending his way through sagebrush and chamisa. Ahead, the uplift of stone beckoned, black against the overcast sky.

He finished hand-drilling the shallow hole in the arch as the sky lightened with dawn. He tamped the charge into the hole, sank the parallel prongs of the detonator into the charge mixture, set the timer for 7:36, and backed off. Needles of wind-driven sleet gathered on his shoulders as he crouched in a sandstone fold two hundred yards from the narrow rock span. The arch soared above a meadow of sagebrush, connecting humped ridges of sandstone.

The first *thump* of the day pulsed through him in his hiding place in the stone crevice at 7:30, right on schedule. A second *thump* followed from the north a few seconds later, then another, and another.

Minutes passed. The pulses continued their slow, inexorable beat. *Thump.* Pause. *Thump.* Pause. *Thump.*

A light *tap-tap-tapping* noise reached him—the sound, propelled by the gusting wind, of running steps. He stiffened and checked his watch. 7:35. He leaned forward, eyes wide, heart pounding.

She appeared a hundred yards beyond the arch, her blue running jacket and black tights silhouetted against the gray clouds. She ran with the light, easy gait of a gazelle, crossing the spine of stone high above the sage meadow, headed straight for the arch.

He very nearly jumped up and screamed at her to stop. But that would have meant giving himself away.

He knelt in place instead, his head ducked. Surely, she would stop before venturing out onto the span itself.

She slowed and edged down the sloping shoulder of sandstone to the point where the arch soared away from the hump of rock into space. Rather than stop, however, she stepped from the solid shoulder of stone onto the bridge of stone.

The digital numbers on his watch flicked from 7:35 to 7:36. He dug his fingernails into his palms, his breaths coming in quick bursts.

She extended her arms from her sides and placed one foot directly in front of the other, walking slowly down the middle of the span. She was fifteen feet out on the arch, surrounded by sifting mist and swirling sleet, when a sharp, concussive crack sounded at the near end of the rock bridge. She dropped her arms to her sides, her gaze fixed on the narrow arc of stone stretched through thin air before her.

The near end of the arch cleaved in two. Dark lines shot like black lightning through the remainder of the span. For an instant, the arch maintained its shape, hanging in the sky. Then it fractured into hundreds of jagged chunks of sandstone.

He leapt to his feet. "No!" he cried out, finally finding his voice.

Too late.

The woman's eyes found his just as the shattered arch fell away beneath her. She screamed and grabbed at the air with outstretched fingers as she plunged amid the falling pieces of the span to the sagebrush flat five stories below.

PART ONE

"A civilization which destroys what little remains of the wild, the spare, the original, is cutting itself off from its origins and betraying the principle of civilization itself."

—Edward Abbey, *Desert Solitaire*

1

Thump.

Chuck Bender quivered from head to toe as the pulsing vibration passed through him.

He lay awake beside his wife, Janelle Ortega, in their camp trailer. Carmelita and Rosie slept in narrow bunk beds opposite the galley kitchen, halfway down the camper's center aisle, their breaths soft and steady.

He didn't need to check his watch to know the time. The NatResources truck had begun its work promptly at 7:30 the previous two mornings. No doubt the crew was on time this morning as well.

Chuck pulled back the curtain over the window abutting the double bed at the back of the trailer. Wind-driven sleet pelted the glass. Dark clouds hung low over the campground. He dropped the curtain. Another thump sounded, followed by another rolling vibration through his body, as the seismic truck pounded the earth outside the park to the north, trolling for underground deposits of oil and natural gas.

He rolled to face Janelle. Her eyes were closed, but her breathing was uneven, wakeful. He drew a line down her smooth, olive cheek, tracing the gentle arc of her skin with his fingertip. Her eyes remained shut, but the corner of her mouth twitched.

"Hey, there, *belleza*," he murmured, lifting a lock of her silky, black hair away from her face.

She opened her eyes. Turning to him, she tucked her hands beneath her small, pointed chin. "*Belleza nadie.* Nobody's beautiful this early in the morning."

"It's not that early. We slept in."

A powerful gust roared through the campground, tearing at the trailer's thin, aluminum shell.

Janelle raised her eyebrows. "That's some storm."

"As predicted," Chuck said. He gathered her in his arms and pressed his body to hers.

Sheets rustled in the lower bunk bed. Janelle raised her head to peer down the walkway past Chuck's shoulder. "Look who's awake," she said. "*Buen día, m'hija.*"

"*Hola, Mamá,*" eleven-year-old Rosie replied from the bottom bunk in her deep, raspy voice. "You two woke me up with all your lovey-dovey talking. Are you having sex?"

Chuck stiffened and released Janelle, who slid away from him to her side of the bed. A snort of laughter sounded from behind the drawn curtain hiding thirteen-year-old Carmelita in the top bunk.

Janelle grinned at Chuck as they lay facing each other. She said to Rosie, "No, honey, we're not . . . we're not . . ."

". . . having sex? But you said that's what people do when they love each other."

"There's a time and place for everything, *m'hija.* I can't say this is exactly the right time and place to be asking about that sort of thing, but I guess it's good you're remembering all the stuff we've been talking about."

"The birds and the bees," Rosie confirmed from her bed. "Sex, sex, sex."

Janelle pulled her pillow from beneath her head, pressed it over her face, and issued a sigh of resignation from beneath it.

Chuck folded his pillow in half, settled his head on it, and looked on as Carmelita drew back the upper-bunk curtain and leaned over the side of her bed. Her hair, dark and silky like her mother's, hung past her head, hiding her face. Rosie lifted herself on her elbows and looked up at Carmelita. Rosie's hair, also dark, was short and kinky and smashed against the side of her skull from her night's sleep.

"You're never gonna learn the right time and place for anything," Carmelita scolded her younger sister.

Rosie flopped to her back on her mattress and crossed her pudgy arms over her thick torso, her hands clenched. "Will, too."

"I wouldn't bet on it."

Chuck broke in. "I would," he said to Carmelita. "Your sister's going to keep on getting smarter and smarter, just like you. I mean, look how wise and all-knowing you've gotten, just in the last few weeks."

Carmelita sat up straight in her bed, her spine rigid. She gathered her top sheet around her waist and narrowed her hazel eyes at Chuck before whipping the curtain back across her bed, closing herself off from view.

Janelle lifted her pillow from her face. "There's no need for that," she whispered to Chuck.

"I couldn't help myself," he apologized, speaking softly. "I can't get used to her, to our new Carmelita."

"We don't have any choice."

Chuck worked his jaw back and forth. Carmelita had been a loving big sister to Rosie and kindhearted daughter and step-daughter to Janelle and Chuck until a few weeks ago, when she'd woken one morning with a scowl on her face and a smirk playing at the corners of her mouth. Since then, as if inhabited by an alien being, she had subjected her little sister to nonstop teasing and had responded with little more than monosyllables and grunts of exasperation to all attempts at conversation by her parents.

Chuck knew Carmelita was simply expressing her growing sense of independence as she entered her teen years. But knowing what was going on with her didn't make dealing with her any easier.

"You can't be the one going on the attack," Janelle insisted, her voice low. "You have to control yourself—which is to say, you have to stop channeling your mother."

Chuck recoiled. "Shonda has nothing to do with this."

Janelle rested her hand on his forearm. "She has everything to do with this. Especially now, for the next two weeks."

He pressed the back of his head into his pillow. "Between the two of them, it's like they've got us surrounded."

"The only way we'll survive is if we stick together. *Juntos.* And we have to keep on being nice to Carm. Just like we'll be nice to your mother." She tapped his nose with her finger. "Remember, this was all your idea—Shonda, your contract, the four of us crammed together into this teeny, tiny trailer for two whole weeks in the middle of winter."

"It's not winter yet. Not quite. Yesterday and the day before were great—sunny, warm. Plus, we've managed to avoid Shonda so far."

"The first two days were the calm before the storm." Janelle lifted the curtain on her side of the bed and peeked out. "Literally."

Chuck stared at the camper ceiling, close over the bed. At seven feet by twenty-four feet, the trailer had seemed palatial when he'd bought it off a used lot in Durango a month ago for their planned stay in Arches. But by the end of their first day in Devil's Garden Campground, at the terminus of the dead-end road into the park, palatial had transformed into cozy. This morning, with the gale raging outside, the camper felt hopelessly cramped.

The four of them couldn't possibly stay inside all day, trapped by the storm. They'd drive each other crazy. Nor could Chuck avoid Shonda forever. Maybe today was the day—finally, after four years—to introduce Janelle and the girls to his mother.

He tensed, anticipating the next pulsing beat from the NatResources truck. Instead, a sharp crack sounded from somewhere just north the campground, much closer than the truck's location outside the park. A thunderous rumbling noise followed, accompanied by a shock wave that rocked the trailer on its wheels.

Chuck clambered out of bed, smacking his forehead on the cabinetry lining the walkway. Janelle threw off the sheets and grabbed her fitted jeans and black T-shirt she'd worn yesterday from hooks in the center aisle.

Carmelita pulled back her upper-bunk curtain. She and Rosie looked on, mouths agape, as Chuck and Janelle tugged on their clothes and hurried past the girls' bunks.

"Wait here," Chuck told them from the front of the camper. "We'll be right back."

He caught his reflection in the small window in the camper door as he bent to tie his boots. His unkempt hair, brown going gray, rose straight up from his grooved forehead. Morning light streaming through the window reflected off his high temples, bared by his receding hairline. Crow's feet cut away from his blue eyes, seared into his leathery skin by the harsh western sun over the course of two decades of shovel and trowel work on archaeological digs—tough, physical work that kept him lean and fit.

He tied his boots, pulled on his rain jacket, and ducked outside. Janelle followed. She matched him stride for stride as they hurried through the campground. Bus-sized recreational vehicles loomed out of the mist, parked in numbered sites on either side of the paved campground drive. Electric generators hummed at the back of the RVs. Blurry faces peered out from behind the vehicles' fogged windows. No one besides Chuck and Janelle was outside.

"Everybody must think the sound was part of the seismic

operations," Chuck said, his head lowered against the driving sleet.

"That's what it sounded like to me," Janelle replied.

"It wasn't, though. It was different. Sharper. And close by."

"It came from the direction of your work site, didn't it?"

"That's one of the things I'm worried about."

Janelle glanced back at the camp trailer. "Will the girls be okay?"

Chuck waved a hand at the watching RV owners. "We couldn't ask for nosier neighbors. Besides, Carmelita's in charge. She knows everything at this point."

Janelle turned her head to Chuck, sending droplets of melted sleet cascading off the hood of her jacket to the pavement. She ticked a finger back and forth at him. "Uh-uh," she warned. She slipped her hand back in her jacket pocket. "One smart aleck in the family is enough. You can't fight fire with fire, not in this case. You'll never win."

"*Sí, señora mía,*" Chuck said, though he wasn't at all sure he had it in him to do as she directed.

No vehicles were parked at the Devil's Garden Trailhead, where the road through Arches ended next to the campground. Like the RV owners in their massive homes on wheels, would-be park visitors were holed up in their motel rooms in town this morning, waiting out the storm.

Devil's Garden Trail headed north from the parking area. Chuck's foot slipped when he stepped from the parking lot onto the dirt pathway. He waved his arms wildly, struggling for balance, his boots sliding like skis in the saturated soil. Janelle giggled behind him as he caught himself, set his shoulders, and continued on the path, his feet squelching in the untracked mud.

The trail passed through a walled corridor thick with sagebrush and opened onto a mile-wide sagebrush flat at the start of a seven-mile hiking loop. The loop path led to five of the sandstone spans that gave Arches National Park its name. The right-hand branch passed Private Arch on the way to Double O Arch. The left branch led northwest to Landscape Arch, just over half a mile from the parking lot, then to Navajo Arch and Partition Arch.

"We should go left," Chuck said as they neared the junction.

A gust of sleet-laden wind blew across the flat, carrying with it the crisp, piney scent of wet sage.

"But your contract site is to the right."

"The more I think about it, the more I think the sound came from one of the arches—and of all the arches in Devil's Garden, Landscape makes the most sense."

Janelle moaned. "Please, no."

"Something made that noise. Besides, the timing's right."

"But it's been there for thousands of years."

"It's the longest, narrowest span in the park—and it's never had a seismic truck pounding away at the ground so close to it before." Chuck hunched his shoulders against the falling sleet. "The freeze-thaw cycle causes most arches to collapse. The most recent arch to fall in the park was Wall Arch, in 2008. It fell in late October, the time of year when temperatures drop below freezing at night and climb back above thirty-two degrees in the daytime." He raised his hand, allowing the sleet to wet his palm. "This is the first real cold snap to hit the park this fall. The temperature dropped into the twenties last night, before the clouds came in. That was the freeze part of the cycle. Then came sunrise and the thaw part, with temperatures rising to freezing or a little above just as the truck started thumping."

"You really think . . . ?"

"Lots of people have been worried about it. That's why they fought the seismic work so close to the park for so long. But the courts finally okayed it. NatResources started pounding the ground outside the park a week ago—just in time for the storm to come along."

Chuck led Janelle down the left branch of the trail. The path angled across the flat and entered a gap between sandstone cliffs. The cliff walls fell back after two hundred yards, giving way to a second sagebrush flat, this one a quarter mile across. Red sandstone bluffs surrounded the flat. Wind whistled off the bluffs and across the ground, shivering the sage bushes. Ice crystals clung to the bushes' tiny, gray-green leaves.

Chuck stopped abruptly at the edge of the flat. He stepped aside and pointed, his back muscles drawing up tight. "There."

On the far side of the opening, a pair of sandstone stumps extended outward from facing rock bluffs a hundred yards apart. The rock stumps marked the two ends of the place where, until this morning, Landscape Arch had soared through space.

Bile built in Chuck's stomach. He'd hiked from the campground to see the arch with Janelle, Carmelita, and Rosie just two days ago, their first day in the park. Upon spying the span, Carmelita had become a little kid again for a few welcome moments, oohing and aahing with Rosie at the spindly rock bridge arcing across the sky. But now the sky was empty, the arch reduced to a line of jagged rocks lying jumbled on the ground between the two shoulders of stone.

Janelle led the way across the flat, her movements stiff. She stopped at a wooden post-and-beam fence that until today had kept onlookers from venturing closer to the overhead span. Chuck halted beside her. The sandstone stumps protruded from the facing bluffs fifty feet above their heads. On the ground below, shards of the shattered arch lay amid smashed clumps of sagebrush.

Thump.

The rolling vibration from the seismic truck caused a chunk

of sandstone the size of a softball to break free from a waist-high hunk of the broken arch. The small chunk of rock came to rest in the mud beside something blue extending upward from beneath the larger piece of the fallen span.

Chuck gripped the top rail of the fence, his fingers cold and white. "See that?" he said to Janelle, his voice shaking.

He vaulted the fence and sprinted toward the waist-high chunk of stone. The pungent smell of crushed sagebrush filled the cold morning air. When he neared the line of shattered rocks, another scent mixed with the smell of smashed sage, something metallic.

The scent of blood.

Printed in the USA
CPSIA information can be obtained
at www.ICGtesting.com
JSHW021517010424
60353JS00003B/53